One

Day one: Berlin, late August; 03.30 hours, Central European Time.

It was raining, and unseasonably cold. The man stood by the side of the road, waiting, it seemed, for a tram that had long gone; or for one that was yet to come. He would have a long wait, if indeed that was his purpose. He had long missed the last one of the night, and was far too early for the first one of the new day.

The soulless glare of the street lamps played with the weak, nascent promise of the light of the day to come, to give a forbidding illumination to the scene. The man looked like the loneliest creature on the planet – and the most vulnerable – as he huddled within his cheap-looking bomber jacket against the rain. There was not even a parked car in sight. It was as if they too, had decided that this was no place for them. The night was not friendly.

The huddled man looked slowly about him, turning his head tortoise-like, as if afraid to push it too far out of the turned-up collar of his jacket. A knitted, woollen hat with a bobble on top was clamped tightly upon his head; and into the pockets of his crumpled jeans – already wet through – he had stuck his hands in useless protection against the downpour. There was one anomaly: the trainers on his feet seemed of remarkably good quality, at odd variance with the rest of his attire. Every so often, he would shift his feet uncertainly. He clearly looked like a man who wanted to be anywhere else but where he had found himself.

1

Then out of the night like spectres of malevolence, the bright lights of a car, approaching at speed, homed in upon the waiting man. As it approached, it seemed to be heading directly for him in a slanting course that would take it off the road and on to the pavement. The man poised himself to run, but the car changed direction suddenly and screeched to a halt some distance away, its headlights glaring balefully. A creature of the night, it had taken on a feral life of its own.

The man stared at it, a rabbit mesmerized by a snake. Nothing happened for a while. Only the sound of the car's engine at idle was loud enough to disturb the night. The man breathed softly, open-mouthed. A weak spume of vapour, sneaking out, marked the exhalation of his breath. The lights of the car played upon the darkness of his face.

At last, four men climbed out of the still-idling vehicle. They slammed the doors like a four-shot burst from a heavy calibre gun. They were all young, shaven-headed, mean, and looking for someone to hurt. The satisfied expressions of anticipation upon their faces vividly betrayed their eagerness. They had found their prey. One had a spiked chain which he swung slowly in growing anticipation. It made a soft, hungry noise. Another carried a baseball bat loosely upon a shoulder. Something gleamed in the light of the street lamps, on the left hand of the third: a knuckleduster. The fourth had a knife as big as a bayonet. With the courage of the pack, they seemed to be smiling, certain of the outcome. The rain gave a menacing sheen to four pairs of boots that seemed to have been manufactured for the sole purpose of kicking another human being to death.

They fanned out, planning to come at the lone man from four quarters. They did not hurry. There was no need. Their prey had nowhere to run to. They had effectively blocked all escape. They came forward slowly. No need to hurry at all.

The huddled man made no attempt to move. Perhaps he was paralysed by fear.

The young men stopped. They did so with precision, as if on parade.

A Cold Rain in Berlin

'*What are you doing in my country, you piece of shit of an asyl?*' one of them shouted at the man suddenly, his voice a snarl of vicious anger. He was the one with the baseball bat. His accent was of the east.

'I . . . I am not an asylum seeker.'

The man's answer was apologetic, diffident. But there was something strange about the way he had spoken. His German was perfect, educated; unlike that of his interrogator.

There was a sudden pause as the young men seemed to take some time to assimilate this unexpected turn of events. But it would not deflect them from their intended purpose. They found a new way to refocus their anger.

'You bastard foreigner!' the one with the knife yelled. 'You come here and our shit of a government educates you! We will kick you all out of Germany! This government too!' He too, had spoken with an eastern accent.

If anyone in the darkened houses had heard this exchange, no one dared to look and certainly, no one intervened. It was doubtful whether they would much care about the fate of a lone foreigner. No lights came on. The houses remained resolutely dark.

As if a switch had been turned on, all four began a sudden rush at the man. It was clear they did not intend that he survive the eventual encounter.

The man, still apparently paralysed by fear, did not move.

Then, at a point when his attackers were at the peak of their headlong rush, he did at last move; but it was not to run.

A remarkable change had come over him. Both hands were out of his pockets and one was diving into his jacket. His movements were swift; too swift for someone paralysed by fear. The running men had still not assimilated this new change in circumstances.

The man's hand was out of his jacket now and held firmly in a two-handed grip was a big automatic pistol. A silencer was attached to its muzzle. The men still did not quite realize what was happening. Perhaps the rain and the night had temporarily blinded them; perhaps the glare from the lights of the car had somehow hidden the swift and surreptitious movements of the huddled man from them. Whatever the reasons, the man had chosen his moment well. It was as if he had been waiting for it.

The gun had zeroed upon its first target and had coughed a single shot into the rainy night before the four young men at last realized what was happening. The game had suddenly changed for them. The hunters had become the hunted.

That first shot took the one with the baseball bat in the throat. He dropped the bat and grabbed uselessly at his wound in a desperate attempt to stop the terrible thing that was happening to him. He gave a strange, high-pitched gargle.

The other three were skidding to clumsy halts to turn to look in astonishment at their now-tumbling comrade.

The man with the gun was quick, and deadly. The second shot took the one with the chain in the head. He died on his feet, the chain flailing out of the lifeless hand. His body was falling slackly when the third shot hit the one with the knuckleduster in the heart. He too died quickly.

The man reserved the fourth shot for the one with the knife.

'Please!' the survivor begged, all bluster having vanished completely.

He dropped the knife in a rapid, jerking movement, as if it had suddenly become too hot to hold, and seemed to have conveniently forgotten what he had been about to do to an apparently defenceless man.

'Don't shoot me!' he pleaded. Courage of the pack had long deserted him.

'Just don't tell me they forced you to do it,' the man said coldly.

The other did not reply. Now it was his turn to be mesmerized. He stared fearfully at the gun.

'At least you didn't,' the man said, and shot him in the stomach.

'Oooh my God!' the young man screamed. '*Oooh my God!*

Shit, shit, shit! Why did you do that? You've killed me! You've killed me!'

As he fell to his knees holding on to his middle, his erstwhile victim leaned down and said emotionlessly, 'It will take you an hour to die. By then, perhaps your friends will have found you. Tell them *we're* hunting you all now.'

The man straightened and turned away, putting the gun back into his jacket.

'Don't leave me here to die!' It was a scream and a prayer. The young man began to crawl after his unknown nemesis, crying as he did so. 'Please! A doctor! Call a doctor!'

The man stopped, and turned round. 'The way you would have got a doctor for me?'

He waited until the crawling man had almost reached him before turning once more to continue walking away in the rain, the cries of the fatally wounded survivor following him in the night.

'Come back!' There was a terror now, in the young man's voice. '*Come back! Please, please! Don't leave me here to die! I can tell you things. I can give you names!*' But when even that had no effect, the fear coalesced into an impotent hatred. '*You shit! You shit of a black bastard! Rot in hell, you fucker! Rot in hell . . .*'

The man kept on walking as the pleading wails recommenced until the cries faded to a whimper and, at last, he could no longer hear them.

A few streets later, he came to where he had parked his car. He got in, and drove for some kilometres until he reached a wooded area on the southern edge of the city. He turned off the road and on to a track that led deep into the woods. When he was satisfied the car was well out of sight of casual observation, he stopped and turned off the engine.

He got out, went to the boot and took a small sports bag out of it. He shut the boot and got back behind the wheel; but he did not drive off. Instead, he placed the bag on the passenger seat, opened it, took out some cotton wool, and a plastic bottle of cosmetic cleansing fluid. He began to work on

5

his face. The dark colour came off on the wad of cotton. Pale skin showed where he had rubbed. He worked quickly.

When he drove away from the woods, his face was no longer dark. It was, he decided, a good night's work.

In the street with the dead and the dying, no lights came on. No one wanted to know. The rain kept on falling, washing the glistening streams of blood darkly along the road surface.

The dying man, breath exhausted by his cries, stared blankly at his silent friends, not wanting to believe what had just happened to him.

He looked up tiredly at the buildings, perhaps hoping someone would look out; but they continued to remain resolutely dark. Perhaps in these fading moments he at last began to understand why he had found himself lying there in the wet street.

Perhaps.

Berlin, 09.00 hours that morning.
It was still raining.

A man looked out of his office window and made a wry grimace. 'God,' he said to himself. 'They ought to sack the meteorologists. They get it wrong every time. One day bright, hot sunshine . . . next day, this shit.'

For a police *Hauptkommissar*, Jens Müller was very unusual; unique even. To begin with, he seemed rather young for the rank. His thick dark hair, with barely perceptible strands of grey lurking deeply, was so long, he wore it in a ponytail. He had blond eyebrows, but his hair was not dyed. He liked designer clothes and today he was wearing a grey Armani suit. No tie adorned his spotless white shirt.

Müller was a tall man – over six feet and solidly built – yet he seemed strangely delicate; an impression he liked to encourage, since the direct opposite was in fact the reality. But the thing that got most people seeing him for the first time and knowing his profession and rank, was that he also wore a single *earring*.

Müller's direct superior disliked most things about him, especially that earring; but this dislike was also laced with a heavy dose of envy. Matters were made worse by the fact that Müller, coming from a rich family, did not depend upon his salary. Müller's boss, Heinz Kaltendorf, a man of severe conservatism, hated this with a vengeance. It was the reason, he felt, why Müller was so insubordinate.

He considered Müller a bad policeman, a man who did not work by the rules. What Kaltendorf could not accept was that Müller's quite exceptional skills and successes were a direct result of his subordinate's unconventional approach.

Unlike Müller, Kaltendorf did not go in for stylish dressing. Though his suits were immaculately clean, they somehow managed to look wrong; and his taste in ties was always the subject of secret hilarity among his subordinates. He was the classic plodding policeman who rose to his rank by patience, and by keeping his nose clean. Müller's accelerated promotion gnawed at him like a rat at his vitals. It formed an acid within his gut that was exacerbated by his full knowledge that Müller was contemptuous of him. He also hated the fact that, being shorter, he was forced to look up at Müller during conversation. It was therefore with great relish that he strode into Müller's office unannounced, carrying a thin red-jacketed file.

'Ah, Müller!' he began gleefully. 'Something right up your street. It seems that some asylum seeker shot four of your friends last night. Dead. The case is yours.' He dropped the file on Müller's desk. He kept his distance, so that he didn't have to look up too far.

Müller glanced at it sourly. 'My friends?'

Kaltendorf was a political animal, Müller knew, who was more worried about hanging on to his position than anything else.

'You'll understand,' Kaltendorf said ominously. 'We want results. Fast.' He strode out of the office.

'"*We*"?' Müller repeated at the closed door. 'I don't need any of your *we are the nation* shit today.' He gave the red file another glance. 'And I don't need this. Pappenheim can handle it.'

7

The door opened again and Kaltendorf's head poked round. 'I know you, Müller. Don't even think of giving it to Pappenheim.' The head withdrew, and Kaltendorf was gone. Müller gave an ironic salute. 'Yes, *sir*.' He stared at the file with distaste. The only reason Kaltendorf had been so openly happy was because this had all the makings of developing into something very nasty indeed. 'Just what I need on a shitty day like this. Things can only get worse.'

He sighed, went over to the desk and sat down. He opened the file and began to study it. Four large black and white photographs had been neatly slotted into a pocket in the inside front cover of the file. He removed and spread them out like a set of cards.

They were of the dead men. They had been photographed in the street where they had fallen. Their clothes blatantly pictured them for what they had been. The fourth had been photographed in hospital.

'As in life, so in death,' he said to the photos. 'Ugly bastards.' There was no sympathy in his voice. 'Ugly in spirit, ugly in appearance.'

He read the information in the file minutely, looking for anomalies. The one who had been left alive long enough to talk had been found not by his comrades but, ironically, by a Turkish taxi driver who had taken him to the nearest hospital, where he had subsequently died, despite the efforts of the medical staff.

'Would you have helped a Turk in the same way?' Müller asked the dead man in the photograph. 'Certainly not. You would have finished him off.'

He read aloud some of the words the fatally wounded man had lived long enough to relay, just as his killer had intended. '*Tell them* we're *hunting you all now*.'

Müller closed the file slowly, but left the photographs where they were.

'So,' he began softly. 'Someone's hitting back. It was only a matter of time. But who? Outside their own ideological world, these people have no friends; so there will be many candidates, some perhaps completely unexpected . . . and that will be the headache. And all mine,' he added dryly. 'Thanks for nothing, Herr Kaltendorf.'

He was about to get to his feet, when Kaltendorf again appeared.

'What now?' Müller snapped irritably.

'Careful, Müller!' Kaltendorf warned with remarkable cheerfulness. He did not seem to mind Müller's disrespectful tones. 'One day, that insubordinate attitude of yours will get you into hot water. But today's not the day. I have a surprise for you.'

'I can live without your suprises, *sir*.' Müller pointed to the file.

'Oh, that. What I bring is much more pleasant.' Kaltendorf seemed unable to stop smiling. 'A companion.'

Müller frowned. 'What companion?' This was not good news.

'Someone to work with you, so to speak.'

The day was getting worse by the second. '*So to speak*? What does that mean exactly? I have my team, I don't need . . .'

But Kaltendorf was standing back to let someone enter. 'May I present,' he began elaborately in American-accented English, 'Miss Carey Bloomfield, journalist from New York, here to research the history of the Berlin police . . . from 1940 to the new century.' He behaved as if he had just handed Müller an award. 'I thought, as you are so well educated,' he continued, switching back to German, 'what better person to show her around?'

Kaltendorf was smiling so hard, Müller thought his face would crack into splinters.

Müller nodded curtly at Carey Bloomfield, but glared at Kaltendorf. 'I have a new case, as you know, *sir* . . .' he started to say in German.

'Which makes the whole thing perfect,' Kaltendorf interrupted smoothly. 'She can see how you work. You'll be an excellent ambassador for the force, Müller, a gentleman like you. We want to ensure that Miss Bloomfield has a correct impression of the Berlin police at the beginning of the new century.' He was back in English as he turned to Carey Bloomfield. 'I leave you in very good hands. Anything you need, just ask Müller here.' He smiled pointedly at Müller, and left before Müller could object further.

Müller stared frustratedly at the closed door, then turned to Carey Bloomfield. 'I'm sorry . . .' he began in English.

'I seem to have come at the wrong time . . .' she commenced in German.

They both stopped awkwardly.

'You speak German,' Müller continued in English.

'All Americans are not stereotyped provincials, you know,' she said, staying in German. 'Some of us can speak other languages.'

Müller smiled and held out a hand.

'Stereotyping is the coin of the world,' he remarked, back in German. 'These days, all Germans are again Nazis. Your German is very good . . . which means you understood that little exchange with my wonderful boss.'

She shook the hand and smiled back at him. 'I'm afraid so.'

'Oh well . . . the day might as well continue as it seems to have begun. Just to save further confusion, do we speak English, or German?'

'German. But I am sure my German is not as good as your English. It sounds *English* English.'

'I was at Oxford.'

'Of course. That figures.'

'Does it?'

She nodded, but did not elaborate. She went over to the desk, and stared neutrally at the photographs. 'Couldn't have happened to nicer people.'

'You approve of this?'

'It's not a question of approval. They had it coming. It was only a matter of time before people started to strike back.'

He stared at her. 'I had that thought just before you arrived.'

'There you go. We'll work well together.'

'Ground rules, Miss Bloomfield . . .'

'Carey . . .'

'Ground rules, Miss Bloomfield,' Müller repeated firmly. 'Me policeman, you journalist. We don't *work* together. You observe, and keep out of my way.' He smiled. 'How does that sound?'

'Just like a policeman.'

'Good. Keep remembering that. Oh . . . and do you smoke?'

'No.'

'Even better. Pappenheim, my deputy, smokes like a chimney. I'll take a bullet for that man, but I hate getting into his car. An ashtray on wheels.'

'You'd take a bullet for him? That's what I call true blue.'

'He took one for me, long ago, when I was young and green . . .'

'You're thirty-five, and young for your rank. You're not old . . .'

'How do you know this?'

'I'm a journalist. Remember? I do my research.'

Müller gave her a speculative look. 'Sometimes,' he went on, 'I feel a lot older. Pappenheim taught me a lot.'

'But you're his superior now.'

'Pappi's a good policeman. One of the best.'

'But?'

'*But* nothing. I'm sorry there's no secret envy from Pappi to whet your journalistic appetite. I call him "Pappi" because, at times, he is like a father to me. You'll meet him soon enough.'

At about the time that Müller was doing his best to accept with good grace the tasks that Kaltendorf had dumped on him, a couple were having breakfast in a café in a rejuvenated section of what used to be East Berlin. While they did not behave like lovers who had spent the night in the same bed, their manner showed they were certainly more than casual friends. Both were dressed casually yet, at the same time, there was an inherent smartness about them.

They had been in the coffee shop for nearly an hour, and for at least half of that time, they had been surreptitiously observed by three men in a car that was parked across the street. The couple seemed oblivious to this, being more occupied with each other. Outside, it was still raining; but the couple seemed oblivious to that too.

The men in the car, a dark Mercedes saloon that was some years old, did not look benignly upon them. The car's engine was running.

The woman was blonde. Her hair, plaited in a cockscomb at the back and neatly tucked in, gleamed as the light within the café shone upon it. To them, she was a supreme example of Aryan perfection and it galled them that her companion was a black man. It never occurred to them to imagine that the object of their admiration would look upon them with contempt, had she been aware of their interest in her. They waited in their car with eager anticipation. They had plans for her companion, none of them good.

At last, the couple got up to leave. The man paid. They left the café, glanced up at the rain and, laughing, began running to where they had parked their car, a red Corvette, further up the street.

The Mercedes started to follow slowly, keeping pace, but remaining behind.

The couple was close to their car now, but before they had time to unlock it the Mercedes raced forwards and slid to a halt alongside, blocking the Corvette. The men rushed out, coming at the couple from different directions, one brandishing the ubiquitous baseball-bat.

'*Neger arschloch!*' he screamed at the man, and swung the bat.

Despite being surprised, the black man was swift. He

ducked to one side. The swing of the bat threw the one wielding it off-balance when it did not connect. He stumbled and tried to regain his footing. In so doing, the bat swung back and, though with much depleted force, struck his intended victim glancingly. The black man dropped to his knees and rolled with the blow.

The woman meanwhile, was doing something quite unusual. Instead of the expected scream of fear and horror, she was swiftly digging into the bag that hung from her shoulder. She pulled out an automatic pistol and fired two rapid shots into the air.

The sudden blasting of the double reports in the rainy street brought the attackers to a shocked halt. They stared at her in disbelief. First uncertainly, then like rabid animals suddenly trapped, they glared at her in watchful defiance as if they didn't believe she would really shoot. But something in her manner began to worry them. Their uncertainty increased.

'*Alright you fucking bastards!*' she screamed at them in English. It was the English of America. She was holding the gun braced two-handedly, and it was very clear she knew how to use it. '*One fucking move and I'll blow your fucking brains out. Move away from him! Move, you shitheads!*'

The shock was now growing by the nanosecond and widening their hitherto defiant eyes. Fear was coming too.

'*Do it!*' she ordered. 'If you don't understand English, you're in shit street, because if you don't move, this thing in my hand is going to talk some more . . . but not into the air.'

They understood well enough. They moved, and quickly.

'Drop your weapons! *Drop them! And step back!*'

They did so, even more quickly. This was not going to be their day, and they knew it.

'We're Americans, you fucking barbarians!' She glanced at her companion, who was slowly getting to his feet. 'You OK, Danny?' She kept the gun pointing unerringly at the three attackers.

'I'm cool, Meg,' the black man answered.

He was standing now. He rubbed the side of his head briefly. There was a slight weal, but no blood. He turned to look at the one who had struck at him, then walked towards the man, who took an involuntary step backwards.

Megan Childes bawled, eyes unblinking in the rain, *'Don't fucking move, I said!'*

The baseball-bat wielder stopped immediately.

The man she had called Danny was taller than his assailant, and looked like someone who exercised regularly enough to stay in peak condition. He went up close to his attacker and stared down, ignoring the dripping rain.

'Enjoyed your fun, did you?' he said quietly. He didn't even seem angry.

Without warning, his fist slammed into the side of the man's head. The blow was so powerful, it practically lifted the other off his feet. He fell heavily to the wet ground. The shaven head slammed against the pavement. His companions, aghast, stared uncertainly down at their fallen comrade, then warily back at Danny Thompson, expecting the same treatment.

'Cool it, Danny,' Megan Childes cautioned. 'Let's get out of here before the local cops arrive. People have come out to look. Someone is bound have called them. You OK to drive?' The gun was still pointing. 'Besides, I'm getting wet.'

'I'm OK.' Thompson stared at the two who were still standing. 'Your lucky day, after all.'

He turned from them, taking the car keys from a pocket. He squeezed the remote and a soft squawk told him the car was open.

More people were coming to look, but keeping well away from what they hoped was gun range.

'Can you get out?' Megan enquired urgently.

Thompson glanced round. 'Can do. Room to reverse.' He quickly entered the car, then leaned across to push open the passenger door. He started the engine. 'Get in!'

'Coming!' She moved rapidly to pick up the dropped weapons with one hand and put them behind the seats, all the while keeping the gun trained on the men. 'I'm just as good with one hand,' she warned them, 'so don't try your luck.' She got into the car. 'Next time you try something like this we *will* blow your fucking brains out . . . if you've got any, you sick assholes!'

Thompson did a fast reverse, then swung out past the Mercedes to accelerate away, trailing spray.

Many of the people who had come out to observe the incident believed they had been watching an undercover police action, although they tried to assimilate the fact that English, American English at that, had been spoken. They could also not quite understand the pairing of the two supposed officers.

'I didn't know we had black undercover police here,' a middle-aged man said to a woman standing next to him. She looked of a similar age.

'We have so many here these days,' she responded sourly, 'why not in the police too? They probably need them to get at the drug dealers and the pimps.' But she didn't really sound as if she believed it. To her way of thinking, all drug dealers and pimps were black. 'They should send them all back where they came from. It was never like this in the old DDR.' They were the comments of one who mourned the passing of the former regime, and who looked upon that time as a golden age.

'Yes it was,' the man corrected. He too, had lived in the former DDR. 'They were invited from places like Africa. We promised their countries more economic and military help than the West, to get them on our side. Comrades together.'

The woman didn't like having her convenient amnesia exposed so bluntly. She snorted with vicious derision.

'Comrades!' she snapped poisonously, years of officially suppressed racial antipathy spilling out in that single word. 'I always hated them.'

But he was not interested in having an argument about

15

past times in the workers' paradise. 'Anyway, the man and
the woman sounded American.'
'Of course they would,' the woman retorted, as if that
explained it all.
Neither commented on the reason for the incident as the
two shaven heads picked up their groggy comrade and got
into the Mercedes, which shot off at speed.
The middle-aged pair don't even look. A few minutes later,
the first of two police cars arrived.
'Late as usual,' the woman remarked caustically, 'now that
the black one and his whore have gone.'

When the call came, Carey Bloomfield was still in Müller's
office. He picked up one of the phones on his desk and
listened without comment, then hung up. His face was
expressionless.
'Trouble?' she enquired.
'I'm always in trouble,' he replied. 'I've got to leave for a
few minutes. Please sit down and make yourself comfortable
on –' he looked at a chair that was well away from his desk –
'that chair. And please, Miss Bloomfield, don't take a look at
the file while I'm out of the office. We've all seen that movie;
and I'm not leaving it there accidentally on purpose so that
you can sneak a look. So don't make that mistake either.'
'I've seen *that* movie too. I won't look. See? I'm sitting
down.' She went to the chair and sat down.
Müller went to the door and looked out. 'Berger!'
'Yes, Chief?' Berger's voice replied.
'In here.'
A smiling young woman with dark, wavy hair, tied loosely
in a ponytail reminiscent of Müller's, entered.
'Miss Bloomfield,' Müller began, 'this is Lene Berger.
Anything you need, just ask her.'
Carey Bloomfield glanced at the file. 'I see you trust me,'
she said.
'What do you expect?' he countered on his way out. 'I'm
a policeman.' A glance passed between him and Berger.

Berger knew exactly why Müller had called her in.

'And with Berger,' he added, pausing at the door, 'you're in good hands.'

'Now where have I heard that one before?' Carey Bloomfield remarked dryly.

Pappenheim's office was a smoke factory, and his desk was a mess. Müller entered, coughing elaborately. It was Pappi who had called.

'Some excitement, eh?' Pappenheim began as Müller took a seat in front of the desk.

'That depends.'

'Droll as ever,' Pappenheim commented, taking a quick pull on his inevitable cigarette.

Pappenheim's clothes looked as if the words *sartorial elegance* were nightmares to be avoided at all costs. They were clean; which was about it . . . except for the fine specks of cigarette ash decorating shirt, tie, and trousers. The strange, perhaps even bizarre, thing about Pappenheim was his taste in ties. Unlike those of the hapless Kaltendorf, they were invariably well chosen; and his solid fingers, though long stained by nicotine, were otherwise scrupulously well tended.

'As long as my tie is good,' he was once heard to reply when asked about his attire by an irate Kaltendorf, 'and my fingers clean,' he had added mysteriously, 'I'm fine . . . sir.'

Kaltendorf had glared at him, searching the words for indictable insubordination, but had been forced into thwarted retreat. Kaltendorf hated smoking and always, at every opportunity, tried to ban it from the unit's offices; but, so far, with little success.

Pappenheim was shorter than Müller, and round with it. At first, his rotundity could be mistaken for an excess of fat caused by the consumption of too much rich food, and generous quantities of beer. While he did indeed have a substantial appetite and liked his beer, he was solidly built. Pushing at Pappenheim when he did not want to be pushed was like being faced by an immovable tank. He was also ridiculously light on his feet when he needed to change direction in a hurry, which was often, given the way he worked. It was one such change of direction that had saved Müller's life when a bullet was headed the younger man's way. Pappenheim had taken the shot in a beefy shoulder, thereby giving Müller the chance to fire an effectively incapacitating shot at their intended killer. Each had been quietly decorated for the action, which had ended in the capture of a highly efficient and equally highly paid professional killer.

They never reminded each other of the incident. As far as each was concerned, there was no need. It was an unspoken and accepted thing between them. Others among their colleagues, however, always talked about it in hushed tones.

'Every time I come in here, Pappi, I feel in need of a gas mask,' Müller now remarked, waving ineffectively at the smoke.

'I'll buy you one,' Pappenheim said cheerfully.

It was an established routine with them.

'You've read the file from the Great White Chief?' Pappenheim went on. Kaltendorf was not one of his favourite human beings.

Müller nodded.

'All my own work,' Pappenheim continued dryly. 'I was about to bring it in to you for a look, when the GWC intercepted me and decided to give the case to you. He truly loves you, that man.'

'The feeling's mutual,' Müller said grimly.

Pappenheim stubbed out the Gauloises Blonde he had been smoking into an already full ashtray, and promptly lit another. He took a long, satisfying drag of it.

'Those things will kill you,' Müller said.

'Of course,' Pappenheim agreed calmly. 'But a bullet will probably do that first, if I keep on in this job.'

This was also a routine of theirs.

18

'Well?' Müller demanded. 'Are we going to talk all day about your addiction? Or are you going to tell me what that phone call was all about?'

Pappenheim took another pull on his cigarette. 'The GWC doesn't know as yet, and he'll probably burst a blood vessel when he finds out I spoke to you first . . . I hope, if there's a God in heaven . . . but as you've already got the case . . .

'Pappi . . .' Müller began warningly.

'Alright, alright, I'm coming to it. Such impatience.'

Which was not strictly true. There were times when Müller's patience could make a statue seem frenetic.

Pappenheim passed a single report sheet to his younger superior. Müller had to shake specks of cigarette ash off it, before reading.

He stared at the paper, then looked up at Pappenheim when he had read it through. 'Two American-sounding *civilians* with guns?'

'The woman had the gun . . . perhaps her friend as well. But all the witnesses who were prepared to speak were adamant only the woman had the gun . . . at least, as far as they could see. Gave those shave-heads a fright, though.' Pappenheim smiled through his wreaths of smoke. 'She knew how to use it, Jens.'

'Which means?' Müller trusted Pappenheim's instincts completely.

'The witnesses thought they were our lot doing undercover work; but couldn't understand why they let the men go. If they really are American . . . perhaps military?'

'A new dimension I don't particularly relish getting into.'

'Didn't think you would. Do you remember Hartmann?' Pappenheim seemed to know so many people, Müller sometimes considered him better than a databank.

'I do. It's been nearly eight years, though, since I met him at an official function. He was with the diplomatic protection unit then.'

'Well he's now boss of the local boys who arrived at the

scene afterwards. He called me, assuming I would find it of interest.'

'And why would he do that, I wonder?'

'He owes me a few favours.'

'Is there anyone who doesn't?'

'No,' Pappenheim admitted shamelessly. 'Not even Kaltendorf. You, perhaps.'

'*Kaltendorf*? I don't believe it.'

'Believe it.'

'You must tell me . . .'

Pappenheim shook his head. 'This one I'll enjoy for as long as possible.'

'And as for me . . . I owe you plenty. You know that,' Müller added, touching on the forbidden subject.

'No. You don't.' Pappenheim's voice reproached Müller for the indirect reminder.

'Sorry, Pappi,' Müller said, knowing he should not have bent their private rule.

A slight nod from Pappenheim indicated he had accepted the apology. 'And as for your Amis – if they *were* really Amis – although the woman is supposed to have shouted, "We're Americans", or something like that. You never know with so-called witnesses. Plenty of bias and prejudice always goes into what they say. Anyway, our supposed fugitives are on the A115 Autobahn at the moment, heading south towards Michendorf. I've got a chopper up. A red Corvette isn't hard to follow.'

'And the number plate?'

'The witnesses all give different versions. One said normal Berlin plates; another swears it was Bremen. One said Bonn, and a middle-aged man claimed the plates were American. Take your pick. But the camera on the chopper will have the truth once they get a good zoom shot.'

'Evasion?'

'None at all. Considering they must have spotted the chopper by now, they're not making the slightest effort to evade; which either means they have nothing to hide, or they're very sure of themselves . . . for whatever reason. After the Michendorf junction, they can go east, west, north, or south . . .'

'Or in any number of other directions, if they choose to go off the Autobahn.'

'My guess is they're heading as fast as they can for a particular destination, and that means they need to use the Autobahn. Shall I have them stopped?'

'No,' Müller replied thoughtfully. 'Let's see where they end up. Liaise with any of the other *Bundesländer* police whose territory they may cross into, and ask for cooperation. We have a certain degree of autonomy.'

'That should be fun. Our autonomy – as you call it – may not be *certain degree* enough to avoid some ruffling of sensitive feathers. You know, here come the Berlin boys thinking they're big shots, giving us orders. That sort of thing.'

'If we do . . . too bad.'

'That should be fun,' Pappenheim repeated. The ruffling of feathers was not new to him. There were those who believed he thrived upon it. 'You've picked up my bad habits. I didn't teach you that.'

'Of course you did.'

Pappenheim grinned from behind his cigarette. 'And you? What do you plan?'

'For the moment, I think I'll follow. See where they end up.'

'They could be going out of the country.'

'I'll still follow . . . Besides, I want to see if there is a possible connection between what happened last night, and this incident. Kaltendorf gave me the case. I'm on it. One day, I might strangle that man, so the further I can get away from him, the better. It's a good way to get the Great White out of my hair for a little while. He can't annoy me if I'm not here.'

'Oh yes, he can. His reach is long, as you know . . . even abroad.'

'Don't remind me.'

'So what are you taking? An unmarked car? Or yours?'

'Mine.'

'Of course.'

'What do you mean *of course*? Even unmarked cars can shout *police*. Mine doesn't.'

'We have many excellent unmarked cars in this unit that don't give the game away,' Pappenheim reminded Müller with a fleeting smile.

'I'm taking my car!' Müller insisted firmly. 'Oh . . . *shit!*' he added testily.

'What? What?' Pappenheim was staring at him, pausing in the midst of lighting a fresh Gauloises from the recent one that was already close to the filter.

'Berger.'

'What has *she* done?'

'Nothing. She's watching that reporter Kaltendorf has landed me with.'

'Poor you. Your reporter friend is . . . well . . . sexy. I saw her with the Great White on his way to your office. She has quite a walk.'

'Shame on you, Pappi. How can you think of such things at your age?'

'All the time, the scientists say . . . when they have nothing better to do.'

'You're hopeless,' Müller said, getting to his feet. 'There is something you can do for me, though.'

'Tell it.'

'I want you to check out Miss Bloomfield. Everything you can find. Use all your many sources.'

'You don't trust her?'

'Do vipers have poison?'

'Ouch! OK, Boss. To hear is to obey. I'll do what I can.'

'And enough of the *Boss*.'

'Yes, Boss.'

Müller shook his head slowly, giving up. 'Try and get into the fresh air more often,' he said, again waving fruitlessly at the writhing tendrils of smoke that came from the cloud surrounding Pappenheim. 'How can you stand it? I'm choking.'

'Easily,' Pappenheim said unrepentantly. 'Think I'd do this if I didn't like it?' He grinned at Müller. 'I'll get the dirt on your sexy New Yorker.'

'Not dirt, Pappi. Just information.'

'Some information can come with dirt attached,' Pappenheim said reasonably.

Müller shook his head slowly once more and was about to leave when he paused, and stared at Pappenheim.

'You're looking smug,' he accused. 'What are you hiding from me?'

His subordinate grinned through freshly exhaled clouds of Gauloises. 'I left the best out of my report. The man is not only a supposed American . . .' Pappenheim let the rest of the sentence hang.

'And?' Müller prompted. 'Are we waiting for World War Three? Or do I get to know today?'

Pappenheim's shameless grin came once more. 'He's black.'

'Ah!'

'And there was a woman witness who lived in the old DDR. Hates black people. Pure vitriol. Gave the officers an earful for employing black police to order good Germans around. If I did some checking I'd probably discover that in the good old days, she informed on her neighbours to the Stasi. She certainly fits the profile. Now, suddenly, she's a good democrat. A leopard would change it's spots first.'

Pappenheim looked as if he wanted to spit and only the fact that he would spit out the cigarette as well seemed to prevent him from doing so.

'God knows how such people look into the mirror every day without puking,' he went on with distaste. 'Doesn't mean anything, of course . . . the black man being there. Our real perpetrator could be long gone. On the other hand . . .'

'His presence could have been pure coincidence.'

'We're the police. We're not supposed to believe in coincidences.'

'Don't quote the Great White at me, Pappi. And put out that grin.'

'Yeah, Boss!'

Müller was about to respond with something snappy, but saw that Pappenheim had already picked up a phone and was talking rapidly into it. The bobbing cigarette in his mouth sent a jerky funnel of smoke upwards, where it flattened out against the ceiling, and laid down its own carpet of nicotine detritus to join the countless others already there.

Müller left him to it and went out.

Two

On the Autobahn, the Corvette was still heading towards Michendorf. The rain had long stopped, and the top was open. The day was warming up, and the road surface was dry.

'Still there?' Thompson asked. They had just passed Potsdam. Megan Childes had been peering upwards at the dot in the sky. 'Still there . . . but they're keeping their distance. Probably hoping we won't notice. But if they've got a zoom on us, they know we know. If we're going to be shadowed all the way, they'll probably keep switching choppers as we cross the state borders. We're outside Berlin's jurisdiction, so they must have decided we're important enough for some cross-state police cooperation.'

'We shouldn't wait to find out how far that cooperation will go. I think we should call base and do our own switching . . . a decoy, and a change of wheels.'

'You got it.' She took the in-car mobile phone out of its bracket, punched in a number and spoke quickly when the call was answered. 'Done.' She held on to the phone. 'We'll do the change just north of Halle, at the *Tankstelle* on the A9. They'll be waiting.'

'OK,' Thompson said. He glanced in the direction of the distant helicopter, adding, 'Now let's see just how smart you flyboys are.' He glanced at Megan.

They smiled at each other as the red Corvette rumbled southwards at an easy pace.

* * *

The rain had also stopped falling in Müller's area of Berlin. He returned to his office to find a less-than-pleased Carey Bloomfield waiting, still sitting in the same chair, and still under the watchful eye of Lene Berger.

'Miss Bloomfield!' he began brightly in English, as if seeing her for the first time. 'So sorry. Plenty to do. I hope Officer Berger looked after you?'

'She got me a coffee,' she replied shortly, in the same language. 'As you can see.'

An empty cup was on Müller's desk.

'Yes,' he said, glancing at it. 'I see. Would you like another?'

'No, thank you.'

'It was not good?'

'It was fine.'

'I am glad. We have very good coffee here.' Müller smiled. 'Not like the bad coffee all the police lieutenants in your Hollywood and TV movies seem to complain about.'

She gave him a sideways look. 'Are you stalling me, *Hauptkommissar* Müller?'

'Not at all, Miss Bloomfield. In fact, I bring some news you might like.'

She was scepticism itself. 'This I've got to hear.'

'The news is good. I promise you.'

'Try me.'

'I am about to follow two suspects. It may take a short time, or a long time. Perhaps days. You can stay here for as long as you like and continue your research with Pappenheim's help, or . . .'

'You're not going to get rid of me so easily, mister. Your boss said *you* deal with me, not your friend Pappenheim. He won't like it if you dump me here.'

Müller's look gave nothing away. 'Then you'd better pack your toothbrush. We'll be leaving Berlin.'

'Can I stop off at my hotel first?'

'But of course. Berger will take you . . .'

'Thank you, but I can handle that myself.' She stood up and said to Berger, 'Nothing against you . . .'

'I speak English . . .' Berger began.

'Good for you,' Carey Bloomfield remarked sweetly, reverting to English. To Müller, she went on, 'Back here in . . .' She paused.

'One hour,' he said. 'No longer.'

'I'll be here one minute before my time's up.' She turned again to Berger. 'Thank you for looking after me, Miss Berger.'

'My pleasure.'

'I'm sure it was, Miss Hawk Eyes.'

'Was that sarcasm?' Berger said to Müller in German as Carey Bloomfield went out.

'I'm afraid it was. She was not pleased with you. What did you do?'

'Watched her, as you said. She tried to divert me by asking for coffee, thinking I would go and get it. But I asked Helmut Franck to get it instead.'

Müller smiled at her. 'Well done, Lene. So she did try something. She was hoping to take a look at the file. Good work. Thank you.'

Berger looked pleased. 'Shall I follow her?'

'No. She might expect it. I never do what others expect. At least, not all the time. So . . . from now on, should we call you Hawk Eyes around here?'

'Don't you dare!'

Müller grinned at her as she left his office, then he picked up one of the phones on his desk.

'Pappi,' he said when Pappenheim answered, 'do you have anyone within the area near Miss Bloomfield's hotel?'

'The Orion? Better than that. I know the manager.'

'You *know* the manager?'

'Of course.'

'Of course. I should have known. So how come?'

'A long story. Too long for now.'

'I'm looking forward to hearing it,' Müller remarked dryly.

'And what do you want me to do?'

'Contact your . . . friend, and ask him . . .'

'Her . . .'

Müller glanced patiently upwards. 'Ask *her* . . . how many exits there are in the hotel.'

'Just that?'

'Just that.'

'OK.' Pappenheim sounded uncertain. 'Consider it done.'

'Thanks, Pappi.' Müller hung up before Pappenheim could say more.

Less than five minutes later, Pappenheim was back on the line. 'Seven,' he said, 'including the main entrance, the kitchens, and the underground garage. Three of the exits are on the same side street. Does that help? Shall I have all seven watched?'

'Just the three on the side street. Who can you get there in time?'

'Reimer. Miss Bloomfield has never seen him, and he looks like a computer nerd. She won't give him a second look. There's a small café right across the street. He can be there in time.'

'Alright. Put Reimer on it.'

'Done,' Pappenheim said. 'Should he follow?'

'Absolutely not.'

'OK.' Pappenheim again sounded uncertain, and seemed to be waiting for an explanation.

But all Müller said was, 'Thanks, Pappi,' before hanging up.

In his own office, Pappenheim stared at the phone before putting it down.

'As you wish,' he said.

Carey Bloomfield went straight to her room at the Orion, packed a small bag, into which she also put a laptop computer, then went straight out again, using one of the exits that opened out on to the side street. She spotted Reimer immediately. She crossed the street, and went directly to his table.

'Hi,' she greeted in English and with a bright smile. 'I'm impressed. I know *Hauptkommissar* Müller's missing me already, but tell him I won't be long. Really.' The smile widened as Reimer stared at her dumbfounded. 'I'm going for a taxi. Do you want to follow? Or you can come with me, if you like. No? Fine. See you later.' She gave him her brightest smile, and walked away down the street.

Reimer put down the newspaper he'd been pretending to read in disgust.

'Shit,' he said to himself, and tried not to think of what Pappenheim would say to him when he reported back.

Carey Bloomfield's taxi took fifteen minutes via a round-about route she indicated to the driver, to stop a street away from the office building she was going to. She waited a full minute after the taxi had gone before continuing on to her destination. She had gambled that her bold move to the man positioned in the café to watch her would confuse him sufficiently to prevent him from following; or that he had not been ordered to follow. In any case, she had decided to take no chances and, as a precaution, had instructed the taxi driver accordingly.

When she got to the building, she went up to the top floor. The sign for the suite of offices identified them as belonging to the *Weekly Courier*, Berlin Office. It was not the name that was on the business card she had given to Kaltendorf.

'Hi, Miss Bloomfield,' she was greeted in English by the receptionist. 'Good to see you again.'

'Hi, Gloria. Enjoying Berlin?'

'After two months it still feels strange to be in East Germany.'

'Not East Germany any more, Gloria.'

'Politically perhaps; but it feels kind of . . . uneasy and . . . schizophrenic. You know what I mean?'

'I think I know exactly what you mean. Is he in?' Carey Bloomfield added.

'Arrived fifteen minutes ago. He's waiting. Go right in.'

'OK. Thanks, Gloria.'

'You're welcome.'

She went past the big, curved art deco desk and along a corridor that eventually stopped at a mahogany door. There was no sign upon it. She knocked; once.

'It's open!' a voice called from within.

'Gloria warned me you were on your way,' a tall greying man said, rising from behind his desk as she entered and closed the door behind her. This was not his usual office, nor even the building it was in. 'Good to see you again, Carey.' He came forward to give her a quick embrace.

'Toby. Where was it last time? Tel Aviv?'

'Tel Aviv it was. Four years, two months, ten days, and counting.' His smile had the fondness of a benign uncle.

'Still in one piece, I see,' she said.

'All in one piece. And you . . . you're looking as good as ever.'

She smiled. 'Flattery, as usual, will get you everywhere.'

'No flattery. The truth. The stateside message said to expect you,' he continued, 'and to give you every assistance, at any time. Name it.'

'Just be there if I should need you; and stall any enquiries that might be made about me, long enough for my purposes.'

'That goes without question.'

'Which is all I need to know. Not much time to reminisce today, Toby. I've got to get back and I'm probably being watched; although I've cleared my tail pretty well for now. This is just to touch base.'

Toby Adams nodded. 'Understood. Have you got your policeman?'

'I could not have worked it better. He's a smart cop, so don't underestimate him. I was assigned to him by his own boss, without my asking. There's a needle between him and the boss-man.'

'Always useful, as we both know.'

'We do indeed.'

'What if he finds out who . . . *what* you really are?'

'If I do this right – and I intend to – I'll be long gone by the time he finds out.'

'I hope so,' Adams said.

'Don't look so worried, Toby. I'll be fine.'

'Just be careful. Don't push the limit.'

'I'll watch it.'

'You do that. I have an aversion to body bags.'

'Me too . . . me too. Okay, Toby. Gotta go.'

They embraced quickly once more and she went out, leaving him watching her exit anxiously.

Reimer, meanwhile, was receiving an earful from Pappenheim. Bravely, he had decided to face the music in person, instead of simply calling in.

'*She spotted you*?' Pappenheim spoke softly and somehow that made it even worse. His eyes, baby blue, were fastened upon Reimer and seemed remarkably clear, despite the wreath of cigarette smoke veiling them.

'Sorry, sir.'

'*Sorry*? That should make me feel better?'

'No, sir.'

'You're one of the best we have, Reimer,' Pappenheim said, relenting slightly. 'What the hell happened?'

'She came right out of the middle exit and walked straight up to me. No hesitation. She *knew*.'

'You gave no sign?'

Reimer looked pained, as if asking how could Pappenheim think it. Reimer had an impressive record of undercover work.

'No sign,' he replied firmly. 'I wasn't even looking in her direction. I scanned the street at irregular intervals, making certain I was not caught looking when one of the doors opened. Out of the corner of my eye, I saw the door move and was already looking at the paper long before she appeared. I even turned the pages normally, in case her room overlooked the street and she looked out to check.'

'She may have paused behind the door to check if anyone was watching.'

Reimer shook his head. 'Where I was positioned, I could

see right through. I would have spotted her if she had been standing there. She came straight out. There was nothing about me to give her warning. Besides, I was one of many people sitting there. Then she gave me that message for the boss.'

Pappenheim sighed. 'And she even suggested you come with her.'

'Yes, sir.'

'Sense of humour like acid.'

'Yes, sir.'

'This means we can't use you again to watch her, now that she's spotted you.'

'Yes, sir.'

'How does that make you feel, Reimer?'

'Like shit, sir.'

'Alright. Off you go.'

'Sir.'

'Oh, Johann.'

Reimer stopped.

'My bark is always worse than my bite,' Pappenheim said, drawing deeply on his cigarette. 'You know that.'

Reimer smiled ruefully. 'No it isn't, but thanks.' He knew it was Pappenheim's way of apologizing.

Pappenheim gave a single nod to show the tenseness of the atmosphere had passed.

Reimer was relieved to get out of there.

About 150 km south of Berlin, well out of the state of Brandenburg and deep into Sachsen-Anhalt, Megan Childes and Daniel Thompson were approaching their rendezvous. Thompson pulled off the Autobahn and into the service station area. First he stopped at the pumps and filled the tank, then he drove slowly towards the restaurant complex and parked the Corvette nose-on, next to a silver-grey Jeep Cherokee with Hamburg plates.

They climbed out and went up the short flight of steps to the restaurant. Inside, they saw a black man and a blonde woman sitting at a table in the no-smoking area. The woman wore her hair in a fashion similar to Megan's. In front of the couple were half-eaten slices of cake on small plates, and two cups of partly drunk coffee. A set of car keys was next to the man's plate. There were two empty chairs on either side of the table.

Thompson and Megan went up to them.

'Are these free?' she asked in German, pointing to the chairs.

The man looked up, smiled, and waved a hand at the chairs. 'Oh. Yes. We are just about to leave, anyway.' His German was good, but there was the hint of an American accent.

'Thank you.'

Megan and Thompson sat down. Thompson placed the Corvette keys next to the other set, and both he and Megan each picked up a menu. No one looked at the keys.

Presently, the other couple stood up. The man picked up the keys to the Corvette.

'Time to go,' he said. 'Have a nice trip.'

'You too,' both Thompson and Megan said together.

The woman smiled and said nothing as she followed her partner out.

Thompson glanced at the keys the man had left. The leather tag had a Mercedes badge, and the licence plate number was on it.

Outside, the man and the woman got into the Corvette and moved off in loose convoy, leading the Cherokee out on to the Autobahn. The Cherokee did not stay close enough to make it obvious that the two vehicles were travelling together, but it remained within visual range. Their planned route would take them off the Autobahn at the Halle exit and on to the *Bundesstrasse* 100; but before reaching Halle itself they would join the A14, to head northwards in the direction of Magdeburg.

'Hope those flyboys enjoy the trip to wherever those guys lead them,' Thompson said. 'We'll stay here for about twenty minutes.' Neither of them had looked out to check the Corvette's departure. 'Give them time to get well away from this place.'

She nodded. 'I'd like some cake, anyway. And don't say I'll get fat.'

'I'm not suicidal,' he said.

She gave his shoulder a playful smack.

The waitress came to their table and Megan ordered Black Forest cake and coffee. Thompson ordered just coffee. When their order was delivered, the cake was a very generous slice. Thompson stared at it.

She pointed her fork at him. 'If you say just one word.'

Thompson said nothing.

She paused, fork hovering over the cake. 'I just like the stuff. OK?'

'OK.'

The required twenty minutes was spent unhurriedly, then he pushed the keys towards her. 'You drive.'

'That's brave,' she said.

'I trust your driving. And besides, switching drivers confuses observation . . . especially when there's only time for a fast look.'

'And I thought you were so looking forward to being driven by me.' She stood up. 'Freshen-up time.'

When she returned, her hair was now brushed down and gleamed about her shoulders. The blue-green eyes seemed bigger somehow. He looked at her approvingly.

'Confusing the observation even more,' she explained; but she had clearly enjoyed the way he had looked at her.

'It works,' he said.

He got to his feet as the waitress came to the table, and paid the bill. As she was about to return his change, he waved it away. The tip was generous enough for the woman, from somewhere in eastern Europe, to thank him profusely.

'That was a big tip for a piece of cake and two cups of coffee,' Megan said as they left the restaurant.

'It's not going to break the bank, and her life can't be very pleasant in Germany right now.' He felt some solidarity with the woman.

'You're right about that for sure,' Megan agreed, remembering their earlier incident in Berlin. 'No chopper,' she added, glancing at the sky as they paused on the steps to check out the parked cars. 'The decoy seems to have worked too. Now I wonder what they left us as replacement for the Vette.'

'There,' he said 'The Merc by that blue Fiat coupé. It's got the numbers on the key tag, starting with GL. Where the hell's GL anyway?' he added to himself.

'Ooh yeah,' she said, looking at the car in question. 'I like. Neat job. No changing your mind now. I drive.'

'You drive. Nice car, though.'

'Tough,' she said, grinning at him in triumph. 'And GL, by the way, is Bergisch Gladbach . . . up near Cologne.'

He stared at her as they went up to the dark-grey metallic coupé, a CLK 320 Kompressor with fat wheels. 'And how do *you* know that?'

'Misspent youth. When I was a kid, my dad was stationed over here. He used to try to keep me from being bored on long Autobahn drives by making me guess the number plates. I got to know nearly all, especially the obscure ones; then I bet the kids at school. No one ever beat me. I made lots of dough from that.'

'You're kidding.'

'I never kid about money.'

'Jesus,' he said. 'You learn something new every day about someone you think you know.'

'It would be boring to know *everything*.'

They reached the car and entered. It smelled of new leather.

'You're not going to get your hands on this before we get to base,' Megan said to Thompson, briefly stroking the steering wheel. She started the engine. It growled powerfully. 'Definitely not,' she added, and reversed out of the parking slot. 'Definitely not.'

'OK, OK,' he said. 'I've got the message. No one's going to take it away from you.'

'Hah!' she countered, knowing he really wanted to drive it.

They rejoined the Autobahn and continued south at speed, Megan revelling in the car's surging power. Before long, they would be crossing into Thuringen. The shadowing helicopter was a long way north, keeping tabs on the open Corvette.

Which was the information that Pappenheim received. He put down the phone he'd been using and picked up another. It gave him direct access to Müller.

'They're approaching Magdeburg,' he said when Müller had answered.

'Magdeburg? Almost all the way to Halle, and back up again? Why the long detour?'

'Lost?' Pappenheim suggested dryly.

'Pappi . . .' Müller began warningly.

'Leading us a dance?' Pappenheim suggested quickly, this time without the humour.

'Most likely. But if so, why? And why still no attempt to evade?'

'They did stop at that *Tankstelle*.'

The way Pappenheim had spoken made Müller pause. 'A switch?'

'Perhaps. But it's the same car, and the same people. The chopper boys confirm the licence plate. München.'

'A hired car, perhaps?'

'Being checked; but probably not. Most hired sports cars are European, unless you go to the specialized companies. Of course, many of the American military like to have their Corvettes, Mustangs, and Firebirds.'

'So we're back to the military suggestion.'

'That's all it is, for now.'

'I am not happy about this, Pappi.'

'God didn't put you here to be happy.'

'Thanks for nothing.'

'Telling it like it is, as the Amis would say. One other thing,' Pappenheim went on. 'The guys in the chopper think the Corvette is possible being followed. But they're not certain.'

'Being followed by what?'

'A Jeep Cherokee, they think. It's not close enough to be obvious, but they have a feeling about it.'

'How far from the Corvette?'

'Sometimes a kilometre . . . sometimes two to three.'

'It may just be going the same way. On that basis, any number of cars could be tagging them.'

'Just an idea.'

Müller always took Pappenheim's *ideas* seriously. 'Alright. Tell them to keep an eye on the Cherokee as well.'

'I already have.'

Müller smiled to himself. He'd expected to hear Pappenheim say just that. 'Let us suppose there was a switch, Pappi . . . the only opportunity must have been at the *Tankstelle*, as it's the only time they were observed to stop.'

'Unless they did it before we got the chopper up.'

'Possibly, but I don't think so. They needed time to organize it. Whatever they were up to, they were not expecting those morons to attack them. So they had to improvise.'

'This could mean that two other people who look like them are driving their car, leading the chopper away, while they continue to their original destination in another car . . .'

'Which we won't find . . . for now.'

'No point in your following then.'

'Even more reason to do so. Those two intrigue me.'

'You may be getting into something deeper than what's in that file.'

'I'm already there. As you said so nicely, the Great White does not love me. I am certain he hopes I'll get so deep, I'll drown . . . or be buried.'

'We can stop the Corvette and at least be sure of something, whatever it turns out to be.'

'No. Let them run their course. Plenty of time yet. Just don't let them disappear as well, if they *are* decoys.'

On the Autobahn, still heading southwards, the Mercedes came to a long stretch that was free of traffic. It was, for the moment, the only car travelling in that direction; and traffic on the opposite carriageway was temporarily so light, it appeared virtually non-existent.

Megan Childes did something extraordinary. She whipped off her rich blonde tresses in a single swift motion to reveal equally rich, but red hair, cropped short.

'If you wouldn't mind putting that into my bag,' she said, handing the wig to Thompson. 'Sorry to lose the blonde bimbo,' she went on as he complied. 'I know you liked her.'

'I like the red hair too, Captain.'

'Why thank you, Major, sir.'

They smiled fleetingly at each other.

The Mercedes continued to head south at speed.

Carey Bloomfield returned to Müller's office at precisely one minute before her hour was up.

'What?' she began as Müller looked up expressionlessly from his desk. 'No Berger?' The red file and the photographs, she noticed, were no longer there.

'You *have* been busy,' Müller said, ignoring the question. 'Going for walks instead of packing your toothbrush. Thanks for the message,' he added with some irony. 'Reimer delivered it.'

She pointed at the small bag she had brought with her. 'My toothbrush.'

He didn't even look at it. 'Do you have reason to evade the police?'

'Do you have reason to have me followed?' she countered.

'I'm a policeman. It's my job.'

'To have people followed?'

38

'If my policeman's instincts tell me to . . . yes.'

'I'm a reporter,' she said. 'Evading the police is sometimes part of *my* job. In some of the places I've been, where the difference between police and criminal is so thin you couldn't pass a wafer through, it's the key to survival.'

'The whole world knows of such places. Berlin isn't one of them . . .'

'Once, it was.'

'I am sorry I cannot indulge your fantasies, Miss Bloomfield. This is not the Berlin of the forties, and my name is not Heinrich—'

'—Müller, Gestapo chief.'

'You know your facts.'

'I do my research.'

'And do you believe the days of Gestapo Müller have returned . . . or are about to?' He sounded as if he thought she had taken leave of her senses.

'You tell me.'

His eyes studied her carefully. She was, as Pappenheim had unashamedly indicated, an extraordinarily good-looking woman. Not pretty in the obvious sense, she possessed a beauty that required a certain degree of perception to appreciate it. When that perception hit the mark, the result was an astonishing revelation.

Deep brown eyes; gleaming dark hair, cut to just past her ears, that appeared to float briefly upwards, whenever she moved her head; strong, naturally crescent-shaped eyebrows, so dark they seemed etched upon her skin; a slim yet fully curved body; loose white shirt and blue jeans; lightweight black leather jacket; and black trainers on her feet.

The deep brown eyes looked right back at him. 'Like what you see? Or are you studying a suspect?'

'Why should I suspect you of anything?'

'Why haven't you answered my question?'

'Which one?'

'About Berlin. *You tell me*, I said. But I'll answer, if you won't. Just over ten years ago, this part of Berlin was in the

39

East. After the Second World War, it went from one police state straight into another without pausing for breath. This building we're in is younger than my nephew, and he's just three. When you united East with West, you imported a political and social virus. The evidence is in that file you didn't want me to see.'

'Neat encapsulation, but that still does not make Berlin a reincarnated police state.'

'Perhaps. But it has all the makings, if you don't stay awake. You're not going to persuade me that people who were happy to shoot their own when they tried to escape, or who built minefields, a wall, and barbed wire in the middle of a city – who *informed* on each other, for God's sake – have suddenly joined the so-called civilized section of the human race. I'll bet some of the informers you use today once informed for the Stasi in the bad old days. There are many old scores to settle. It takes more than a few years . . .'

'There are no former members of the East German police in this unit.'

'What about former East Germans?'

'The few we do have were too young—'

'Like those in the photographs? *Kids* used to inform—'

'No, Miss Bloomfield,' Müller replied patiently. 'Not at all like those in the photographs. Our personnel have been through very exhaustive psychological tests. Anyone with extremist tendencies – right or left – is spotted very early. No one can fake their way through them.'

'Oh come on, Jens Müller, Graf von Röhnen. The really smart ones can fake through any test . . .'

His astonishment was genuine as stared at her. 'You *know* my full name?'

'As I said before, I always do my research. I know more than you think. A blue-blood masquerading as an ordinary man; a cop at that.'

'It's no masquerade. I believe in what I am doing.'

'Quit while you're ahead, Müller. Where are we going, anyway?'

Despite himself, Müller smiled ruefully. 'You have nicely turned the tables, Miss Bloomfield . . . for now. I am still interested in knowing where you went. But we shall leave that for the time being. As for the really smart ones, *they* are too smart to be extremists . . .'

'Of course they are. They're very good at hiding in the woodwork. Those who want to control the mob always *are* smart enough; smart enough, at least, to fool those dumb enough to be willing cannon fodder, and too dumb to know better . . .'

'And as for your latest question,' Müller continued in his patient manner, rising to his feet, 'we're going after two suspects. Americans.' His smile widened. 'Shall we go? My things are already in the car. I'll introduce you to Pappenheim on the way.'

He went to the door and opened it for her. This time, she was the one with the expression of surprise. He enjoyed that.

In the event, there was no need to go to Pappenheim's office, for they saw him coming towards them in a corridor. He was not smoking. This was a great sacrifice on his part; but the large number of red circles with a diagonal bar across a graphic of a lighted cigarette adorning the walls gave the answer. Kaltendorf's decree made every corridor in the building a smoke-free zone.

Pappenheim walked with an economy of movement that clearly indicated his potential for swift reaction.

'Pappi,' Müller began as his deputy came to a halt before them. 'Miss Carey Bloomfield, journalist from New York. She is here to research the history of the Berlin police.'

Pappenheim smiled at her as if he had never heard of her before and held out a welcoming hand and shook hers warmly. 'A great pleasure, Miss Bloomfield. You will write good things about us, I hope. Jens will look after you well; but if he doesn't, come to me.'

He grinned at Müller, who, out of Carey Bloomfield's eyeshot, glanced heavenwards at Pappenheim's shamelessness.

'I'll take the invitation seriously,' she said. 'Thank you.'

'Any time at all.' Pappenheim beamed at her. 'I'll make him jealous,' he added, glancing at Müller's pained expression.

'Let go of her hand, Pappi,' Müller said firmly. 'We've got to go.'

'Do you see, Miss Bloomfield? Jealous.'

'Evidently,' she agreed, playing along.

Pappenheim released her hand reluctantly. 'Don't let him lead you astray.'

'I won't.'

Pappenheim gave her a slight nod and walked on, after a sly glance at Müller.

'I like him,' she said as she and Müller continued along the corridor.

'Everyone likes Pappi.'

'Except your boss.'

'There's always an exception.'

'But I don't trust him.'

'My boss?'

'Pappi.'

Müller glanced at her.

'I didn't just arrive in the big city from hicktown, Müller,' she told him dryly. 'I didn't fall for that smooth talk, and he knew it. You saw one operator talking to another.'

'Then I'm the innocent around here.'

'Sure. And snowballs make good hamburgers. Come show me your car. This I've got to see.'

At the end of the corridor were the sliding double doors of a lift. They slid open just as Müller and Carey Bloomfield arrived. Two women in jeans and loose t-shirts got out. Each had a jacket slung over a shoulder; each wore a pistol in an underarm holster. They smiled broadly at Müller.

'Girlfriends?' Carey Bloomfield's question was mildly barbed.

'Police officers,' Müller corrected.

'Sure.'

They entered the lift. The doors began to slide shut; but

not before Kaltendorf, coming from one of the doors in the corridor, spotted them.

'Ah, Müller!' he called.

'Shit!' Müller swore softly.

He was about to press the button that would halt the sliding of the doors, then decided against it. They hissed shut.

'*Müller*!' came Kaltendorf's outraged voice faintly, accompanied by heavy banging as the senior policeman slammed his fists against the doors.

Then the lift began to descend.

Carey Bloomfield looked at Müller. 'You'll be a popular man.'

'I can live with it.'

'You enjoy being the bad boy.'

'It's not a question of enjoying. Kaltendorf is . . .' Müller paused, looking at her. 'I must remember you're a journalist.'

'As if you'll forget. OK. Don't tell me. I'll switch subjects. Let me guess the kind of car you drive.'

'Does your mind ever pause?'

'Never.'

'I am duly warned.'

'So? Do I guess your car?'

'Please go on,' he said.

'You're wearing an Italian suit, but I don't see you as a Ferrari man. Are you rich enough for a Ferrari?'

'You tell me.'

'Throwing my words back at me? OK. Not a Ferrari. Not a Bimmer, either.'

Müller listened to all this with an amused expression, and said nothing.

'So,' she continued, 'we have a rich cop . . . insubordinate . . . well, your boss clearly thinks so. Rich cop, unconventional, what would he buy? Either a car that looks like an old garbage truck, or some kind of super sports car. To needle your boss, you would buy the sports car. Definitely not a fancy sedan.'

'Are you quite finished?'

'Am I right, or what?'

The lift halted at the underground garage.

'We're there,' Müller said. 'Time to find out. And for your information, I never buy a car for any other reason except that *I* like it.'

The doors slid open. The lights in the garage came on automatically.

'It's the sports car, right?' she persisted as he stood back for her to get out.

'You'll see,' he said, following. The doors slid shut behind them. 'But we should hurry. I would not be surprised if Kaltendorf is after us. I am not in the mood for a stupid argument with him. Come on.'

They hastened to where his car was parked. She stopped to stare when she saw the gleaming, seal-grey metallic Porsche Turbo. 'Well . . . if you're going to buy a sports car . . . you buy a sports car. It looks ready to fly. Is it new?'

'It is.' Müller held the passenger door open. The smell of expensive leather wafted out. 'Please get in,' he urged. 'I am sure Kaltendorf is on his way.'

She climbed in. 'Even I can appreciate this,' she said, looking around the car.

Müller squeezed the door shut, went quickly round to the driver's side, and climbed in. 'Put on your seat belt.' He started the car. The powerful boxer engine roared challengingly within the confines of the garage. 'And here he comes.'

They were moving just as Kaltendorf, too late to stop them, seemed to erupt from the doors of a second lift, arms waving furiously, mouth open in an unheard shout.

Three

K altendorf barged into Pappenheim's office, fury rising
by the second.

'Pappenheim!' he barked. 'Are you in contact with Müller?'

Pappenheim, squinting at his superior through a veil of
smoke, remained seated. 'Not at this moment, sir. No.'

'Don't play any of your word games with me, Pappenheim!'
Kaltendorf snarled. 'I want an answer!'

'I gave you one, sir,' Pappenheim replied calmly. 'I am
not in contact with him.' He spoke the words carefully, as
if to a child having difficulty in understanding. 'He went out
with Miss Bloomfield. He is following the suspects, and I am
certain he will call in when he needs to. And if you remember,
sir, you ordered him to look after Miss Bloomfield . . .'

Kaltendorf was turning a perilously sick tinge of purple by
this time. 'Don't tell me what I order and whom I order! I am
perfectly capable of remembering my own commands! And
at least put out that damned cigarette when I am in here!'

Pappenheim, who had not even removed the cigarette from
his mouth when Kaltendorf had entered, now put it out with
uncharacteristic obedience. It was only half smoked.

'As you wish, sir,' he said in the same calm voice.

This did not totally satisfy Kaltendorf, who suspected
Pappenheim was only humouring him.

'Why is Müller following the suspects?' he snapped,
waving exaggeratedly at the tendrils of smoke that had
drifted his way. 'He can have them stopped.'

'The *Hauptkommissar* does not believe this is the correct thing to do at this time. He has his way of working, sir, as you know.'

'I know it!' Kaltendorf raged. He made it sound like a curse. 'You and Müller may believe you're fireproof . . . but you're *not*!'

He stormed out of Pappenheim's office, slamming the door shut.

Pappenheim looked at the stubbed-out cigarette and sighed. 'Definitely losing it, that man. Waste of a good smoke.'

He lit another, and inhaled thankfully.

Müller's Porsche had all the trimmings and 420 bhp of boxer motor was propelling it at seemingly rocket-like velocity along the southbound A9 Autobahn. Santana's singing guitar in 'Smooth' was on the CD player, and pouring out through ten speakers. Carey Bloomfield relaxed in her seat, eyes closed.

Müller glanced at her, and turned the music down.

'Don't do that,' she said, eyes still closed. 'I was listening.'

'I thought you were asleep, and did not wish to disturb you. You either feel safe with my driving, or you're too frightened to look.'

'I feel perfectly safe, and I wasn't asleep. I was listening to the engine, and to the music. Turn it up again.'

'To hear is to obey,' he said, and turned up the music. 'But we'll be stopping soon. We'll be at the *Tankstelle* in about twenty kilometres.'

She glanced as an Autobahn sign, indicating Dessau, flitted by. 'There's a town that will go down in history for all the wrong reasons.'

'Too many towns and cities in the new *Länder* are becoming famous for all the wrong reasons,' Müller said. 'It is not a happy thought.'

The Porsche and Santana's guitar sang their way to the service station.

At 15.30 and exactly twelve hours after the killings, Müller pulled off the Autobahn and into the service station where Daniel Thompson and Megan Childes had refuelled their Corvette. He stopped at a pump, did likewise to the Porsche, then was about to go off to pay when he paused to open the driver's door.

He poked his head into the car. 'Please wait here while I go to pay,' he said to Carey Bloomfield.

She made a great play of looking about her. 'I always run off at gas stations.'

He ignored the sarcasm. 'You know exactly what I mean.' He withdrew, shut the door, then went off to pay for the fuel, knowing she was following him with her eyes.

He entered the shop. Only one of the two cash desks was occupied, and this had a queue of four customers. Other people were checking out maps and choosing packets of sweets and bottles of soft drinks or water for their onward journey. He patiently waited until all had left, before going up to the cashier.

He paid for the fuel, then quickly showed the man his ID.

'*Hauptkommissar* Müller,' he began. 'Were you here this morning?'

The man, in his late twenties, nodded. 'Since eight.'

'Did you serve a couple in a red Corvette?'

'Couldn't miss it,' the man replied. 'Just like your Porsche. It stood out.' He looked in the direction of Müller's car, noting the bright yellow brake calipers. 'Ceramic brakes too. They must pay the police well,' he went on, turning back to Müller. 'I'm in the wrong job. Have you any idea how many hours—'

'I could stand here and swap stories about long hours with you all day,' Müller cut in firmly, 'but neither of us has the time. Please tell me about the Corvette.'

'Couldn't miss it, as I said,' the cashier remarked, a little miffed that Müller had cut him short. 'A black man and a blonde woman. The black man was the driver. It's all on the security cameras if you need—'

Again, Müller cut him short. 'Thank you, Herr . . .'

'Graumann. Helmut Graumann.'

'Thank you, Herr Graumann. If we need it, we'll definitely be in touch. Meanwhile, can you tell me what happened next?'

'Not in trouble, is he? He was a nice guy. I have nothing against black people, you know . . .'

'No one is saying you have, Herr Graumann.'

'Terrible things that are happening. Bad for the name of Germany . . .'

'I happen to agree with you, Herr Graumann, but please, can we continue?'

'Oh. Yes. They went to the restaurant.'

'Are you certain?'

'Of course. I went out to look. I love American sports cars, you see. I have a Mustang just like the one in *Bullitt*. Worked on it for years. Just me. Now, it's like new, engine chromed and everything. I've got it parked if you want to see . . .'

'Herr Graumann, *please*.'

'Yes. Well. My colleague, Frau Nassim, was at the other cash desk and, as there was only one customer, I went out to have a look. That's how I saw the Corvette stop in front of the restaurant. It made a great sound when it moved. Powerful V8—'

'Thank you very much, Herr Graumann. You have been very helpful. If we need your cameras, someone will definitely be in touch.'

'Always happy to help the police.' Graumann, still miffed that his narratives had been interrupted, decided to add a barb. 'Even those who drive Porsches.'

Müller smiled at him, and left.

He was still smiling when he entered the car. He started it and blipped the engine loudly as he moved off.

'A joke I should know about?' Carey Bloomfield suggested. 'And if we're about to take off, I don't think the runway's long enough.'

'He likes the sound of sports cars,' Müller explained.

'Who?'

'The man at the cash desk. He particularly likes *American* sports cars.'

'A discerning man.'

'He's something.'

Müller pulled into a parking space in front of the restaurant.

'We're stopping to eat?' Carey Bloomfield said eagerly. 'Great. I'm starved.'

'I'm stopping to investigate. You can eat.'

'You say such nice things, Müller. At least this time you're not going to leave me in the car like some weak tit of a woman while you go about man's work. Can I watch you carry out an interview this time?'

'You're upset because I talked to the man in the *Tankstelle* without your being there to watch?' he asked in disbelief as he switched off.

'I'm supposed to watch you work, remember? What would your boss say?'

'It's no use trying to threaten me with Kaltendorf. You know it won't work. Nothing you could tell him can make me look worse in his eyes. To him, I am a lost cause.' He got out of the car. 'Coming?'

She got out and he secured the Turbo with the remote.

'What do you expect to find?' she asked as they walked the short distance to the restaurant.

'I'll know when I find it,' he replied mysteriously.

She said nothing as they climbed the steps that Thompson and Megan Childes had trodden that morning.

They entered the restaurant and took a table with a window view, in the no-smoking area.

'Feel free to order anything you want,' he said to her.

'I shall,' she said, scanning the menu. 'I'd like a good salad, if I can find one. Ah. This looks OK. Well . . . sort of . . .'

'Americans,' a voice said in English. A waitress was smiling down at them.

'I am,' Carey Bloomfield said. 'He isn't.'

'Were Americans in here today?' Müller asked in German.

'Yes. Four of them. Over there.' The waitress had switched to German and helpfully pointed to where Thompson and Megan Childes had been sitting, three tables away.

'Did you serve them?'

'Not me. My colleague.' The waitress frowned, distancing herself. 'Why do you want to know?'

Müller did the swift ID-showing routine. 'Müller. *Hauptkommissar*. Where is your colleague now?'

'She is finished for the day and is getting ready to leave . . .'

'Please ask her to stop. I must speak with her.'

The waitress looked uncertain.

'This is serious police business,' Müller said firmly.

The tone of his voice galvanized her. 'I'll . . . I'll go right away.'

'Thank you.'

'Shall I ask her to come here?'

'No. We'll do this without fuss. I will see her in an office. Tell your manager.'

'Yes. Yes.' The waitress hurried off.

'You frightened her,' Carey Bloomfield accused.

'I did not. I was very gentle.'

'If you say so.' She was glancing around and paused when she saw the sign for the toilets. 'I won't be long,' she said, getting to her feet. 'Don't conduct that interview without me.'

'Then you should hurry.' He smiled at her.

'I don't trust that smile. I'll hurry.'

As she left, it was not the waitress who returned but the manager.

'*Hauptkommissar* Müller,' the man began quietly, clearly not wanting the other customers to know. 'I am Karl Dacher, the manager. Is there some trouble?'

'No trouble at all, Herr Dacher. I simply wish to speak with the person who served some people this morning.'

Dacher nodded quickly, eager to please. 'That will be Fatima. She is ready and in my office. Please follow me.'

Müller stood up. 'When my companion returns, please have her shown to your office.'

'Of course.'

They went to the back of the restaurant, where the manager had his office. The woman who had served Thompson and Megan Childe was there, perched, rather than sitting, on a chair, looking anxious, hands tightly clasped between her knees. She wore olive-green trousers with a matching jacket over a thin beige sweater. Her deep-black hair was tied tightly into a bun. Open-toed, low-heeled shoes were on her feet. Dark eyes looked uncertainly at Müller.

'Please don't look so worried,' Müller said immediately, to put her at ease. 'I'll be as quick about this as possible. Alright?'

She nodded and smiled hesitantly, but didn't relax.

Müller turned to the manager. 'I'd like to do this in private, if you wouldn't mind. I shall observe her rights.'

Dacher clearly minded, but Müller's look was unambiguous. The manager got the message.

'Of course,' Dacher said reluctantly and left, closing the door quietly behind him.

'Alright, Fatima. Please relax. So, you served those people this morning?'

She nodded once more, settling a little more comfortably on her chair. 'They were very nice people. Two black men, and two blonde women . . .'

'*Two* of each?'

'Yes, *Hauptkommissar*. The first two were already here. Then the other two joined them at their table. They didn't seem to know each other, because they asked if they could sit. Then they just talked a little, and the ones who were here before left.' Fatima, a little more at ease, had now unclasped her hands.

'Was this a long time after the others arrived?'

She shook her head. 'No. They had already finished, so they didn't stay long.'

Müller understood exactly how the switch had taken place.

'Now, think very carefully,' he said to her encouragingly. 'Did you see what car the second couple drove?'

'I didn't see when they arrived, but I saw them leave.'

Müller gave no indication of the excitement he felt. 'Why were you able to see them leave?'

'The man was very kind. He gave me a big tip. I was curious to see what he was driving. Sometimes, those who give the worst tips drive the most expensive cars. People with the smaller cars seem to be more sympathetic, as if they appreciate what this kind of work really means.'

On such small things . . . Müller thought ironically, restraining the wry smile he felt coming. 'Can you think of anything else about them that took your interest? It does not matter how unimportant you may think it is.'

'Well . . . the second blonde woman went to the toilets. Her hair was tied up when she went in. When she came back, it was brushed down to her shoulders . . .'

Just then, someone knocked.

'Enter,' he said.

The restaurant manager, looking hopeful, pushed the door open to let Carey Bloomfield in. Müller did not realize the manager's hope.

'Thanks for waiting,' she said to Müller pointedly in English, when the disappointed manager had shut the door again.

'I did say you should hurry,' he reminded her in the same language. 'I have some interesting information. I shall tell you later.'

'All of it?'

'What I think is necessary.'

'No surprise there.'

'May I now continue?' Müller asked patiently. 'This young woman has to leave and I don't want to delay her any longer than is necessary.'

'Of course.'

'Thank you. Now, Fatima,' Müller continued in German. 'What car did you see?'

'I went to the steps to look,' Fatima went on, 'expecting something like a Polo . . . you know . . . the size of the tip . . .'

Müller nodded. 'I quite understand.'

'Well . . . it was a surprise . . . A big, dark car. Grey but shining . . .'

'Metallic?'

Again, Fatima nodded. 'Yes. Like that.'

'You are *very* sure?'

'Oh yes. And it was a Mercedes.'

'A Mercedes, dark-grey, metallic,' Müller remarked softly. 'Please tell me more about it. Did it have two doors on each side? Or was it a coupé, with one on each?'

'A coupé. Definitely. I remember thinking it was very beautiful, with big fat wheels.'

'Big fat wheels? Are you a fan of sporting cars?'

Fatima shook her head. 'My younger brother is always going on about such cars. He wants to own one when he is old enough to drive. He has many pictures on the walls of his room. The Mercedes looked like one of those pictures . . . even the colour.'

'Finally, one last question – and I realize this may be more difficult. Did you see the number plate?'

Fatima looked disappointed, as if she had let Müller down. 'I'm sorry—'

'No matter,' Müller assured her quickly. 'You have done very well. Thank you, Fatima. You are a very good witness.'

She got to her feet, brushing down the sides of her thighs reflectively. 'They will not get into trouble, will they? The man was so nice . . . Not like some people, who behave as if you are their servant . . .'

'Don't worry. You have done nothing wrong. You may go.'

'Will you be calling me again for—'

'No, no. This is all finished. You will not see me again. Once more, thank you for your help. I do appreciate it.'

Müller opened the door for her. She gave him a warm smile as she left.

'Why do all the women smile at you?' Carey Bloomfield asked when Fatima had gone.

'I'm a nice man.'

'Hah!'

Then the manager was knocking hesitantly.

'Come in, Herr Dacher. We are finished here.'

Dacher entered, looking curious. 'Any problems?'

'None at all, Herr Dacher.'

'I'd like to eat,' Carey suggested hopefully.

'We would both like to eat now,' Müller amended to Dacher.

'Of course, of course. Please.' Dacher stood back to allow them to leave.

He accompanied them all the way back to their table and was so eager to please, he ensured Carey Bloomfield got exactly the salad she wanted.

Müller and Carey Bloomfield had finished eating and were about to pay when, in Berlin, Pappenheim stubbed out a cigarette, picked up his phone and made a call to New York. High-speed relays were silently switched through. The call went from New York to Washington, then via a secure satellite connection back to Berlin. It all took place so swiftly, there was nothing about the transmission to alert Pappenheim.

In his real Berlin office, Toby Adams picked up the call. 'Editor in Chief,' he answered in English.

'*Oberkommissar* Pappenheim calling from Berlin, Germany,' Pappenheim said, clearly fluent in the language. 'I am enquiring about someone, possibly one of your journalists, who is at the moment with us on an assignment. This is the number we have for your offices.'

'Ah, yes. You mean Carey Bloomfield. Not in trouble, is she?'

'Absolutely not. This is a routine enquiry. In our business, we have to be certain that people really are who they tell us they are. She is on research here, and this is simply a routine check of her bona fides.'

'I quite understand. Carey Bloomfield is one of our very best people, and I have every confidence in her. I assigned her to the job, so ask anything you want.'

'Not necessary, Mr . . .'

'Jameson.' Toby Adams responded smoothly. 'Paul Jameson.'

'Of course. We have your name with the information she supplied.' Pappenheim made it sound as if it had slipped his memory. 'As I was saying, Mr Jameson, it is not necessary to go further with this. I was just making sure. Blame it on being a policeman. You know how it is. Bosses to keep happy.'

Adams chuckled. 'I quite understand. Do not hesitate to call if you need anything else.'

'There won't be a need, but I thank you.'

'Then goodbye, *Oberkommissar*, and thanks for the call. Have a good day, and say hi to Carey for me.'

'I will do that. Goodbye, Mr Jameson.'

Pappenheim hung up, knowing he would say nothing of the call to Carey Bloomfield.

He put the phone down slowly. 'Neat,' he said in German. 'Very neat.'

He took a fresh cigarette out of the pack and lit it, drawing upon it as if he had not had one for days.

'Neat,' he said again, blowing a stream of fresh smoke at the ceiling.

In his office in the same city, Adams put down his own phone slowly.

'Very smart, Mr Pappenheim, but we were waiting for that one. And I'm certain you won't say a word about our conversation to Carey.'

He got up from behind his desk and went over to a large window. From eight storeys up, he looked down upon the Friedrichstrasse.

'You watch your step, kid,' he said to the distant Carey Bloomfield softly.

At about the same time, the Corvette was leading the shadowing helicopter a merry dance through the eastern German countryside. Staying off the as yet not fully constructed A14 Autobahn, the couple who now drove it had used the back roads. After refuelling at Stassfurt, they had travelled non-stop to Calbe, Aken, Zerbst, Barby, back to Calbe then up to Schönebeck, across to Wanzleben, back across the Elbe again, this time to Gommern. They still did not stop, continuing to play their game on the outskirts of Magdeburg. But their apparent aimlessness had a pre-set destination.

In the helicopter, the pilot was getting impatient. 'What the hell are they playing at?' he grumbled to his observer crewman. 'A mystery tour?' He glanced at his fuel gauge. 'We're going to have to land soon. I'm not going to crash because I've run out of fuel. I'd be grounded, assuming we survived. We need the other chopper on-station *now*. Tell base.'

'I'll tell them,' the observer said. He sounded uncertain. 'Remember Krause's ship had a problem. He's our relief.'

'Tell them anyway.'

The crewman called base and made the request.

The reply was less than welcome. 'There's still a problem. Can you wait for forty-five minutes?'

'Did you get that?' the crewman asked his pilot.

The pilot briefly tapped at once of his headphones. 'I got it. *Forty-five minutes*? Are they crazy? The engines will be sucking air by the time he gets here. What do I use for fuel? My piss?'

'So, what do we do?'

'Do? We've got just forty minutes of fuel left; enough for five more minutes on-station, and to make it back in a straight line with a small reserve for emergencies. And that's pushing our luck. We should have been relieved and back at base by now, with thirty minutes of fuel *still* on board. I'll tell you what we're going to do. We give them the five minutes, then we leave. I will not endanger my ship, and lose my licence for good measure. The regulations are clear.'

'So much for the infrared shots, if we don't know where the Corvette stops. The Berlin boys . . .'

'Fuck the Berlin boys. I'm not going to get myself killed—'

'And me.'

'—And you, for this fucking Corvette. OK. Our five minutes are up. We're going home.'

On the ground, the woman in the Corvette watched the helicopter bank away.

'There they go,' she said. 'Finally heading home for juice. I thought the damned thing would fly for ever. No relief chopper in sight as yet. This is the break we've been waiting for.'

'Right. How far to the truck?'

She consulted a folded map. 'Ten kilometres north. We'll make it.'

They had spoken in English; the man American-accented, she British.

When they got to the waiting truck, with its long pantechnicon, there was still no helicopter shadowing them. The truck, refrigerated, and with its ramp down, was deep in some woods. Next to it was the Cherokee. Three men in casual dress were there. Two by the truck, one by the Cherokee.

The couple drove the Corvette up the ramp and into the empty refrigerated container. The woman grabbed at her hair and tugged. The blonde wig came away to reveal short, dark hair. She dropped the wig into the car. They quickly climbed out of the Corvette and hurried back down the ramp, which was beginning to retract even as they ran. They jumped off, went to the Cherokee and got in. By this time, the rear doors of the truck were closing.

The Cherokee began to move. The truck was already doing so. Each went in different directions.

Throughout, no one had spoken.

The distant Carey Bloomfield, meanwhile, was walking out of the restaurant with Müller.

'My ears are itching,' she said. 'Someone's thinking about me.'

'I wonder who,' Müller said.

'Me too. Me too. Does this rocket ship use a lot of gas?' she went on as they stopped by the car. 'How much did you pay back there?'

'For the kind of power it has, it's very economical. I paid eighty marks. The tank is full. I never let it get too low.'

'You guys have seriously expensive juice.'

'We don't have your oil wells.' Müller squeezed the remote to unlock the Porsche.

'Nothing to do with oil wells. Even allowing for that, you still pay too much. If everyone decided to pay exactly what they did before a price hike, you'd soon bring it down again. No extra gas sold, no extra money made. Much better than blockading gas stations, and the effect lasts much longer. You also deny asshole politicians the opportunity of scoring points off each other for votes. You make your displeasure known with your wallet. No commercial enterprise – nor the politicians, for that matter – can resist that kind of pressure and survive. It's simple: price too high, don't buy. They all *need* your money.'

Müller stared at her. 'Did you spend the last hour thinking of this?'

'I've been doing it for years back in the States – paying the same amount for gas, I mean. When prices go up, I get a little less juice for the same money. That's for my own car, of course, not the company car.'

'Of course,' he said dryly.

'It works,' she insisted. 'Imagine the effect if a few million car owners over here did that. Imagine the *whole* of the EC. Out of three hundred and forty million people, there must be about two hundred and forty million drivers of all kinds of vehicles that need gas – at the very least. That's one hell of a market. A lot of gas not sold every day; a lot of money not made, and a lot of tax lost. You'd soon get your prices back down.'

'I get the point,' Müller said. 'But first, all car, truck, motorcycle owners and others would have to mobilize; and that won't happen. Most people are only interested in how things affect them individually. That is why demagogues can always fool them. Luckily, not all politicians are assholes . . .'

'You shouldn't be surprised just how many *are* . . .'

'I'm not. Now please get in. I have a call to make.'

'You've got that fancy all-in-one navigation and communication system in the car. Why not make it from there?'

Müller tapped at his breast pocket. 'I've got a phone here too.'

'And I get the drift. You don't want me to hear.'

'Miss Bloomfield—'

'Carey.'

'Miss Bloomfield, please get into the car.'

'Jesus! We're going to spend enough time together. Stop being so goddamned German.'

'But I *am* German.'

'Jesus!' she said again; but she entered the car.

Müller walked a little distance away, then took the slim mobile out of his pocket and quickly dialled a number.

Pappenheim answered. 'Yo, Boss.'

'And you can stop that as well,' Müller said.

'We are in a good mood. Babysitting getting you down?'

'Pappi . . .'

'OK, OK. So? Anything? The hunch work?'

'It did, and we have something.'

'Aha! That will please the Great White . . . *not*. He came in here bursting several blood vessels, the poor man. Seems you didn't stop for a chat. He wanted to pull in the Corvette. So? Are you going to tell me?'

'As soon as you stop talking.'

'Aha!' Pappenheim said again, pausing; and Müller knew he was taking a pull on a cigarette.

Müller used the pause to quickly tell him about the switch of cars and the information supplied by the man at the pumps and the waitress.

'You've done it again, Jens,' Pappenheim said when Müller had finished. 'This will eat at the Great White's guts.' He sounded as if he actually wanted to see Kaltendorf's guts being eaten. 'So, where will you be, if he asks?'

'You don't know.'

'And where will you be if *I* ask?'

'Continuing south. I want to find that grey car. We don't have the number plate, but check with the Autobahn patrol boys. You never know. They might spot it. There can't be all that many big-wheeled Mercedes coupés of that colour to choose from, in the same general area.'

'On the other hand, they could be as thick on the ground as flies up a cow's—'

'Pappi . . .'

'Got it. I've also got some news.'

'And?'

'Your passenger appears to be what she says she is.'

'Appears?'

'I called her New York office, and I got the Editor in Chief. He verifies her.'

'But something is still itching at you.'

'Yes. So far, my other sources have come up with nothing suspicious; but I'm still itchy.'

'Then keep at it, Pappi.'

'You know me. Dog with a bone. I never stop.'

'As ever. Well . . . we've got something of a trail, so I'll follow that. And don't let Kaltendorf pull in that Corvette. Not yet.'

'I'll sit on his head, if that's what it takes.'

Neither could know it was already too late.

'I'll wait to hear from you,' Pappenheim continued. 'Enjoy the babysitting.'

Pappenheim was chuckling when Müller ended the call.

Müller put the mobile back and returned to the Porsche. Carey Bloomfield was looking less than pleased.

'Don't sulk,' he said as he climbed in. He started the engine and it growled hungrily. 'It does not suit you.'

'This is not a sulk, believe you me. You're treating me like an idiotic bimbo.'

'I am most certainly not. I would never make that mistake. Others, perhaps; but not this one.'

'Should that please me?'

'I have no idea.'

Müller began to reverse out of the parking space. 'Is all this a preliminary to something else?' He stopped, slipped into first gear and began to slowly drive out of the parking area, heading for the Autobahn.

She said nothing further until they were again on the Autobahn, and at speed.

'So, where are we off to?'

'Continuing south,' he replied. 'Music?'

'Talk.'

'About what?'

'About what you haven't talked about throughout the time we were eating. For example, what the waitress said before I joined you.'

They drove on in silence for some minutes, then Müller said, 'We are following our suspects south, although the Corvette they were known to have been driving has gone north towards Magdeburg. Note, I have said *suspects*, not fugitives.'

'The Americans.'

He nodded. 'The Americans, in the Mercedes.'

'How do you know they're going south?'

'It's what I would do if I switched cars . . . and I know myself very well.'

'That still doesn't mean they're heading south.'

'That may be so; but I'm playing my hunch. I've been a policeman for perhaps too many years now,' Müller went on, 'but it never fails to amaze me how much people do actually see, even when they think they haven't. People are a living network and database . . . If they decide to talk to the police at all, that is. No wonder the Stasi tapped into it.'

'Uh-oh. Where have we heard this be-the-eyes-and-ears-of-the-state philosophy before?'

The Porsche shot past three huge, articulated, double-container trucks, which were travelling at more than 100 kph each, at the very least, as if they were standing still.

He glanced at her with a quick smile. 'Don't worry, Miss Bloomfield. I am not about to advocate a new Stasi system. I am merely pointing out how a particular method of questioning can solve many a mystery. There is always someone who has seen or heard something; just as these days there always seems to be someone, somewhere, with a video camera to record an incident when it occurs. Of course,' he added ruefully, 'not always when you really need it.'

'So, the man you spoke with in the gas station, and the waitress, both gave you enough to make you go south?'

He nodded. In short sentences, he gave her an abbreviated version of the conversations he'd had with the two at the service station. He said nothing of his call to Pappenheim.

'It's always the little things,' he went on, 'that put pieces of the puzzle into place. Who would have expected that the man at a *Tankstelle* on a Sachsen-Anhalt Autobahn would be an American sports-car freak? Or that a fat tip would make a waitress with her own philosophy about tippers take an interest in the car that her generous customer drove? That's why I love this job. You learn something new every day.'

'Doesn't everyone learn something every day?'

'No. And even if they know what is happening, they don't always learn from it; otherwise there would be no wars, no crime, and—'

'No police.'

'Exactly. But as we both know, human beings are so imperfect, there will always be work for people like me.'

'All this love-my-job earnestness . . . You're kidding me, right?'

'I'm kidding you; but the premise remains.'

'Alright. Let's assume I buy that . . . How far south do you plan to go?'

'For today, only as far as a beautiful little place I know not too far from here. It is near Saalburg on the river Saale. It's on the edge of the Thüringerwald. Very beautiful area. We'll be staying the night. I've already made arrangements.'

'And the Mercedes?'

'It will stop somewhere, for fuel at least.'

'You're very calm about it.'

'For a start,' Müller said, 'they don't know we're following. They won't try to dodge, because they think they're safe.'

'And?'

'I have a small insurance. Pappenheim has people looking.'

'So, it was Pappenheim you talked with on the cellphone,' she accused. 'But you're not going to tell me about it.'

'Would you expect me to?'

'I guess not,' Carey Bloomfield admitted.

Berlin, 17.30 hours.

Pappenheim was barking into his telephone. 'What the hell do you mean they *lost* them near Magdeburg? When did this happen?'

He paused as the person at the other end explained. He removed his cigarette and tapped it impatiently on his desk by the filtered end. A spark shot upwards and landed on a sheet of paper, which began to smoulder.

'Shit!' he exclaimed, stuck the cigarette back between his lips and brushed at the paper. 'No, no. Not you. Go on.' He paused again. 'So, they lost it nearly an *hour* ago. When did *you* get the news? Oh. Alright. Thank you, Johann. Sorry I bawled at you. I seem to be apologizing a lot to you lately. You OK? Alright. Look, get those assholes to do some work. OK. I'll talk to you later.'

Pappenheim put the phone down. '*Shit!*' he said again. 'Ran out of fucking fuel. Shit, shit, *shit!*'

He stubbed out the cigarette, and did not immediately light another.

'Trouble?'

Pappenheim looked at the door with a sinking heart. Kaltendorf, he decided, was like a shark and could smell blood at great distances.

Kaltendorf's expression as he entered showed he expected Pappenheim to lie to him. 'No cigarette. It must be big trouble.' He sounded almost gleeful.

Contrary to Kaltendorf's expectations, Pappenheim went straight to the point. 'Madgeburg.' He remained seated.

'What about Magdeburg?' Kaltendorf asked dangerously.

'They lost the Corvette,' Pappenheim answered, staring expressionlessly at his superior as a cold silence descended.

Even the residue of smoke in the room seemed to hang, unmoving, as if frozen in space forever.

'They lost the Corvette.' Kaltendorf spoke the words as if each were an entire sentence by itself. 'I did not hear that, did I? *Did I*? I just had a bad dream. That's it, isn't it?'

Pappenheim continued to stare at him, keeping his own counsel.

'No,' Kaltendorf muttered to himself. 'It wasn't a bad dream. I really did hear it. Where, precisely, and how did they lose it?' Kaltendorf demanded in cold fury.

'To be precise,' Pappenheim began in even tones, 'an area between Magdeburg and Gommern.' He went on to explain the whole, sorry sequence of events, as relayed to him by Reimer.

'Let me see if I have got this correctly,' Kaltendorf said when Pappenheim had finished. 'The helicopter on station was *low on fuel*, while the relief was *still on the ground with problems*?'

Pappenheim nodded. 'That's about it.'

'That's about it?' Kaltendorf snarled. 'I told you to bring in that Corvette. But *you* said the almighty Müller said no. And where is our smart boy now? Showing off his expensive toy to that journalist woman—'

'Whom you ordered him to—'

'*Don't interrupt me!*' Kaltendorf raged. 'Get Müller, and do it fast! I know you two always keep contact, so don't try to pull the wool over my eyes. Just get him!'

'With respect, Herr—'

'*Respect*? You wouldn't know how to respect a superior if your life depended upon it! I don't want any of your excuses, Pappenheim. Just find Müller, and tell him I *order* him to give me a report *personally* by morning. And as for that Corvette, you had better find it again. I warned you before, Pappenheim. You are not fireproof, and neither is Müller!'

Kaltendorf stormed out without waiting for any response from Pappenheim, slamming the door so hard it shuddered. Pappenheim sat there for some moments, savouring the sudden quiet.

'He likes making those exits,' he said at last, and lit a cigarette. 'It's a dog's life . . . for me, and f–' he picked up a phone – 'for you,' he added to the person he was about to speak to.

He punched in some numbers. The response was immediate.

'Johann?' he said. 'Me again, I'm afraid. Krause's chopper was the one on the ground, right? Where is he now? In the air. OK. Can you speak with him directly from where you are? Good. Well, you tell him he knows I know his boss, but if he doesn't find that Corvette by the time it gets dark, he won't have to worry about his boss at all. He'll have to worry about *me*, frying his balls . . .'

'I can't say that, sir,' Reimer protested. 'Not exactly like that. We don't have jurisdiction—'

'Johann,' Pappenheim interrupted softly.

'Sir?'

'The sooner you get my message across to Krause, the sooner you get to see your girlfriend tonight. Do you understand?'

'Oh, very clearly, sir.'

'I knew you would.' Pappenheim hung up. 'And I didn't even raise my voice.'

At that moment, he had another visitor; this time, more welcome.

'Aren't you going home, sir?' Lene Berger enquired. 'The night staff are coming in.'

'That time already? Who's in charge tonight?'

'*Kommissar* Neuss.'

'Ah yes. Marina. Well, I think I'll stay a while longer. She can get on with the night's business while I continue to hold the fort while Müller's away. The big boss gone yet?'

She nodded. 'He's got one of those functions.'

'He would. Ever the political animal. And you did not hear me say that.'

'No, sir. I can stay behind too . . .' Berger started to add hopefully.

'No, no. Off you go. Enjoy all the time you can away from this place. In this business, it soon becomes a twenty-four hour job, if you let it.'

Berger didn't move.

He peered at her through his screen of smoke. 'You hard of hearing, Berger?'

'No, sir.'

'Well then . . .'

'I can get pizzas . . .'

Pappenheim squinted at her through the veil. 'Why?'

Berger stood her ground, keeping her eyes firmly upon his. 'You haven't had lunch . . . except coffee and cigarettes. I don't call that lunch . . .'

'Are you trying to tell me what's good for me, Berger?'

'No, sir . . .'

'Because it won't work. Many have tried, and failed.' He

squinted at her a second time. 'Not feeling sorry for me, are you?'

'No, sir!'

'That's alright, then. Since you insist on punishing yourself, I'll have a deep-pan with ham and pineapple.' He reached into a pocket. 'Here's some money . . .'

'My treat,' Berger said with a broad smile, and went out quickly.

Pappenheim shook his head slowly. 'I'm too old for you, Berger,' he said softly, 'and it's far, far too late for me.' He looked at the phones on his desk. 'And Jens Müller is not going to like the news I have to give him.'

Four

The helicopter was beating its way in a spreading search pattern centred on Gommern, when Krause's observer coughed.

Krause glanced at her. 'Something wrong?'

'Message for you,' she said. 'I think you should take it.'

'Message? From whom?'

'Take it,' she repeated.

'Alright.' Krause gave her another glance, this time the eyes behind the tinted visor of his flight helmet were questioning. 'Switch it over.'

'Switching.'

'Krause?' Reimer's voice began in the headphones.

'This is Krause.'

'A message for you from my boss, *Oberkommissar* Pappenheim.'

'Fire away.'

Reimer told him, word for word.

Krause's eyes widened as he listened. 'He *said* that?'

'This is not something I would joke about. Besides, I'm looking forward to dinner tonight with my girlfriend.'

'Your girlfriend—'

The observer made urgent cutting motions across her throat with a hand, indicating to Krause that he should bite back what he was about to say.

'You have delivered your message,' Krause amended. 'Krause out.' He cut transmission. 'Those Berlin boys really believe the sun shines out of their backsides,' he added to the observer testily.

'We'd better find that Corvette.'

'Shitty Corvette. Why didn't they pull it in when they had the chance?'

'Do I have holes in the palms of my hands?'

'Don't get smart with me, Engels. If you hope one day to sit in the pilot's seat instead of spending all your career as an observer, this is not the way to go about it.' But he was smiling tightly at her.

'Yessir, pilot, sir,' she agreed, smiling back.

'So we'd better find their stupid car for them.'

'I think we should.'

The Porsche was just 5 km from the Saalburg exit. 'After Hours' by Swing Out Sister oozed its way from the ten speakers, softly filling the car with the retro supper-club sound. Despite at times meeting with heavy traffic heading towards Bavaria, a deluging fall of rain and encountering time-consuming standstills, Müller had still managed to maintain a high average speed. The 130 or so kilometres from the service station had taken less than an hour.

The rain had stopped, but the road surface was still damp. The car sped along it, fat low-profile tyres gripping surefootedly. Moody clouds, however, gave a gloomy tinge to the day, which made it seem darker than the actual time warranted. Müller drove with his lights on.

The music was interrupted by a *ping* and the multi-function display on the central console changed from CD information to a read-out of an incoming message.

Don't shoot the messenger, it displayed in German.

'Bad news?' Carey Bloomfield commented in English as Müller glanced at it.

'It is not good. That's from Pappi. He will first have tried my mobile and, finding it switched off, will know I am driving; so he has sent this to alert me. I'll call him when we have left the Autobahn.'

The message faded, and the music returned. A short while later, Müller filtered into the exit lane and left the Autobahn. He turned on to a minor road with views that would have been stunning on a brighter day. Even so, the landscape, despite the brooding atmosphere, was still impressive.

Müller soon found a spot off the road to park safely, and stopped. He left the parking lights on and began to climb out.

'You don't have to leave to make your call,' Carey Bloomfield said pointedly. '*I'll* get out. I can admire the view, doomy as it looks, while you have your little chat.'

'Humour me,' he said. 'You can change the CD if you want.'

'Gee, thank you, kind sir.'

Müller said nothing and gave her a tight smile as he left the car.

Her eyes focused expressionlessly upon him as he walked a short distance from it. He got out his mobile and made contact with Pappenheim.

'Give me the bad news,' he said as soon as Pappenheim answered.

Pappenheim did not waste time in preamble, but gave it to him in succinct phrases. Müller listened without interrupting.

'Is it raining up near Magdeburg?' Müller asked when Pappenheim had finished.

Slightly taken aback by the question, Pappenheim had one of his own. 'Why?'

'Trust me. Has it rained at all over there?'

'I don't think so, but I can double-check. Again . . . why?'

'Infrared. If it hasn't rained, there may still be some heat traces. Get the chopper to make infrared scans of the general area between Magdeburg and Gommern. There may still be something left, if we're lucky. And if we're really lucky, the trace may be big enough to identify shapes and sizes.'

'Sizes?'

'From what you've said, Pappi, it's clear they've switched again. We might find out where that took place, and how many vehicles this time. And one more thing: that Cherokee the first chopper spotted which *seemed* to be following the Corvette . . . was it seen again?'

'Funny you should ask. It disappeared for quite a while, only to show up again near—'

'Magdeburg?'

'You're so smart, Jens,' Pappenheim said, putting a fake tremor into his voice. 'I'm blinded by your light . . .'

'Have your fun, if you must, but tell Krause to keep an eye out for it. Again, it could just be coincidence and it's just a bunch of people admiring the countryside, but . . .'

'You don't think so.'

'I could be wrong . . .'

'But you could be right, and we wouldn't want to cost the Great White more blood vessels . . . talking of which, he *orders* you to give him a report *personally* tomorrow. His emphasis. Isn't that nice? What do I say when he asks?'

'You passed on the message. That lets you off the hook.'

'Will you call him? I'm not pleading, you understand.'

'I understand. I'll think about it.'

'Of course you will,' Pappenheim said cheerfully.

A munching noise sounded in Müller's ear.

'Are you *eating*, Pappi?'

'Finishing off a pizza Berger brought in.'

'Berger. It would be. When are you going to respond to her? She's been soft on you for so long now, it's plain to everyone.'

'I'm too old for her, Jens. She should find herself a younger man.'

'Pappi, never tell a woman such a thing. You, of all people, should know that. She made her mind up long ago.'

'I'm still too old,' Pappenheim said firmly.

'You wouldn't be saying that in her presence, so I assume she's gone home.'

'Er . . . no. She's checking on something for me. I decided to stay on and she—'

'Said she would as well.'

'You know how it is.'

'I know how it is,' Müller said. 'Sometimes, Pappi—'

'Yes, yes. I know. Anything exciting comes up, I'll call you.'

'Alright.'

They ended the call simultaneously.

'Pappi, Pappi,' Müller said to himself as he put the phone away. 'Damn,' he added, as a call of nature urged.

He walked away from the road and into the woodland, looking for a discreet place that would be well out of sight of the car.

In the Porsche, Carey Bloomfield watched him go. 'Now what?' she remarked, shaking her head slowly. 'Does he think I can hear him from this distance?'

She worked her way through the CD selection until she found a classical piece, *Concierto de Aranjuez* by Rodrigo. She selected the second movement, the Ádagio, and raised the volume. As the mournful guitar and strings filled the car, she thought that, although the music was Spanish, it somehow suited, rather than conflicted with, the darkling atmosphere outside.

Müller, who had meanwhile entered deeper into the woods, noticed how a fine mist hung between the trees and cloaked the shrubbery, giving it, in the strange twilight, a primeval air of foreboding. He actually felt the hairs on the back of his neck rise.

'Come on, Müller,' he admonished himself. 'You're only going for a piss. This is not somewhere in prehistory, and dinosaurs are not going to come at you out of the bushes. You're a police *Hauptkommissar*, not a child scared of ghosts.'

Even so, he felt strangely uneasy. He looked about him slowly, but could see nothing to explain this. He decided to do his business quickly and went behind a big tree, which he felt gave him sufficient privacy. As he began to relieve himself, he heard the sound, which had been of spattering on leaves, suddenly change to that of a more solid impact. He paused to look down and saw before him the round toe of a boot.

All the need to urinate suddenly left him. He quickly tidied himself, fastidiously wiped his hands with a paper handkerchief from a side pocket, crumpled it tightly and returned it to the pocket. He then looked for and found a thin, short length of a long-broken branch. With it, he carefully moved aside the covering of leaves and foliage that had been hiding the boot, and which had at first been displaced by the gravitational force of his urine. At once, he began to understand the strange foreboding he had sensed when he had first entered the wood.

As he worked, a jeans-clad leg was disclosed. Then the smell of nascent putrefaction which had been stifled by the screen of deliberately broken foliage and leaves, suddenly hit him. He reeled back slightly; but, holding his breath, worked a little more.

A second boot appeared, then a third, and a fourth. They were a very familiar type of boot. Two bodies, at least; perhaps more dispersed within the woodland. He stopped. They should not be further disturbed until the forensic team arrived.

He moved away from the gruesome find and immediately called Pappenheim.

'Pappi . . .' he began as soon as Pappenheim answered.

'I can tell by your voice,' an instantly alert Pappenheim remarked.

'I've found two bodies. There may be more, but I'm not certain.'

'Jesus! Where?'

Müller told him the location. 'They've been here for some time, I think. More than a week, at least. The forensic people will tell us more precisely.'

'And are they—?'

'At first look, they seem to be.'

'Jesus,' Pappenheim repeated softly. 'So, our friend has been at work before last night's little fun and games.'

'If it *is* his work, yes. But we can't say that until we know more. However, it certainly adds a new dimension. We could be looking at group activity. Remember, he is supposed to have said, "*We* are hunting".'

'This will give the Great White a fit. How come you found them, anyway?'

Müller told him.

'You're joking,' Pappenheim said. He sounded as if he was about to burst into laughter. 'Well, you'll not forget that piss in a hurry. How do you want to play this?' he went on. 'Do you call the locals? Or do I arrange it from here?'

'Better if you do it. Arrange all the formalities. I don't want to have any stupid arguments with the local forces.'

'I'll get on to it right away. This is turning into something very strange, Jens. Do you think there could be more of these in other parts of the country?'

'Who knows, Pappi. Who knows. I'll wait here for the locals. We'll talk later.'

'Right.'

Müller ended the call. As he made his way back to the car, he quickly called the place where they would be spending the night to warn of the delay, without stating the reason.

At the same time, Krause's helicopter was making infrared scans of the area Müller had suggested to Pappenheim. They found plenty of traces, but nothing that gave any indications of the Corvette.

'This is like fly shit in the wind,' Krause remarked sourly to Engels. 'What will they come up with next?'

'Ours is not to reason why.'

'*What?*'

'I'm misquoting an English poem . . .'

'You *read* English poems?'

'Why not?'

74

'I'll be damned . . .'

'You already are . . . sir . . . Ah!'

'You've got something?' Krause asked hopefully.

'I . . . think . . . so . . .'

'Don't think it, Engels! Anything down there?'

'Definitely something down there,' she confirmed positively. 'Two traces, one bigger than the other, but close together. One could have been a truck.'

'A *truck*?'

'I'm not completely sure, because the trace is weak; but how best to hide a car? Put it *inside* a truck.'

'Engels, you're an angel.'

'That's my name. I suggest we land.'

'I accept your suggestion. Let's show the Berlin prima donnas they are not the only smart ones around.'

They had found the spot where the Corvette had been loaded into the refrigerated truck.

Krause put the helicopter down smoothly in a clearing, not far from where Engels had indicated she had found the traces. They hurried out of the machine and, with torches in the fading light, discovered tyre impressions. The ground was just soft enough. They discovered three sets: the truck's was obvious. The second, a short distance to the side, was too wide to be the Corvette's. Then Engels found the set that was directly behind the truck's.

'When it gets to here,' she said, indicating with the torch, 'it disappears. But look at this.' Her torch showed a straight indentation. 'That's a ramp. They loaded the Corvette here. We can make casts of each of the different tracks, just to be sure we've got the right ones. This could just as easily be a car-smuggling switch point. There's something strange about that truck too. The trace is—'

'Whatever it is, let's make the casts,' Krause said. 'Engels, you're smart enough to be a pilot.'

'I'm smarter,' she said with a straight face.

In the Porsche, Carey Bloomfield peered about her, studying

the approaching gloom and wondering what was keeping Müller so long in the woods. No other vehicle had as yet passed in either direction. She glanced at the ignition and remembered that he had taken the keys.

'Oh great,' she said. 'Anything happens to him and I'm stuck here.'

She had changed the music to something by Bon Jovi, when she saw him approaching.

'At last,' she muttered with relief. Then she noted the grimness of his expression as he drew closer. 'And now what?'

Müller entered the car; he did not insert the ignition key. 'We'll be staying for a while,' he said to her in English.

She glanced outside. 'Well . . . I guess this place probably looks romantic on a bright, sunny day; but right now, it reminds me of the atmosphere in one of those *Friday the 13th* type movies . . .'

'Appropriate,' Müller cut in. 'There are bodies in those woods. I have just found them.'

'That figures.' She stared at him. 'You're kidding me. Right?'

'I'm kidding you . . . Wrong. No, Miss Bloomfield. I am not kidding you this time. We're in the state of Thüringen, so the local police are on their way.'

'*Bodies?*' She spoke the word as if she did not trust it. Conflicting expressions shifted across her face, seemingly uncertain whether she could believe him, yet knowing by his expression that this was not something he would joke about. 'Bodies on a romantic *Strasse*,' she continued dryly. 'Great. Why the hell not. What kind of bodies?'

'Like the ones you saw in the photographs on my desk.'

'No shit,' she said after some moments. 'So, that incident was not the first.'

'It seems like it.'

'How did you find them? You couldn't know . . .'

'A call of nature. And there they were, almost at my feet.'

She giggled suddenly – a release of tension, or the incongruity of the way he had made his discovery. 'Sorry. I . . . I don't mean to be frivolous, but it *is* kind of funny. You go for a pee and bingo . . . there they are.'

'Pappenheim was there before you. I could hear him trying not to laugh as I told him.' Müller started to get out again. 'The first of the local people should be here soon.'

She started to get out as well.

'You, Miss Bloomfield,' Müller said, 'stay put.'

She climbed out. 'The hell I do. Not this time, Müller. I'm a reporter. I've seen dead bodies before.'

He stared at her. 'Are you going to make an issue of this?'

'You bet your German ass I am.'

Müller sighed. 'I could easily compel you to remain in the car . . . but I have neither the time, nor the inclination for the aggravation. Just keep out of the way.'

'Sir, yessir!' she agreed.

'And stop that.'

'Sir—'

But flashing lights beyond the trees made her stop to look.

The green and white patrol car, the first to approach the scene, was two bends away from where the Porsche was parked. There were two uniformed officers in it.

'Did I hear this right?' the driver began to his partner. 'A Berlin *Hauptkommissar* finds bodies on our patch?'

'You heard the same thing I did.'

'What the hell was he doing out here?'

'Why don't you ask him when we get there? Perhaps he'll be nice and tell you all about it.'

Whatever retort the driver intended to make was cut short as they came round the last bend at speed and their lights framed the Porsche.

'Watch it!' the partner shouted. 'Hit that car and you'll be paying for it for the rest of your career, if it lasts long enough.'

The patrol car slid to a halt a safe distance from Müller's Turbo.

'What *do* they pay these Berlin boys?' the driver asked.

'A lot more than you or me,' his partner answered sourly. 'We're Easterners.' There was a lot of resentment in that last remark.

'And look at him,' the driver continued. *'That's a Hauptkommissar*? He looks like a bloody designer's model. All that hair.'

His partner was looking in Carey Bloomfield's direction. 'And we know what he was doing in the woods,' he said, a little enviously. 'Imagine having your fun in the company of rotting stiffs.'

'Coitus interruptus. But their clothes don't seem dirty.'

They laughed softly.

'Designer's model or not,' the partner said urgently, 'here he comes. Let's not ruffle his feathers.'

They got out as Müller reached them, doing so with the casual arrogance of certain types of policeman everywhere. The lights on the car continued to flash.

'Hauptkommissar Müller?' The driver, short-haired and like his partner a native of Thüringen, sounded as if he felt his eyes were deceiving him.

Müller showed his ID and both patrolmen immediately straightened their stance.

'Thank you for getting here so quickly, gentlemen,' Müller said. His eyes studied them neutrally, giving nothing away.

'We were nearest, sir,' the driver responded, more cautious now, sensing he might be close to making a serious error of judgement. 'The others are on their way. I can't believe there are bodies in there.'

'Believe it . . . And they don't smell too good.'

The driver, slow to learn, shot his partner an amused glance as Müller looked away. More flashing lights were beginning to show beyond the trees.

Müller again looked at the two policemen. His eyes raked them without emotion. 'Wait here till your boss arrives.'

'Yes, sir,' they both said together, discretion finally winning through and making them more wary of their superior officer.

Müller moved away from them without a backward glance.

Soon, the country road began to fill up with police and other emergency vehicles. An unmarked car went past to park in front of the Porsche. Two men in civilian clothes got out. The older one approached, and stopped before Müller.

'*Hauptkommissar* Müller?'

Müller nodded.

'Klee, sir,' the other said. '*Kommissar*. The eager young man by the car is Eugen Jöst.' Klee had a generous moustache, and looked older than Müller.

They shook hands. Müller nodded in Jöst's direction.

Müller turned to Carey Bloomfield. 'Miss Bloomfield, a reporter from America.'

Klee shook hands with her. 'Miss Bloomfield.' His eyes, however, still clearly readable in the encroaching gloom, were questioning.

'Miss Bloomfield is under my authority,' Müller said to Klee as they began walking towards the scene of the bodies. 'The crime scene is all yours. Look upon me as an observer.'

Klee seemed unsure. 'I was told to give you every cooperation . . .'

'You will be doing just that, if you see me as an observer.'

'Yes, sir.' Klee still sounded unsure, but he immediately took charge of the operation. He turned to his subordinate. 'Get those patrol boys to keep any press out of the way. Use a second car as first stop.'

Jöst went off to talk to the patrolmen.

As the paraphernalia for a crime scene – floodlights, tents, body bags, etc – invaded the woods, more vehicles and people arrived until the narrow road began to look like a car park.

Throughout the careful recovery of the bodies, Müller did not interfere with Klee's work, preferring instead simply to observe what was being done.

Carey Bloomfield also made herself inconspicuous, while at the same time ensuring she missed nothing of importance. Though she kept her distance, she could not avoid seeing the first of the bodies. It was not a pretty sight; for though it had been in the woods for a relatively short time, a substantial part of it was a writhing mass of crawling life that had to be patiently cleared away. She felt her stomach heave, but managed to control the reaction. She did not watch the recovery of the second body.

Müller noted the stillness of her face and understood what was going on. She may have seen many dead bodies, but clearly not quite like this. There was always a first time. The soulless glare of the lights cast elemental shadows upon her face.

He looked about him. The bright lights that gave an alienating, forbidding air to the woods; the people going about their grim tasks; the almost hushed tones of conversation; the police searchers working in spread pattern within the immediate area, looking for more bodies; their probing lights flickering amongst the trees and shrubbery like giant fireflies in the deep, unsettling gloom of some tropical forest. There was an unreal quality to it all that gave the impression of a scene from a past century, where strange, secret rituals were being enacted; which, in a way, he decided, they were. Only the century was different.

'It's spooky,' a voice said.

He turned to see Carey Bloomfield approaching. 'Seen enough?'

She nodded. 'All I want to.'

'I thought you'd seen many dead bodies before.'

'I have, and in some of the worst asshole spots of this beautiful, sick planet of ours; but I never could take this kind of stuff. I've seen kids who've been blown away by mines; political prisoners riddled by police machine guns; people crushed by tanks . . . You name it, I've probably seen it. I can show you people who think I can be a hard-assed bitch at times. But things crawling on bodies . . .' She shivered.

'Intimations of mortality,' he said.

'You mean, I can't imagine being blown apart, but I can see the worms on my own body.'

'Something like that.'

'Ugh. Thanks for the nightmare.'

'I didn't give it to you. You had it long before we even met.'

'Ugh,' she repeated, shivering again. 'No thanks for reminding me. It's getting close to midnight. Are we going to stay here till the bitter end?'

'No. We'll be leaving soon. Klee and his people can get on with it.'

'Thank God for that,' she said with relief. 'And talking of Klee . . .'

Müller saw the *Kommissar* coming towards them. Klee stopped, then glanced at Carey Bloomfield before speaking.

'It's alright,' Müller told him.'

'So far,' Klee began after another uncertain glance at Carey Bloomfield, 'there seem to be just the two bodies. Clean shots in the back of the head. A professional job. I'll have a full report by tomorrow, when the lab people have done their bit. We're still looking, of course. In the morning I'll have the search widened. You never know.'

Müller nodded. 'I'll get out of your hair. Talk to Berlin when you're ready with your report.'

'I don't contact you directly?'

'You'll be doing so by contacting Berlin.'

'And my boss? And *his* boss?'

'Nothing for you to worry about. They've already been told this is the chain of communication.'

'That's why I'm here in these woods, I suppose,' Klee said ruefully. 'I don't thank you for this, sir.'

'I wouldn't thank me, either,' Müller said.

The unexpectedness of this made Klee smile wearily in the strange twilight created by the crime scene's illuminations. 'Yes, sir.'

'You're doing good work. Sorry I cannot tell you more at this time.'

'I see.' Klee paused. 'I have my own ideas about this, given what has been happening recently. All these hate attacks on—'

'Then I suggest you keep them to yourself . . . for now. With one exception . . . Any thoughts you may have on this, no matter how outlandish, pass on to Berlin.'

'And my bosses?'

'Directly to Berlin,' Müller insisted. 'I'll take any responsibility, if you have trouble from above.'

Klee turned to look back at the lighted area among the trees, particularly at a brightly lit tent.

'To tell you the truth, sir,' he said, 'I'm not sure I really want to know.'

'I didn't want the case, either,' Müller said. 'But I've got it.'

Klee made a sound that was suspiciously like a snort. 'Always someone else on top, to give the orders.'

'Your curse, my curse.'

'Everybody's curse,' Klee said philosophically. 'Well, I'd better get back. Goodnight, sir . . . Miss Bloomfield.'

Müller held out a hand. Klee shook it, then returned to his unpleasant work.

'Always someone else on top to give the orders,' Carey Bloomfield repeated as they made their way out of the woods and back towards the car. 'You always obey orders, Müller?'

'Not always.'

They reached the grassy edge of the road and stepped on to it. There seemed to be even more vehicles.

'Now, why does that not surprise me?' she asked rhetorically. 'No wonder your boss loves you so much. And if so much love could kill—'

Müller gave a harsh chuckle. 'I'd be long dead.'

'Life's a bitch.'

'Not so long ago,' Müller continued seriously, 'a lot of people got into a lot of trouble for blindly obeying orders, then later used it as a defence.'

She nodded in the direction of the lights. 'Some people don't seem to have learned that lesson, or we wouldn't be out here tonight and all this would not be happening.'

'Who says people ever learn? But tell me, Miss Bloomfield—'

'Gawd,' she exclaimed impatiently. 'Are you ever going to quit this Miss Bloomfield—'

'Tell me,' Müller repeated, ignoring her question as they neared the car. 'Why are *you* really here? Are you really doing research on the Berlin police?'

She stopped and turned so suddenly to face him, he nearly stumbled into her. 'Now, what do you mean by those questions, Müller?'

'I'm a policeman,' he responded mildly. 'I'm supposed to ask awkward questions. The car,' he added. 'We're here. Please get in.'

'Jesus!' she said in frustration.

'And please don't slam the door.'

He expected her to do it, just to spite him. But she didn't.

'Thank you,' he said to the darkened heavens before he climbed in. 'Small mercies.'

Jöst had arranged for a second patrol car, lights flashing, to block the road further back. This left the first to act as back-up near the recovery vehicles, in case any unauthorized press and camera teams managed to sneak through on foot. Other police, also on foot, prowled the nearby area with the same purpose in mind.

The driver of the first car watched as the Porsche's engine started and Müller began to manoeuvre out of where he had parked, in order to get past Klee's vehicle.

'There goes the Berlin pretty boy with his piece of stuff,' the driver commented rancorously. Apart from his partner, no one else was close enough to hear. '*He* discovers the shit, but he leaves us with it. These Wessies think they're the sunshine gods.'

'They won,' the partner said bluntly. 'We lost.'

'They won,' the driver said caustically, 'with a little help from NATO . . . which really means big American money.' He spat as he said that.

'So, what do you want? The DDR back?'

'People like you and me would have some real power,' the driver countered balefully, 'and our senior officers would not look like that rich pretty boy with his long hair and fancy sports car.'

The partner watched as the Porsche's lights disappeared round a bend.

'No,' he said. 'They would have had fancy limos instead.' He was not old enough to have been a policeman before the wall came down.

The driver glared at him in silence.

The Porsche turned off the road and on to a curving driveway illuminated by ground-level spotlights, to pull up before a floodlit mansion of medium size. It looked new.

Despite her sense of frustration with Müller, Carey Bloomfield peered at it through her window in admiration.

'Hey,' she began. 'This is a nice chunk of real estate. Whose is it?'

'It belongs to my aunt,' he replied, turning off the engine. 'On my mother's side. It was once the family home before the days of the DDR. They escaped to the West just after the partition when she was a child, in just the clothes they were wearing, and with very little money. My mother was born in the West that same year. She was very young when I was born – just eighteen.

'The Party took over the house, just as it did with nearly everything else. This one became one of those holiday homes for high Party officials and their cronies. Over the years, misuse and lack of repairs wrecked it. By the time the wall came down, it was so derelict and overgrown, no one wanted it. It had been deserted for years.

'My aunt inherited it. She was luckier than many people who have tried to reclaim their old homes. At least she found it still standing. She and her husband – from western Germany – began to restore it. They had done well in business, so they could afford to; but they also did much of the work themselves. For my aunt, it was a labour of love. There were many memories to preserve. It took a long time to get it back to this standard. It also used up much of their money, so now part of it is a luxury hotel. It's working for its living.'

'I admire her stamina. She and her husband did one hell of a job. It's beautiful.'

'You can tell her yourself. I am certain she would appreciate that.'

'And her husband? Don't tell me they broke up after all this.'

'He is gone, but not the way you think. He died three years ago, before they opened for business.'

'Oh hell . . . I am sorry to hear that.' She looked out at the building again. 'To think he didn't live to see it like this, after all that work . . .'

'Sorry to interrupt, but we should get out now. The staff know the car and someone will have told her we are here. I will tell you more about the house later.'

'Sure.'

Müller was proven right, for almost immediately a tall, elegant woman with short grey hair had appeared at the colonnaded entrance and was coming towards the car, beaming in welcome.

'Jens-Müller!' she greeted him warmly as they climbed out. She gave him a quick embrace and kissed him on both cheeks. She turned to Carey Bloomfield. 'Ah . . . Miss Bloomfield,' she said in English. 'A pleasure to have you in our home.' Her command of the language was perfect, and British accented.

She extended a hand, then, as it was being shaken, kissed the astonished Carey Bloomfield on both cheeks, as she had done with Müller.

Müller looked on with an amused smile.

'And so, Jens-Müller,' she went on to her nephew, staying in English as a courtesy to Carey Bloomfield, 'why has it taken you so long to come and see us? And only because of police business. Shame.'

'Aunt Isolde . . . you know how it is.'

'Excuses, excuses,' she said, and glanced at Carey Bloomfield. 'You see, Miss Bloomfield—'

'Carey, please.'

'You see, Carey? He is hopeless.'

'Tell me about it,' she said, glancing triumphantly at Müller.

'And do call me Isolde, or Aunt Isolde, if you prefer.'

'Thank you. I will.'

A member of the hotel staff, in a smart uniform that was strongly reminiscent of a late-nineteenth-century hussar without the busby, was in attendance, though keeping a respectful distance.

'And have you any luggage?'

Carey Bloomfield tapped at her small bag, which she had taken out of the car. 'Just this.'

'In that case, we'll go in. Jens-Müller knows his way. Besides, he never lets any of the staff park his car. It seems that once in London, a staff member of some hotel was parking a guest's Porsche, lost control and did very expensive damage to the one he was meant to park, and to several other expensive cars to boot. Seven in all, I believe. Jens-Müller has since taken that as a warning.'

Carey Bloomfield glanced at Müller. 'Oh really,' she said. 'Who would have thought it?'

Aunt Isolde winked at her. 'Come on, my dear. Let's leave him to it.'

As they went off, Carey Bloomfield glanced back at Müller. *She called me Carey*, she mouthed at him.

The staff member pretended not to notice. 'May I take the bags, Herr Graf—' he began in German.

'No need, Christian. Thank you.'

'Good to see you here again, sir.'

Müller went up to him and shook his hand. 'Only for a short while, but it's good to be back.'

'If you don't need me . . .'

'No. It's quite alright. Thanks.'

'Sir.' Christian gave a slight nod and re-entered the building.

Müller was just about to get back into the car to park it, when his mobile phone rang. It was Pappenheim.

'You don't have to stay there all night, Pappi,' Müller began. 'Let Neuss hold the fort. Get some sleep.'

'I can do that here, and Neuss is busy.'

'Berger still there too?'

'She is.'

Müller shook his head slowly. 'Alright, Pappi. Is the news good?'

'It is indeed.' Pappenheim went on to tell him about Krause's and Engels' find, then went on: 'The tyre casts clearly identify the makes. One is common for the Corvette, including tread width. The second . . . get this . . . the Cherokee. And the third is of course standard for trucks of that size.'

'This is very good work, Pappi. Thank Krause and Engels.'

Pappenheim gave a slight cough. 'From the way the report reads, it seems that much of this was Engels' work. She—'

'*She?*'

'She. Very smart woman. Krause used to be a military assault chopper pilot in the days of the DDR. He flew what NATO calls the Hind; that's the Mil Mi-24. Looks like a giant mosquito with a bad case of nastiness . . .'

'I know the type you mean.'

'Well . . . to tell you the truth, I think Krause is a bit of a macho asshole. Now Engels, on the other hand, uses her brain. She hopes to be a pilot one day. I think we should steal her for our unit.'

'If anyone can do such stealing, Pappi, you can. You have my support. I'll go on your recommendation.'

'I'll do it. But you'll have to get it past the Great White.'

'Leave that to me,' Müller said.

'With pleasure. Engels has an interesting theory about the truck,' Pappenheim continued.

'Which is?'

'She believes it's a freezer truck.'

'*What*? How did she arrive at that conclusion?'

'The heat trace. She says the infrared display registers a trace that is barely larger than the one for the Cherokee, and if they hadn't landed to check – her idea, by the way – and seen the long tracks for the truck, she would only have been making an educated guess. But for a vehicle big enough to be a transport truck, there were no traces for the axles, which generate strong heat signals. That, she decided, could mean a freezer container *above* the axles, masking the heat trace. She insists it's only a theory; but I think we should not overlook it.'

'I agree. You're right. She uses her brain. Steal her from that chopper unit, if you can.'

'There is no "*if*". I'll do it. Just keep the Great White off my back.'

Müller chuckled. 'I will. That's a promise. As for my little find out here, Klee will give you a full report tomorrow. He seems a good type.'

'I don't know him personally—'

'Someone you *don't* know?'

'I will soon enough,' Pappenheim remarked smoothly. 'But I have heard of him. He is supposed to be good. Don't tell me you want me to steal him as well.'

Müller gave a quick laugh. 'No, Pappi. At least, not yet. I'm assuming you have upgraded the search for the Cherokee, and have now added a freezer truck to the list.'

'You have assumed correctly. Nothing yet on the Mercedes, but that net is still trawling.'

'Alright, Pappi. Thanks. And you really should do something about Berger.'

'And you enjoy your babysitting,' Pappenheim countered with a laugh as he ended the call.

Müller put the phone away. 'Babysitting,' he muttered, glancing at the entrance to the mansion hotel, through which his aunt and Carey Bloomfield had gone. 'And I still need to finish my piss.'

He got into the Porsche and drove it up to an electronic gate at the side of the left wing of the building, behind which was the owner's private parking courtyard and garages. The coded signal had long been installed in the car and the gate opened automatically. He drove through, triggering a floodlight as the gate shut behind him.

He parked, climbed out, collected his bag, then locked the Porsche. A side door had been left open for him. He went through, and pushed it shut. By the time the electronically controlled locks had slid home with a soft hiss, the light in the courtyard had switched itself off.

The time was exactly 0.15.

Day two: Magdeburg Cathedral, 0.16 hours, Central European Time.

The man, in a long coat, was kneeling on the cathedral steps, and seemed to be praying. He had been there for at least half an hour. He was almost in total darkness, and he was the only person around.

Then three people appeared, still some distance off, on a course that would take them directly to the steps. As they drew closer, they turned out to be heavily set young men with shaven heads. They were talking loudly, with the truculence of people who had drunk more than was necessary, and were looking for some diversion. They found it in the lone figure on the cathedral steps.

He did not move when they came up behind him.

One of them tapped his shoulder roughly. 'Hey you! No use praying. *He's* not going to help you.'

Another climbed the steps to move round in front of him. This one peered closely, then grinned hugely, not believing his luck.

'A fucking *nigger*!' he shouted in glee. 'So black, he is invisible! And he's praying out here in the night. To which god, nigger?'

The man did not speak.

The one behind jabbed at the shoulder again, this time much harder. 'Answer him, asshole! No god is going to help you now. Pray you're still alive when we've finished with you, you fucking immigrant!'

The third, who had remained silent throughout, had moved back some paces. He braced himself, then began to run at the kneeling figure, intending to deliver a crippling kick to the unprotected back.

He never made it.

The kneeling figure had risen suddenly to its feet and, in a sweeping motion, had brought out a silenced automatic. The first of the coughing shots hit the running man, who simply kept running until, with stiffening strides, he came to a standstill upon the steps before collapsing. He never had time to be surprised.

The second shot hit the shoulder-tapper fully in the heart. He sat down abruptly, stared up at the man with the gun and died where he sat.

The last man, the one who had been taunting his intended victim from the front, turned to flee. The third shot took him in the middle of his back. A spurt of blood gushed out of his mouth from a ravaged lung. He fell headlong upon the steps, then rolled until his body was stopped by the one which was still sitting. The sitting corpse slowly fell to its side, as if of sheer tiredness.

It had all happened so quickly, time had barely passed, it seemed.

The man worked swiftly. He took something out of a pocket of the long coat and carefully placed it by the bodies. It was a note. From another pocket, he placed something else upon the note, like a paperweight.

Satisfied, the man left the cathedral steps without a backward glance and vanished into the night. No one had come to look. The object he had left on the note was a very unusual paperweight.

It was a small statue of the Black Madonna.

Five

The hotel section of the building consisted of the main central part and the entire right wing. This had thirty generous bedroom suites, each with Carrara marble bathrooms. The left wing was the owner's private quarters, consisting of a vast drawing room, sitting room, dining room, breakfast room, a big study, and a huge modern kitchen. It also contained six guest bedroom suites, plus the owner's master suite, all with similar marbled bathrooms.

The owner's residence was totally sealed off from the hotel section, save for a single arched doorway, which led through a short, enclosed corridor to a second arched door. This door opened into the hotel management offices. Each door was secured by an electronic keypad. The doors were for the private use of the owner and no member of the staff, without exception, was allowed access; not even the manager, himself the son of a long-standing business friend, was permitted. However, he had the door access codes, in case of emergencies. He had never used them.

Members of the staff who were required to remain overnight had their own lodge within the grounds. The lodge, which could sleep eight, was itself barely less luxurious than the hotel itself.

Carey Bloomfield had seen a small part of the ornate interior decorations of the owner's residence as she had been shown up to the room she'd been given for the night, by Aunt Isolde.

'If moths bother you, pull down the insect screens,' Aunt Isolde had advised.

Carey Bloomfield now looked about her in the high-ceilinged bedroom.

A huge double bed in cherry wood dominated the richly carpeted room. To one side was a large chest of drawers, also in polished cherry wood, with black lacquered edgings. In a corner was a writing desk and chair, in the same finish. An antique reading-lamp with a green shade was on it, next to a large writing pad. Two elegant, upholstered armchairs were positioned in another corner. Soft wall lighting, operated by dimmer switches, gave the room warm illumination. A full-length mirror formed the central door of a floor to ceiling wardrobe that, again, was finished in polished cherry wood. A closed door led to the bathroom suite.

'This is some pile of bricks,' she said to herself.

Something glistened beyond the partly opened double-glazed windows, and the murmur of flowing water intruded softly. She went to one of the windows, opened it fully and looked down. The lights of the building played upon the darkly moving surface of a wide stream. A screen of tall trees beyond the stream speckled the lights from the nearest village, a good two kilometres away.

She breathed in the night air. 'Some little place, Müller,' she said with irony.

Then she moved back quickly as something large smacked against the window. A huge moth, trying to get in. She reached up and pulled at a toggle. The insect screen rolled smoothly down to click securely into a slot in the lower frame of the window.

'I don't like things that flutter in the night when I'm trying to sleep.'

She went to her bag and took out her mobile phone. The dull gleam of an automatic showed briefly just before she shut the bag again. She quickly dialled a number.

'Toby,' came Adams' voice immediately. His own mobile

phone was blinking her number telling him it was a secure transmission, and alerting him to the identity of the caller.

'Sorry to wake you.'

'I wasn't asleep,' he said.

'Can't make this long,' she continued with lowered voice, eyes on the door of the bedroom. 'He discovered two bodies near here. This evening.'

In fast, terse sentences, she gave him a quick briefing on the incident.

'That's what you can sometimes find if you go out in the woods to pee,' Adams remarked drolly when she had finished.

'He sure as hell didn't find a teddy bears' picnic.'

Adams chuckled. 'Enquiries are being made about you,' he said, serious once more. 'I fielded a probe from Pappenheim.'

'Müller's been making some attempts of his own. Sudden, unexpected questions.'

'Trying to catch you out?'

'Doing his damnedest. He's no dummy.'

'Do you want to pull out?' Adams enquired.

'Not a chance,' she said. 'I'm here to do a job and I'll do it.'

'If you're certain.'

'I'm certain.'

'OK.'

They ended the call. Immediately after, a knock sounded. She quickly returned the mobile to her bag.

'Are you ready?' came Müller's voice faintly through the solid door. 'Aunt Isolde has something prepared.'

She saw that the large chest of drawers had keys in every lock. She checked and saw that each key was different. She put the bag into one and locked it, slipping the key into a side pocket of her jeans.

'On my way,' she called, going to the door.

She opened it. Müller was standing there, smiling at her. He had removed his jacket.

'What?' she began, looking at his shirt, which he had changed. 'No shoulder harness? No gun?'

'What makes you think I carry a gun?'

'Come on, Müller,' she said, closing the door behind her. 'Your suits are made in a way that hides your gun well; and your fresh shirt does not show the creases of a harness. But even though I never saw it peep out of that designer jacket of yours, you've got a gun.'

'You know of these things, do you?'

They began walking along a wide, polished landing covered with expensive rugs from east of the Caucasus. The square landing led to a sweeping central staircase.

'I've met a lot of cops in my job. They all have their own ways of carrying. I call it gun signature.'

'And what is my gun signature?' He seemed amused by all this.

'Subtle,' she replied. 'But it's there.'

'Subtle,' he repeated, seeming to savour the word. He continued looking at her with the same expression of tolerant amusement. 'And now that you've told me all about my way of carrying a weapon, how do you like your room?'

'You don't just like a room like that,' she answered. 'You wear it. I love it. And I've even got my own stream outside my window.'

Like the rest of the owner's wing and the hotel itself, the walls of the landing were adorned with artwork. The landing seemed reserved for family portraiture. They had reached the staircase and she paused to study a portrait of a blonde-haired young woman. The picture overlooked the staircase. At the bottom and directly over the entrance to the hall, was a Derrenberg shield with the family coat of arms. Crossed sabres were fixed to it.

'Well, you certainly appear to have hit it off with Aunt Isolde,' Müller said, watching her interest in the painting neutrally. 'It's her favourite room after the master suite.'

'She's a sweet lady. So elegant . . .'

'But also very down-to-earth, and tough when she needs to be.'

'I can believe that. Rebuilding and restoring a mansion

like this so completely is not the work of someone without guts and staying power. So, where's your room?' She was still looking at the portrait.

'On the other side of the landing, directly opposite your door. It's the one I always use when I am here.'

'This is some place. And you called it *little*?'

'Relatively.'

'Oh yeah. Sure.' She at last turned from the portrait to look at him. 'That's your mother, isn't it?'

'Yes.'

'There's a strong likeness. You've got her eyes. She's very beautiful.'

'Was.'

'*Was?*'

'It's a long story.' He clearly had no intention of saying more.

They began making their way down the staircase.

'Do you like smoked salmon?' he asked, firmly changing the subject.

'Smoked salmon? Are you kidding? I'd kill for it.'

'Despite what you saw in the woods?'

Her lips briefly turned down in a wry grimace. 'I couldn't look at spaghetti right now. But smoked salmon . . . and you've got a customer.'

'Then this is our lucky night.'

'What do you mean?'

'Smoked salmon is waiting for us in the breakfast room. You don't have to kill for it, and I don't have to arrest you for the crime.' He grinned at her.

She paused again as they reached the marbled floor of the lofty hall, and stared at him. 'There's a message in there somewhere . . . right?'

'In what I've just said? Now what gives you that idea?'

She studied his expression for fleeting moments, then glanced speculatively at the shield over the entrance. 'Do you fence, Müller?'

He too glanced at the shield. 'With swords? Or with words?'

She favoured him with one of her sideways glances. 'Let's go eat, Müller,' she said. 'I could eat a horse, and I like breakfast after midnight.'

'You word is, of course, my command,' he said.

They walked on in silence.

They found Aunt Isolde waiting. No one else was in the breakfast room. The large table seemed overladen with food. The centrepiece was a large oval dish containing generous slices of smoked salmon. Two opened bottles of white wine stood in silver chillers. Three chairs had been placed – two opposite each other, one at its head.

'Ah!' she greeted them both. 'There you are.'

She spoke English. Despite having already been informed by Müller that Carey Bloomfield was fluent in German, she insisted on doing so as a courtesy. Müller believed she was herself also keen to use the language. Over the years before the wall came down, she had spent long periods in the United Kingdom, the US, and Australia; in some cases, years. In spite of this international mixture, her accent when using English had remained resolutely British.

'We'll never eat all this!' Carey Bloomfield protested.

'Nonsense,' Aunt Isolde countered. 'Of course you will. Do sit down. You're opposite me, and Jens-Müller is at the head.'

Carey Bloomfield flashed Müller a glance that was full of comment about the hierarchical seating arrangements, which Aunt Isolde appeared not to see.

'Do help yourselves,' Aunt Isolde urged as they took their seats. 'We shan't stand on ceremony. Carey, you first. I insist. And none of that eating like a bird nonsense. If I want to feed birds, I put crumbs out for them.'

'Then I won't argue,' Carey Bloomfield said, and began to load her plate.

Müller waited until Aunt Isolde had put some food on her own plate before attending to his.

'The wine,' Aunt Isolde said. 'Will you serve, please, Jens-Müller? It's French. Very unpatriotic.' She smiled, clearly at a secret joke, and raised her glass in a toast. 'To you, Carey. It is a pleasure to welcome you to our home. It's Jens-Müller's too, you see. Oh, I know he has his own family home in the West; but this is also his. Our side of the family.'

'Thank you for the very generous welcome, and the wonderful room. I love it.'

'I am glad you do. It is my second favourite.'

Carey Bloomfield nodded. 'I know. I feel privileged,' she added with unaccustomed humility.

'Don't,' Aunt Isolde told her briskly. 'Simply enjoy it. And now, the toast.' They drank the toast then Aunt Isolde continued, 'Let's get down to the serious business of eating!'

'This is delicious,' Carey Bloomfield remarked admiringly as she had her first mouthful. 'You must have a great chef.'

'Thank you,' Aunt Isolde said. 'You see, Jens-Müller? She does like the way I prepare food.'

Being a hard-nosed worldly-wise person did not prevent Carey Bloomfield from blushing to the roots of her hair.

'God!' she said, annoyed with herself. 'Trust me to put my foot— I . . . I just imagined that . . .'

'Someone who lives in a place like this, and owns the hotel, would have an army of people to do such work?' Aunt Isolde finished for her.

'Well . . . I guess so. Yes.'

'An understandable viewpoint. There are people who work here, yes. The residential part of this house is a little big to have its upkeep tended to by one person; but I usually prefer to do my own cooking. Unlike some so-called nobility, I have better things to do with my life than go to openings, give some gloss to politicians and the rest, have people fawning over me, and get my picture in glossy magazines. I'm a lowly, defunct baroness who works for her living, and enjoys it. Just as I enjoy doing my own cooking. My staff are mainly for the hotel. Some of them have contracts that enable them to interchange with the hotel; but they are certainly not my servants.'

'Well, that puts me in my place.'

'Nonsense, my dear. An honest mistake. No one here is going to hold it against you. And if Jens-Müller teases you about it, tell me and I'll tweak his ear.'

'She would do it,' Müller confirmed to Carey Bloomfield. 'She's tweaked my ear before.'

'You were a lot smaller then,' Aunt Isolde confirmed. 'But you're not too big now.'

'There you are, Miss Bloomfield,' he said. 'As formidable as when I was a boy . . .'

'Aunt Isolde, will you tell your nephew to quit calling me Miss Bloomfield all the time? I've tried to get him to call me Carey for . . . oh, I've lost count of the number of times.'

'I can tell you precisely how many, if you'd like,' Müller said.

'Aargh!' Carey Bloomfield said, giving up.

Aunt Isolde smiled at them above the rim of her glass. 'So sweet,' she said.

The extremely late breakfast was over. The bottles were empty, the smoked salmon vanished, and coffee was on the table.

A satisfied Müller leaned back in his chair. 'Aunt Isolde, as usual, that was fantastic.'

'Took the words right out of my mouth,' Carey Bloomfield said. 'I can't believe I ate and drank so much.'

'Thank you both,' Aunt Isolde said, pleased. Then she added to Carey Bloomfield, 'You've got a healthy appetite. What's wrong with that? Enjoy your life, my dear. Everything is always so short,' she added, to herself it seemed, as she got to her feet.

They both stood up with her.

'No, no,' she said, waving them back down with a hand. 'You two stay as long as you please. And do leave the dishes. Ilse will clear them away when you've finished. I have a few details to check with the hotel.'

'The *hotel*?' Carey Bloomfield asked in surprise. 'When do you sleep?'

'I get enough. Sometimes, I sleep during the day.' Aunt Isolde smiled. 'After all, I am my own boss. But tonight,' she went on, 'there's a special reason. All the guests currently in the hotel are leaving tomorrow. We're expecting a big conference group from America in two days, and their advance guard of three will be here sometime in the morning. The conference group will fill the place to capacity and we need the extra day to get everything prepared.'

'From America?' Carey Bloomfield said.

'Why yes. We're a very popular conferencing location for western businesses, and from the Far East. We also get a fair number from the old Eastern Bloc. The westerners – especially people from the NATO countries – like the idea of hosting their events in a former East German mansion, and the scenery is quite splendid. The people from the Far East, mainly the Japanese, like the idea of this kind of building in a land just emerging from the long darkness that fell after the Second World War. Same reasons, in a way, but with subtle differences.

'But our very best customers by far are the Americans. We are booked out months in advance; either privately, or by companies. They come from many different states. Many of the men in these companies served at one time or another in the US forces in Germany during the Cold War. I suppose it gives them a kind of frisson just to see the ground on which they would have fought the former potential enemy. I once had the vice-president of an electronics firm, who was once a young communications lieutenant at Checkpoint Charlie in Berlin, staying here with his wife. He said he'd always wondered what he would have done, had the balloon really gone up. He looked at this house and said, "Thank God we were smart enough not to push the button". He really meant that.

'I have kept a room just as it used to be during the days of the DDR, including the spy holes that were used for cameras and microphones. The comrades didn't even trust each other. The room is a big hit with the guests, as you may imagine.'

'I'll bet it is,' Carey Blomfield said. 'I'd like to see it myself.'

'I'm sure Jens-Müller will be happy to show you. He knows where it is.'

'And will you be happy to show me, *Hauptkommissar* Müller?' Carey Bloomfield said with an exaggerated docility that was clearly lubricated by the excellent wine.

'Your wish,' he said amiably, 'is my command.'

Aunt Isolde looked from one to the other with amusement. 'I can see you two are having fun. Goodnight, children.' She moved round the table to kiss each on a cheek.

'Goodnight, Aunt Isolde,' they called out together as she went out.

A silence descended within the room. Carey Bloomfield looked at the wine bottles.

'I can get another,' Müller offered.

'Are you saying I'm a drunk?'

'I would not dream of it.'

'You let me drink,' she accused, 'while you had scarcely any.'

'I had some. But, as you know, I am on a case that grows more complex by the hour, and I drive a very powerful car. It would not look good for a police *Hauptkommissar* to be caught drunk at the wheel . . .'

'Jesus, Müller! Relax a little. Don't be so goddamned correct . . .'

'I am relaxed,' he assured her mildly.

'Just for once,' she reasoned, 'in this very wonderful house, after this very wonderful meal, drop the guard. Be . . . oh, I don't know . . . more easy-going.'

'I am easy-going . . . too easy-going, according to Kaltendorf.'

'To hell with Kaltendorf! We're not in Berlin right now. We're in your family home . . . Well . . . one of them. Your aunt treats you like a son. You know that?'

'She has no children. And she has been very good to me.'

'Especially after your mother died?'

A sudden hardness came to his face before vanishing as quickly as it had appeared. He said nothing.

'Sorry. I should not have mentioned—'

'It's alright.'

This brought another silence.

'God,' she said after a while. 'I'm killing the evening. Look . . . can we go for a walk, if it's not raining? I think I should walk some of the food off before I go to bed.'

'It's a good idea. The grounds are quite pleasant at night.'

'Right then. We walk.'

'What about the coffee?' he asked.

She looked at the sealed jug. 'Will the *Hauptkommissar* shoot me if I say no thanks?'

'The *Hauptkommissar* will not.'

'In that case, let us retreat and leave the room to Ilse.'

'Your wish is my command.'

'I'll strangle you one day, Müller.'

'That should be interesting.'

'Aargh!' she said in frustration. In the event, it was not raining and the night, while cool, was not uncomfortably so. Their shadows fled around them as they walked past the floodlights of the hotel grounds. Every so often, a sharp explosive hiss marked the demise of a mesmerized moth against the hot filaments.

Müller took her to the stream. Lights had been positioned so that a long stretch of it was illuminated.

'Hell,' she said. 'It's bigger than I thought. It's almost a small river. I'd hate to fall in.'

'I'm sure you can swim,' Müller said with a brief smile. 'It is really a tributary of the Saale that lost its way,' he went on to explain. 'Some time in the past – early in the last century – it changed track, and came through the grounds of the house. Right through to the late twenties the grounds were flooded each time the river itself rose; until someone had the bright idea of building a run-off; a sort of storm drain.'

The ground had been steadily sloping upwards as they

approached the stream. They arrived on the bank, and she saw that it was quite high up from the water. Just within sight to the left was a solidly built, arched wooden footbridge.

'They built this raised wall all along the banks,' Müller went on, 'and a little to your right just under our feet, is the entrance to what we call the pipeline, but is in fact a small tunnel lined with concrete. The entrance is quite wide; big enough for two large men to crawl through side by side. Then, some distance later, it narrows to the width of one, before opening out again to more than double. It keeps that size all the way to the main river. The shape makes the water flow much faster. Because the outflow also points downstream, the river current accelerates the process. If you look— Careful! I don't want to have to drag you out . . .'

'Not suggesting again that I'm drunk, are you, Müller?'

'Absolutely not. But still, be careful. There . . . can you see it?'

She was leaning cautiously forwards and peering down, and could just make out the gaping circular shape, quite high above the surface.

'Yes,' she said. 'It's high up.'

'It's a good indicator of the threat of a flood when the water reaches it.'

She straightened, and stepped back slightly from the edge. 'Has the water ever risen over it?'

'Never. This run-off seems to be sufficient to keep the water level from rising further. Even during the DDR days, when maintenance was very haphazard, it continued to do its job. A pity. Some of the comrades might have drowned.'

'That's a harsh comment.'

'I don't think so. According to a distant cousin who embraced the entire DDR ethos and even came here during those days, more than one out-of-favour comrade made a one-way trip through that tunnel.'

'You're kidding.'

'That was the story he told. No one has yet been able to verify it and, certainly, no remains were ever found around here during the renovation. But that does not mean it never happened.'

She stared at the stream with renewed and somewhat morbid interest. 'Imagine it. Some poor bastard may have once floated outside my window.'

'Outside mine too. We share the same stretch of water, and the bridge. There's a floodlight on the wall that usually shines on it. At Christmas, it's decorated with small lights.'

'It must look great from the window, with all the lights shining on the water. So who is this cousin?'

'Very distant, and not at all welcome in our family – on either side. We believe he betrayed many people in his time; although we can't prove that, of course. But his character makes it likely. He came here again soon after the rebuilding was complete, and noted that Aunt Isolde liked French wine. Very unpatriotic, he told her. Suddenly, this man who had spent most of his years being a staunch Party member had become a patriotic, democratic western German.'

'Your Aunt's ironic little joke at the table. Now I understand.'

'Exactly. Even though he was quite happy to make use of it in the DDR days, in reality he despised this house and everything it stands for.'

'That figures.'

'It was a class thing. He resented the family, and all things *bourgeois.*'

'That figures too,' Carey Bloomfield commented drily. 'It's OK to use the trappings, as long as you despise them as well.'

'Exactly,' Müller repeated.

'So, where is he now?'

'If anyone could tell, Pappenheim is the most probable. He has so many contacts in the darkest of places, but personally, I don't want to know. Aunt Isolde could not stand the idea of that man being in her house, either during the days of the partition, or more recently. Only God and his own conscience, if he has one, know the truth of what he has done in the name of the DDR.'

'Why haven't the authorities taken any action against him?'

'First they would have to find him, even if they wanted to take any action. He has covered his tracks very well. There's nothing official against him. I believe he knew the entire house of cards would come down one day, and he prepared well in advance.'

'Smart man.'

'Indeed. But who knows? One day, one of his many enemies might get him, wherever he's hiding.'

They began walking along the bank. The stream murmured strongly, its surface sparkling intermittently in the glare of the floodlights. Beyond the reach of the lights, the rest of it was a rushing sound on the darkness.

'Your aunt is quite something,' she said. 'There's the spirit of the rebel in her. I like that.'

'She'd be intrigued to hear you say that,' Müller remarked. 'In her youth, she was quite . . . wild. She never really did what was expected of her. Yet, she has turned out to be a very special person. You could put your life in her hands and she would never let go, no matter what.'

Carey Bloomfield knew he was talking from personal experience, but she did not probe.

'She's travelled widely,' Müller went on. 'Probably to places where you as a journalist have never been, nor will ever go to. She's been politically active, has attended demonstrations and, once, just missed having her head split open in Paris by the baton of a French policeman. She ducked in time. She has very little respect for most politicians of virtually any country, because she sees them as self-serving scoundrels. After all, her own home was vandalized by some of the worst examples. Though she belongs to it, her respect for what she calls the so-called nobility is minimal. She feels that because they were blessed by an accident of birth, they should do more in just about every human endeavour without needing public praise for it.'

'Is that why you're in the police?'

'I can't deny she has influenced me. But I am a policeman because I truly want to do the job. I believe in my country, and it gets to me when people abuse it, whether as criminals, politicians, or fake patriots. The last refuge of the scoundrel,' he added.

'The what?'

'Dr Johnson. English philosopher. He once said that patriotism was the last refuge of the scoundrel.'

'Meaning some no-brain asshole with a mean streak wraps himself in the flag and tries to fool people into believing he has all the answers.'

'Graphically put, but yes.'

'I could show you a few people on my side of the world who fit that description exactly,' she said dryly.

'And we have many of our own here,' Müller told her. 'Too many for the good health of my nation. Not all politicians are feckless idiots, of course; but there seems to be a depressingly low number of the astute ones around. Ah,' he continued, stopping to look up. 'There's my window, and of course, the bridge. See? The stream curves round and goes right past. I've done plenty of thinking at that window.'

'About cases?' she asked, looking up.

'About many things.'

They walked on in silence for some moments, listening to the rush of the stream. They stopped by the bridge, but did not use it.

'You didn't tell Aunt Isolde about the bodies you found,' she said.

'In my place, would you?'

She thought about it. 'I guess not,' she admitted. 'She's got a very British accent,' she went on. 'Don't tell me it's Oxford too.'

'Sandhurst,' he said. He seemed to be smiling as he said it.

'What do you mean?'

'Her first husband.'

'Her first? But I thought . . .'

'Dear old Uncle Helmut was not her first husband. He came after Major the Honourable Charles Wilton-Grenville. That's where her Sandhurst accent comes from. She picked it up from him. Sandhurst is . . .'

'I know. The British West Point. Officer College.'

'That's the one. But don't let anyone British hear you call it their version of West Point. And especially not Aunt Isolde. It's the other way round . . .'

'OK,' she said quickly, making pacifying motions with her hands. 'I'm forewarned. What happened to the major?'

'Dead, I'm afraid. He was the kind of man who liked danger; which, of course, attracted her. He was a member of a special-duties unit. He died on a mission. Then she met solid old Helmut. Nothing like her dashing Englishman; but he was exactly what she needed, especially after—' He stopped suddenly. He cleared his throat. 'Anyway, that's the very basic story of my unruly aunt.'

'She's not unruly at all. She's quite a lady. Full of power. I approve.' Carey Bloomfield did not ask why he had ended his story so suddenly. Then she gave a sudden shiver. 'A cold breeze must have come off the river.'

'Then I had better get you back inside.' He was clearly relieved she had not asked him to continue. 'It is quite late and we may have a very busy day to come.'

She nodded. 'Yeah. I could do with the zizz-time. I'd like to see that room with the spy holes, but it will have to wait. Do we have an early breakfast?'

'It's not pre-set. Come down when you're ready . . . Unless, of course . . .'

'All we've got time for is a cup of coffee.'

'Precisely.'

'Who'd be a cop?'

'Who'd be a journalist?' he countered. 'Want to try the bridge?'

106

'Not tonight. Tomorrow, perhaps.'

The grounds were totally deserted as they made their way back; and though they knew there were many guests within the hotel, it was as if they were the only ones around. No more explosive hisses came from the furnace-like heat of the lamps. Even the moths, it seemed, had decided to stop committing suicide.

'Quiet, isn't it?' she said in a hushed voice.

'Not if you really listen,' he told her. 'You can hear more than you would at first believe.'

'You know this from long practice?'

'Long hours on police stake-outs when I was a lot younger,' he replied. 'There were times when I could hear the blood rushing about my body. Or my partner snoring softly when he was supposed to be awake. And here we are.'

They had reached the front entrance of the residential wing. The 8 cm-thick door had a central splice of two full-sized sheets of light, but strong, steel. The arched door was protected by an illuminated keypad.

Müller tapped swiftly at the numbers. The door swung smoothly open and they entered. It swung shut again, locked itself with muted sibilance as the electronic locks slid home.

'Thanks for the walk,' she said as they reached the landing.

'My pleasure,' he said.

'Pleasure? Or duty?'

'I did enjoy our walk,' he said patiently.

'OK.'

'Goodnight, Miss Bloomfield.'

'I don't believe it,' she said in exasperation. 'Goodnight, Müller.'

She turned away and walked on to her room. She did not look back as she opened the door and entered.

The first thing she did was to check the drawer in which she had put her bag. It had not been disturbed. She paused.

'What the hell,' she said to herself. 'I'll get up early so that there's time to check out that room.'

107

She went back to the door and began to open it quietly, intending to go over to Müller's room to tell him. When it was just barely open, she stopped.

Müller was still on the landing at the top of the stairs, standing before his mother's portrait, hands behind his back.

She shut the door very softly. She remained behind it, straining to hear sounds from without. Very soon, she heard the sound of footsteps, muted by the Persian rugs. She waited for some time before peering out again.

Müller had gone.

She squeezed the door shut again, and carefully let the lock click soundlessly home. She then went over to the window to look out at the stream.

'Bodies floating,' she said to it. 'You look different to me now.'

She got the bag with the gun out of the drawer and placed it by the bed. She then undressed, and went into the bathroom. All she needed was there, including a long, luxurious bathrobe. She had a very hot shower, then went to bed naked.

The bag with the gun was close to hand.

Outside, the kamikaze moths had returned. Darting and pirouetting about one particular light, they swooped and dive-bombed into explosively hissing oblivion.

Schlosshotel Derrenberg, 06.30 hours.

Müller came sharply awake to the urgent summons of his mobile. It could only be Pappenheim this early, he thought as he grabbed it off the bedside table.

'Yes, Pappi,' he said into it.

'Good morning!' came Pappenheim's voice cheerfully. 'Sleeping well?'

'I was. *You* sound as if you haven't all night.'

'No rest for the wicked,' Pappenheim said. The sound of his deep drag on the inevitable cigarette came clearly.

'Smoking already?' Müller chided. 'Or just continuing from yesterday? Your lungs will look like the inside of a truck's exhaust pipe one of these days.'

'Don't be ridiculous,' came Pappenheim's still-cheerful retort. 'A truck's exhaust pipe is a lot cleaner by far.'

'You're hopeless.'

'Of course,' Pappenheim admitted unrepentantly. 'So give up. And what about the baby? Still tucked up nicely?'

'Alright, Pappi. You've had your fun and done the job of bringing me fully awake. I'm ready for the bad news.'

'Which do you want first?'

'There's more than one?'

'That depends, to quote you. Some bad, some not so good.'

'There's a difference?'

'That depends,' Pappenheim repeated, 'on your point of view.'

'Forget the point of view, Pappi. Let's have the first punch.'

'More killings.' Pappenheim had reverted to the indefatigable policeman he really was.

Müller shut his eyes briefly. 'Shit,' he said grimly. 'I really needed this. Where? When?'

'Magdeburg.'

'*Magdeburg?*'

'The very same.'

'And the victims?'

'As before. Like the ones you found last night; like the first four the other night. This time, there are three. They could be clones, they're so similar. People do say if you keep a dog long enough, you begin to look like it. I suppose if you share the same warped ideas, you begin to look like each other . . . if you get my meaning.'

'I get your meaning.'

'Our friend, whoever he may be, has a fine sense of theatre. He killed them on the steps of the *Dom* . . . and, for good measure, left a note this time. Then, to add a sense of occasion to it all, he weighted the note with a small statue of the Black Madonna, next to the bodies.'

'It gets better and better. Kaltendorf will make a nice meal out of all this. What did the note say?'

'"This time",' Pappenheim began to quote, '"the potential victims are armed and dangerous." Nice sense of irony, that. It goes on: "Any attacks will from now on be met with a multiple response." I think he means more than one for one. We've got a real joker here, Jens.'

'When did this news come in?'

'About 06.00 hours. Didn't want to wake you before I'd checked out some other factors. They were found by a routine patrol. The officers in the car couldn't believe their eyes. One of them got religion and said the bodies looked like sacrificial offerings. He'll probably start going to Church again,' Pappenheim added with ghoulish cynicism. 'He didn't say that. I just did.'

'I worked that one out.'

'The ballistics report is not in as yet, of course. Interesting to see whether it's again the Beretta 92R, the weapon used for the first killing, and favoured sidearm of the American military, the Italian Carabinieri, and a certain policeman I know who chooses it as his personal weapon, instead of the standard German issue. Interesting to see whether there's also a match with the bodies you found. The Great White hates you so much, he'd love it.'

'Even he wouldn't dare attempt to pin a murder on me on such a flimsy excuse.'

'He could try,' Pappenheim remarked dryly. 'He could try. Even though he couldn't place you in both places at the same time. Do you want me to tell him the latest news when he comes in?'

'Give me the rest of the bad news and I'll let you know after that.'

'The Mercedes coupé. The Autobahn police found three of the type in Bayern. Two were stopped, but were quite innocent. The third one got off the Autobahn . . .'

'Shit!'

'Don't worry. It was still spotted. Unfortunately, it's military.'

'*What?*'

'*American* military,' Pappenheim added with relish. 'It was seen entering a base. The soldiers at the gate saluted. That means officers. Nice little pot we're getting into.'

Müller began to get out of bed. 'What the devil have the American military got to do with all this?'

'At this moment in time, I can't tell you. But I can try a few sources . . .'

'See what you can find out, Pappi . . . assuming anyone will be prepared to say anything. I don't fancy getting entangled with a military operation; but they can't just shoot guns off in my district, whatever my sympathies. Where is this base?'

Pappenheim told him.

'Alright,' Müller said. 'I'm going out there today. See if you can smooth things to get me in. I must talk with the officer in command.'

'Surely, Jens, you can't believe the Amis are going about shooting . . .'

'I'm keeping all options open. One of them used a gun in an open street. I'm not saying they've shot anyone, even though the latest killings have occurred in Magdeburg . . . which just happens to be within the area where the Corvette disappeared. But the way the car switch was carried out shows practised organization, *with the resources to carry it out*. That tells us there *is* an operation running. The question is what, and why. I intend to find out.'

'The Great White will just love this. He wants to be President of Police one day, and will hold you fully responsible if he doesn't make it.'

'So, what else is new? I'm already a condemned man.'

'Here's something to cheer you up.'

'Anything.'

'That female witness to the incident yesterday . . . the one

111

who went on about foreigners. I decided to see what might be in her past, if anything. I asked Berger to get an old contact of mine to do some checking of old Stasi files. The woman, a Frau Hauser, has a very interesting history and a very fat file. Not only was she a hardcore informer, but for someone who hates foreigners, she had a nice taste in Russian soldiers . . . over a period of twenty years, at the very least. There was one particular Russian she was very fond of. Nice, eh? I think I'll pay her a visit. I want to play a game, just to see the look on her face.' The contempt in Pappenheim's voice was palpable.

'Just be careful, Pappi. Someone like that, now that she is in a democracy, will easily forget what she used to be and try to accuse you of police harassment. That kind can be very nasty.'

'Oh, I can be very nasty indeed, when I want to be,' Pappenheim said in a carefree voice. 'But I'll take Berger with me to ensure I shall be as good as a choirboy. Besides, I might get some more information out of this Frau Hauser. She might have recognized those nice democrats who attacked the Americans. Once an informer, always an informer.'

'Are you really going to go through with this?'

'Yes,' Pappenheim replied. 'People like that should always be reminded of their ghosts, whenever they start acting whiter than white. Talking of white, have you decided if you want me to say anything to the GW?'

'Not yet.'

'And are you going to call him with a personal report as he asked – sorry – *ordered*?'

'Not yet.'

'Oh, we do like playing in the fire.'

'The condemned man can eat as much as he likes.'

'But he still gets fried,' Pappenheim said with a chuckle.

'Not always,' Müller countered. 'Oh, and call me as soon as Klee makes his report.'

'Will do, and I'll also let you know if anything comes in about that container truck.'

'Alright, Pappi. Thanks.'

'I'll be in touch. Sorry to spoil the morning.'

'It was spoilt the moment that person fired those shots two mornings ago.'

After they had ended their conversation, Müller quickly showered and dressed, slipping on the unobtrusive shoulder harness that Carey Bloomfield had correctly assumed he wore. The gun in the holster was the Beretta 92R 9mm automatic. With his jacket on, there was no obvious indication that he was armed.

He went down to the breakfast room and found hot bread rolls, a buffet, and fresh coffee waiting; but no one was there. If normal practice were anything to go by, Aunt Isolde was already in the hotel management offices. He began to serve himself, just as he had done on previous occasions. When he had completed his choices, he sat down and began to eat.

It was 07.30 hours.

As he ate, he seriously considered leaving without Carey Bloomfield.

In her room, Carey Bloomfield was already awake, showered, fully dressed and almost ready to go down to breakfast.

She had acted upon her decision to wake early enough, in order to have the time to visit the DDR room. She also instinctively felt it quite likely that Müller would consider dumping her here at the hotel and leaving without her, if the thought crossed his mind. If he were determined to do so, threatening him with Kaltendorf would not work. She wondered if he had already gone down to breakfast.

She went over to the window and looked out. The new day was overcast, and threatened rain. She looked down at the stream and thought it seemed to have risen and was flowing faster.

She turned away and went back to where she had put her bag. She took her mobile out of it and called Toby Adams.

'Why didn't you give me the full background, Toby?' she began as soon as he had answered.

113

'No *Good morning, Toby*?' he countered. 'You don't sound happy, Carey. Bad night?'

'Bad information,' she said. 'Why didn't you tell me about his mother?'

A long silence followed.

'Hello,' she said caustically. 'Anybody there?'

'How did you find out?' he enquired at last.

'Difficult not to, considering there's a big portrait of her right above the staircase. I asked about her. He told me she was dead, then clammed up. Which leaves several unanswered questions. Why keep me in the dark, Toby? I nearly screwed up by asking the wrong question.'

Clearly embarrassed, Toby Adams cleared his throat. 'We didn't want you to get too close by feeling too much sympathy . . .'

'*We*? Who the hell's *we*, Toby?'

There was another embarrassed silence. 'Um . . . you know how it is . . .'

'No, Toby,' she interrupted in a low but furious voice, watchful eyes on the bedroom door. 'I *don't* know how it is. We've worked together for years. Don't let me begin to think I can't trust you.'

'Of course you can trust me!' The tenseness in his voice showed he was wounded by the remark.

'Then what the hell's this? Lack of correct information nearly blew this thing out of the water. Do you call that smart? I *need* to know, Toby. *Give*.'

The absolute determination in her voice told him she would not back down. He sighed, giving in.

'Alright. Just so you know, it was not my idea. I was not happy with leaving gaps in the briefing . . .'

'Then why the hell didn't you fight for me?'

'I did. And I'll have to justify telling you what I'm about to. So, calm down. OK?'

'OK.'

'It's quite a tragic story. She married very young and was deeply in love. However, some years later, the father began

114

to stray. She put up with it for as long as she could, until one day when he thought she was away, he took someone home. She came back early and found them together . . .'

'Jesus. So much for the nobility . . .'

'It gets worse. He pleaded with her to forgive him. It was a mistake . . .'

'Which . . . screwing the woman in the marital bed?' Carey Bloomfield remarked with razor-edged sarcasm. 'Or just screwing around?'

'Stay neutral on this, Carey,' Adams cautioned. 'He promised to stop completely, and suggested they both fly to Tuscany in their small private jet for a long second honeymoon. They were both pilots, so they flew without a crew. Somewhere over the Alps, the plane went in. Both were killed . . .'

'And?'

'And what?'

'I know there's more. How did it happen?'

He sighed once more. '*She* was at the controls. She simply pointed the thing at the ground and held it like that until it hit.'

'Jesus!'

'The voice recorder got it all. The man was screaming over and over. "*What are you doing*! *You'll kill us*!" She never replied. He tried to regain control from her, but she got the strength from somewhere. He never made it. The incident made headlines at the time, of course. The scandal rags had a field day, especially those that had it in for people of that class.'

It was now her turn to be silent. 'Good Christ,' she commented softly, after a while. 'What shit for a twelve-year-old. No wonder he didn't want to talk about it.'

'Carey,' Adams warned. 'Stay neutral!'

'I'll stay neutral. I've got a job to do.'

'He inherited everything, including his father's title,' Adams continued. 'The aunt brought him up. But get this . . . she was known as the Red Baroness.'

'She what?'

'I kid you not. She was political . . .'

'I know.'

'You *know*?'

'He told me.'

'*He*— How come?'

'We were talking, and he mentioned she was active during her younger days.'

'Still is, in a way. Her leanings are more left than right. Kind of centre-left.'

'I gathered that by what he said. So why the Red Baroness?'

'The reports we have were compiled by the sort of people who went in for those kinds of sobriquets in those days. If you were not on the far right, you were a commie.'

'That figures,' Carey Bloomfield commented dryly.

'She nearly got her head busted in Paris . . .'

'He told me that too, and about her first husband.'

'My, my. You *have* been chatting. Do you know how the English major died?'

'Just that he died on a mission.'

'It was the rescue of a British diplomat from the clutches of tribesmen in some hellhole. The mission was a success, but the major didn't make it back to the pick-up rendezvous. His body was never found. Speculation was that he was wounded and captured, and hacked to pieces.'

'God!'

'These things happen, as we both know.'

'It does not make it any less gruesome.'

'That's certainly true. But the point is, no one knows his real fate, as no evidence was ever found. Perhaps for reasons of his own, he faked his own death. Perhaps he had a mental breakdown, discovered a change of sympathies, and didn't want to return to the old life. Perhaps he converted to a different religion. Who knows? It's not the first time in history any of those things have occurred. Perhaps he really is dead. The place where it all happened is now a democratic nation, is a friend of the West and makes lots of dough from oil.'

'Money always talks.'

'Sad, but true. Watch your step, Carey. Got that gun your brother gave you?'

'Got it.'

'Just remember—'

'Yes, yes. I know. Don't get too close.'

'Just remember it.'

'I will.'

'And be careful.'

'I will be.'

When they ended, she put the phone away, then took the gun out of the bag and checked it. It had a full magazine, and she had reloads.

The gun, an automatic, was a Beretta 92R.

Six

Day Two: Schlosshotel Derrenberg, Saaletal, 08.00 hours.

Müller was still at breakfast when she entered.

'Hi,' she greeted him brightly. 'You're up early. Mmm! Coffee smells good.'

'Good morning, Miss Bloomfield,' he said, rising to his feet. 'Did you sleep well?'

'Very well, thanks. And you don't have to stand just because I've entered the room, Müller. This is the start of our second day together, can we relax the formalities a little?'

'I am relaxed,' he said, regaining his seat.

'Yeah,' she remarked, scepticism personified. 'Sure. Where's Aunt Isolde?'

'I haven't seen her, so I am assuming she is busy getting things ready at the hotel, for that conference group she's expecting. Please help yourself to anything you would like.'

She studied the buffet. 'This is being seriously spoilt for choice.'

'No need to hurry. Take your time.'

She looked at him suspiciously. 'Oh no, you don't. *Take your time* reads to me like I'm going to stay all day here while you take off somewhere. No go, Müller. Where you go, I go. Got it?'

He smiled briefly. 'I expected you might say that. Alright. I leave in fifteen minutes.'

'Hey! That's not fair! You've had plenty of time for breakfast! And I've still got to go upstairs for my bag.'

'As you've just said,' he began mildly, 'I got up early. If you want to accompany me, be on time.' He patted the edge of his mouth briefly with a napkin, and stood up. 'You can have a leisurely breakfast, spend a very pleasant day with Aunt Isolde, check out the DDR room, and I'll pick you up later; or . . . you can meet me at the hotel entrance. That's the deal. Take it, or leave it.'

He went out with the barest of smiles, while she stared furiously at him. Then she quickly returned her attention to the table.

'I guess I'd better eat fast,' she muttered to herself.

'This is the manager,' Bulent Landauer said in English into the phone, in response to the American voice in his ear. 'Yes, sir. Everything is being prepared. When can we expect your representatives to arrive?'

Aunt Isolde had called Landauer into her office to discuss the day's arrangements; then the phone had rung. She had indicated that he pick it up while she checked out something on her private computer. She now glanced up at him with mild curiosity before continuing what she was engaged upon, leaving him to deal with the customer.

'I have a rather delicate question to ask,' the voice said tentatively.

'Ask away, sir.' Landauer's own English had more than a hint of American overtones.

The person at the other end seemed to hesitate, then began to speak in an awkward rush. 'You see . . . er . . . some of our people are . . . well . . . black. We wondered whether your hotel . . . er . . . you know . . . with all these attacks by—'

'If you do not mind my interrupting, sir,' Landauer said with cheerful bonhomie. 'Please do not worry about such things. Our hotel has no problem at all. For example, I have a Turkish mother. If this hotel practised what I believe you are delicately hinting at, *I* would not be working here.'

He looked briefly towards the door as Müller entered,

closed the door quietly, and walked on silent feet to Aunt Isolde's desk.

'Yes. Yes. I see.' The voice in Landauer's ear was uncertain. 'But will they be safe? I mean, they will not be attacked?'

'Absolutely not, sir. These people are a minority—'

'You do understand, if our people are not safe, we are likely to cancel and go elsewhere.'

Both Müller and Aunt Isolde were now looking curiously at Landauer.

'I assure you, sir, you will have no need to worry.'

'Alright.' There was still some hesitation in the voice. 'Our representatives will arrive later today. Their plane was delayed.'

'Don't worry, sir. We will be happy to receive them whenever they arrive.'

'Thank you, Mr . . .'

'Landauer.'

'Thank you, Mr Landauer. Will you be there when we arrive?'

'I will ensure that I am.'

'Then I look forward to meeting with you.'

'It will be a pleasure, sir.' As he hung up, Landauer saw that Aunt Isolde was looking hard at him.

'What was that all about?' she asked in German.

'Our conference client. He says, as some of his people are black, he was worried whether we would welcome them.'

'Because of these damned attacks?'

Landauer nodded. 'He even asked if they would be safe, and suggested they might cancel if they feared for their safety.'

Aunt Isolde made a sound full of angry frustration. 'My God. That's all Germany needs. Businesses pulling out as if we were some banana republic, because of those wretched people. They call themselves patriots; but what they're doing will destroy Germany. We've been there before, and we certainly don't want it again. *Ever*. People never seem to learn, do they?'

'There are a lot more good people here in Germany than there are bad,' Landauer said. 'It won't happen again.'

Aunt Isolde stood up and went to a window. It overlooked the stream. She passed a hand slowly along the window sill.

'I hope you are right,' she told him quietly, staring at the risen stream. 'There were good people before; but they were not strong enough, and not enough of them to make a difference when it was needed. This gave the other kind the opportunity to create a chain of events that wrecked Germany, and once cost my family this house. I do not intend to lose it again.'

Müller, noting that Landauer was frowning slightly, broke his silence. 'What is it?'

'I know this might sound strange,' Landauer began after a moment's hesitation, 'but I thought he was overdoing the concern.'

'What do you mean?'

Again, the manager hesitated. 'I just felt he was . . . exaggerating . . . being a little . . . theatrical. I could be wrong, of course.'

Outside, the first spots of rain spattered the surface of the water.

Carey Bloomfield was waiting by the Porsche, complete with bag, when Müller came out of the hotel.

'Well done, Miss Bloomfield!' he greeted her cheerfully. 'I've just been saying goodbye to Aunt Isolde. I explained that you'd be coming with me and, as we're in a hurry, there was little time for you to say goodbye personally. On the other hand, she'd be delighted to have you stay . . . No? As you wish. And you shouldn't frown. It causes wrinkles.'

'Aaah, shaddup!' she said.

He grinned at her as he unlocked the car. 'I take it that means you're coming with me. Don't worry. Aunt

Isolde expects us back for dinner. It's not a long drive, but it could be a long day. So, please get in, if you are coming.'

She entered the car without speaking.

He got in behind the wheel, started the engine and drove slowly away. Once out of the hotel grounds, he rocketed the Porsche along.

'Watch it,' she warned. 'If my hasty breakfast repeats, you could get a great mixture of coffee and everything else I wolfed down, all over your nice leather interior.'

'I doubt it,' he said calmly. 'You're made of stronger stuff.' He did not slow down.

She said nothing to that and instead glanced upwards at the gloomy sky. 'Looks like rain soon. I thought the stream looked swollen this morning.'

'It's been raining heavily in the mountains during the early hours; and that will have raised the river level, which will also have affected the stream. More rain is expected, this time over the whole region. But don't worry. This car grips like a leech on wet roads.'

'I'm not worried.'

'But you are angry.'

'I'm not angry. Why should I be? And where are we going?'

'To a place not far from Schweinfurt,' he replied. 'An American military base.' He glanced at her. 'It is alright to look surprised.'

'Why should I be surprised? I'm just a reporter observing how you work.' But she was surprised. 'How long will it take us to get there?'

'It's about one hundred and ninety or so kilometres. Allowing for traffic, and if we keep up a high average speed . . . just over an hour.'

'We're going to *average* a hundred and ninety *an hour*? Are you nuts?'

'Not the last time I looked in the mirror. I'd be happy to take you back—'

'Forget it, Müller. You're not going to frighten me out of this seat.'

'Then sit back and enjoy it.'

They had now reached the Autobahn access. If anything, once they had joined the A9 heading southwards in the direction of Bayreuth, the Porsche gathered speed and seemed to launch itself forwards.

Watching the road turn into a fast-flowing ribbon of asphalt, Carey Bloomfield was determined not to look anxious.

'Music?' Müller asked.

'No!'

'As you wish.'

'What . . . What did you mean when you said it could be a long day?' she asked as calmly as she could muster.

'There have been more killings.'

She turned her head slowly to look at him. 'Where?'

He smiled without humour. 'Magdeburg. This person, whoever he *or* she may be, is playing a dangerous little game with us.'

'Or she?'

'Why not? A woman is just as capable of committing these murders.'

'Murders?'

'What else would you call them?'

'Some people might think he *or* she is taking out people who are already murderers, or are murderers-in-waiting . . .'

'Not until they themselves have actually committed the crime. Whatever you or I may think or find sympathy with, these killings are a crime. It is my job to ensure the person committing them is caught and punished. Street justice is just one step up from the descent into anarchy. Revenge killings may start and then the whole thing escalates. Before we know it, we've got a civil war. With your country's own history, you know how nasty that can get. We all know about Yugoslavia. Whoever the killer is, I believe that is exactly what he or she may be aiming for.'

'Oh come on, Müller. *Civil war*? In *Germany*?'

'Civil wars have started for less reasons. It is just over ten years since the eastern *Länder* once more became one with the rest of Germany. We are particularly vulnerable at this moment in time . . .'

'Come on,' she repeated. 'This country has a strong constitutional structure.'

'Has it? The western part had nearly fifty years of practice before the unification. The eastern part was a dictatorship throughout that time. There is a strain that is painfully obvious. The difference between what we call civilized behaviour and barbarism is very small; and barely over sixty years ago, the whole country experienced that dark side. A tiny spark is all it takes. Look around the world. He – I will say he, for practical purposes – left a note this time. *The potential victims are armed and dangerous. Any further attacks will be met with a multiple response.* I am quoting precisely.'

'Meaning any one attack on a foreigner will result in two or more of the attackers, or their co-ideologues, being killed in response.'

Müller nodded as he overtook three cars at high speed. 'And he can choose any reprisal number he likes – two, three, ten . . . He is daring them to strike back. He *wants* it. Do you see where this leads?'

'I can see. But do you really believe the victims' buddies will actually do that? They have no idea where he could strike next.'

'My hope is that they will be cautious for a while; perhaps even fearful. That might give me the time to put a stop to this dangerous insanity before it gets even worse.'

'He could be responding to something terrible that was done . . . perhaps to him, or a member of his family. Perhaps his home was firebombed and the perpetrators got away with it because the authorities did nothing . . . except debate about what to do, and he got pissed about it . . .'

'So he takes the law into his own hands? Don't misunderstand me. When I saw the photographs of the first killings, my gut reaction was that they deserved it. But I'm a policeman. It is my duty to stop such criminal acts, from whichever quarter. I believe in that duty. I would hunt *them* down, if the situation were reversed.'

'Would you really?'

'Of course. How can you ask?'

'Then why are so many attacks happening . . . with apparent immunity?'

'I am one policeman, not the government. You are the journalist. Ask them. Make your questions hard, and take no excuses. You might get a sensible answer, if you're lucky.'

'Wow! Kaltendorf know you think like this?'

'Of course he knows. My attitude is no secret.'

'So, looking at this the hard way, he'd like to see you fall flat on your face.'

'Among others, yes. If this killer succeeds in getting away with more and more killings, it would please Kaltendorf. He would remove me from the very case he dropped into my lap, and do so very publicly. I have no illusions about that man. He is hungry enough for power, and will happily sacrifice my head to the gods of his ambition.'

'So, he's really set you a trap.'

'And I am already in it.'

'Aren't you worried? Talking to me like that?'

He glanced at her speculatively. 'No.'

'Trusting me?'

'No.' He did not elaborate. 'The killer added a finishing touch to the Magdeburg killings,' Müller continued before she could say anything. 'He left a small statue of the Black Madonna by the bodies; as a paperweight for the note.'

'An ironic, theatrical flourish . . .'

'Those are almost Pappenheim's words. Intriguing.'

'Why intriguing?'

'Humour me.'

'And what has all this to do with the American military?'

'The car we're looking for was seen entering the base,' Müller said. 'The guards saluted. Officers in the car.'

'So, you're telling me this may all have something to do with an intelligence operation?'

'I don't know. But it's an anomaly. I don't like anomalies. I want this one cleared up quickly. If there is a connection between those deaths and your military, I will be a very unhappy man. Not a pretty sight, I have been reliably informed. Pappenheim swears Genghis Khan is a pussycat by comparison. But that's Pappenheim for you. He tends to exaggerate such things.'

She said nothing to that as the Porsche continued southwards at high speed. It was 08.30 hours, fourteen minutes after they had left Schlosshotel Derrenberg.

In Berlin it was cool, but not raining. The unmarked car pulled into the dreary street that was once part of East Berlin, made cheerful by the warm lights of the café where the incident with the Corvette had taken place. Berger was driving. Pappenheim peered at the houses that had not yet received their westernized facelift.

'There,' he said. 'That one. That's the number.'

Berger stopped the car. 'Shall I come with you, sir?'

'Yes. You should enjoy this too. And besides, I promised Jens you would be there to keep me in check.'

'And could I keep you in check?'

'Not if I didn't want you to.'

'That's what I thought, sir.'

Pappenheim made a sound that could have been a chuckle. Incredibly, he had not smoked in the car. But that state of affairs would soon change.

'Come on, Berger,' he said, getting out of the car and lighting up. He inhaled deeply, welcoming the end of his brief spell of abstinence.

They walked up to the three-storey building, which had been divided into six apartments.

'She must have been living here for some time,' Pappenheim observed. 'Compared to those high rabbit-warren blocks, this would have been relatively classy by DDR standards. We know why, and how, she managed to get it,' he added grimly.

The name, they saw, was on the top floor.

'Shit!' Pappenheim swore. 'Now we've got to walk up.' He jabbed at the button.

Nothing happened.

He tried again. Still nothing. He stepped back to look up at the top floor. No one was looking out.

'The old DDR habit must still be strong,' he commented wryly. 'When the doorbell goes, it must be the police. Pretend you're a mouse and stay quiet.'

He tried a third time.

A short while later, the main door to the apartments opened. A woman in her fifties appeared. She had a pinched face and eyes that had been betrayed and themselves betrayed others so often, they had long since forgotten what it was like to have a soul. They were dead stones in her face.

'Yes?' she snapped, looking at Pappenheim and Berger. 'What do you want? I am on my way out.'

Pappenheim, when he wanted to, could smile so beatifically, he looked like a cuddly teddy bear. The guile was known to work wonders on recalcitrant witnesses. Knowing what he did about her, he forced back his contempt and gave her one of his best examples.

'Frau Hauser?'

She frowned at him suspiciously. 'Who are you?'

'*Oberkommissar* Pappenheim, Frau Hauser. You were very kind to help us out yesterday . . .'

She brightened suddenly, but her face still remained mean.

'Ah! Yes. Always happy to help the police.'

'I'll bet you are,' Berger murmured to herself.

Frau Hauser, ears finely tuned through years of listening-in on the conversation of others, caught the murmuring, but not the words. She glanced sharply at Berger.

Pappenheim pretended he'd heard nothing.

'Would you mind telling me what you saw?' he asked the woman.

She first looked about her to see if her neighbours were observing her. One or two were looking. An expression of self-importance came over her ravaged face.

'I told the other policemen—'

'Forgive me for interrupting, Frau Hauser,' Pappenheim said smoothly, 'but I'm searching for something more specific; something no one but you might have noticed.'

This made her feel even more important. The *Oberkommissar* believed she might have seen something worthwhile!

'I know you are a good German,' he went on, driving home his advantage.

'I am!' she said proudly. 'I am. Not like those foreigners . . . Shooting their guns in our streets.'

'Yes. Quite. What about the others?'

'What others?'

'The ones who started it. Can you tell me anything about them? Were they local?'

Frau Hauser began to look suspicious again. 'Why do you want to know about them? They did not have the guns.'

'Gun, Frau Hauser,' Pappenheim corrected. 'Only one gun was used . . . and only because they were first attacked.'

'So?' She had no sympathy with the victims. 'If they were not here, they would not be attacked.'

'I see,' Pappenheim remarked so softly it was barely perceptible. When Pappenheim spoke so quietly that it was difficult to hear him, he was at his most dangerous. 'Tell me, Frau Hauser, have you heard from Captain Mikhail Derinov recently?'

It was a body blow. Frau Hauser's face whitened, then seemed to crumple. Her entire frame seemed to reel as if in a strong wind, and her breathing had suddenly become laboured. The dead eyes actually showed fear.

'Who . . . who are you?' she whimpered.

'I have just told you—'

'No! No, you're not. They've sent you after me. They—'

Pappenheim took a long drag on his cigarette, stared briefly down at his shoes, as if to check if they needed cleaning.

'Relax, Frau Hauser,' he said, looking back at her through freshly blown smoke. 'We are not from your old friends . . . Although, with the friends you had, if I were you, I would not need enemies. We are normal, German police. But I thought you should know that if we need to question you further about the incident, we expect truthful answers. Is that clear?'

All bluster had gone out of her. She nodded, as if in a dream. 'Yes. Yes.'

'Thank you, Frau Hauser. Goodbye.'

Pappenheim turned and, followed by Berger, returned to the car. He extinguished the cigarette before entering.

Just as they were about to drive off, Berger said, 'She's going back in.'

Pappenheim turned to look. 'I must have ruined her day,' he said unrepentantly. 'I wonder how many days she ruined in her time.'

'That was like an execution,' Berger said as she put the car into gear and drove off.

Pappenheim's voice was devoid of feeling. 'It might make up for some of the poor devils she betrayed. Let her live with their ghosts.'

The Porsche was at the Bayreuth/Kulmbach intersection when the rain, which had been a heavy drizzle for some kilometres, hit with a vengeance. It was as if the very heavens had opened up and let fly with a deluge. The surface had suddenly become a streaming watercourse. The raindrops splattered themselves against the windscreen with the impact of bullets. The day seemed to have become night.

Carey Bloomfield twisted in her seat to look behind. A high tail of spray billowed in the car's wake.

'Worried?' Müller asked as they joined the A70 to head for Schweinfurt.

'Not . . . exactly,' she said, settling back in her seat. Surreptitiously, she tightened her seat belt.

Müller noticed the movement and smiled briefly. 'I see.'

She watched as the car's powerful Litronic headlights lit

up the wet gloom. The rain speared slantingly down, and it seemed to her that the wipers were having a fight of it. This was not really so, for they kept the windscreen brilliantly clear.

She heard a change in the sound of the car's engine. He was slowing down.

'You don't have to slow down,' she said quickly.

'You trust my driving?'

'Of course.'

'Good. I am a fully qualified police pursuit driver, you know.' Their lane was clear of traffic for a long distance ahead.

'Great . . . but . . . but do you think *he* knows that?' Her voice had risen to a squeak.

Someone in a white van had decided it was a good idea to swerve out without indicating. It was clear that the driver had not even bothered to first check his mirrors. The van was swaying on the wet road.

Müller, she noted, had already swiftly dabbed at the brakes. The Porsche slowed massively, and without drama. By the time they were near the van, they had matched its speed, and were a safe distance from it. There was plenty of time to read the number plate, which had BM index letters.

'Bergheim,' Müller explained. 'That's in the state of Nordrhein Westfalen; up near Cologne. He should be more careful. He's a long way from home, and should be prosecuted for such dangerous driving,' he added mildly. 'He's an accident waiting to happen. I ought to give him a warning.'

'Can you do that?'

'Strictly speaking, as we're now in Bavaria, this is the Bavarian police jurisdiction. Officially, I have no writ here.'

'And unofficially?'

'I'm still a policeman.'

Müller patiently waited until the van, struggling at the limit of adhesion and speed, had safely passed the car it had pulled out to overtake, before accelerating past.

A young couple were in the van. The man was driving. As the Porsche went by, he stuck up a middle finger.

'What an asshole,' Carey Bloomfield said.

In the van, the driver remarked sourly to his companion, 'Because he's got a fucking Porsche, he thinks he's a big shot. *Blödes Arschloch.*'

He drove the van as fast as it could go on the wet road.

'Be careful!' the young woman with him warned fearfully. 'It's a long way home.'

'I'm a good driver,' he said to her sharply.

'I was going to let him off,' Müller said, 'but he clearly has his brain in the wrong gear.'

'You're going to stop him?'

'No. I have a better idea.'

Müller touched a button on the navigation and communication console. The button activated a pre-programmed sequence and, within moments, Pappenheim's voice came through on the car speakers.

'Trouble?' it asked.

'No. A favour.' Müller spoke into a highly sensitive microphone that was housed behind a small, circular grill on the instrument panel.

'Ask it,' Pappenheim said.

'We just passed a dangerous idiot on the A70, direction Schweinfurt. Get the Bayern people to alert a patrol. Give the driver a sharp warning. It's a white van with Bergheim plates.' He gave Pappenheim the number.

'Will do,' Pappenheim said. 'I'll call you on the mobile when there's news about the other.'

'Yes.'

'And you are expected at your destination.'

'That was quick work.'

'I'm quick.'

'No bureaucratic problems?'

'A few . . . But nothing I could not handle.'

'Thanks, Pappi.'

'Nada, as the Americans would say.'

'I think it's the Mexicans.'

'Whatever.'

'Neat,' Carey Bloomfield said as the conversation ended, pointing to the console. 'But you guys still don't trust me. Pappenheim was talking in staccato sentences.'

'It's just his way.'

The outside lane was again clear for a long distance.

'Oh sure.' She glanced behind. The high tail of spray was once more trailing the Porsche. 'And I guess the guy in the white van is in for a shock.'

'Just a small one . . . but it might save his life one day. And that of whoever might be with him.'

'Talking of which,' she said, peering out at the seemingly endless rain, 'I know I've got to go someday; but I'd hate it to be on a German freeway; or any other freeway for that matter.'

'Point taken,' he said, slowing down slightly.

'I didn't mean—'

'Yes, you did.'

They drove for some kilometres in silence. Then, up ahead, they saw flashing blue lights. Traffic began to slow down. Müller slowed. A patrol car was on the hard shoulder, waving the vehicles on. The traffic gathered speed.

Carey Bloomfield again twisted round in her seat to look at the patrol car as they too were waved on. Presently, the policeman waving the traffic through held up a wand with a red disc on the top. He was stopping someone. It was the white van.

'Yep,' she said, turning round again. 'They got him.'

The young woman in the van watched anxiously as the policeman held up the stop sign.

'I told you to be careful!' she whispered sharply.

'Don't be stupid,' he said crossly. 'I haven't done anything.' He pulled on to the hard shoulder.

The patrolman came up to the van. His partner stood a careful distance away, alertly watchful.

'Please get out,' the one by the van said.

The driver climbed out.

'Licence.'

The driver handed it over. The policeman inspected it, then handed it back. His partner sternly waved curious drivers on.

'Thank you,' the one by the van said. 'You may drive on.'

'That's it?' the driver began truculently. 'You stop me just for this?'

The policeman looked at him coldly. 'Be thankful I don't do a full safety check of your van. You could be here all day. In future, drive more carefully when you overtake. You are not the only one on the road.'

He turned away and went back to his car. Both policemen got in, and the car rejoined the traffic. The flashing lights went out.

The van driver climbed back in slowly. 'It was that bastard in the Porsche. He called the police.'

'You don't know that. They always stop people at random.'

'Not like this. Bastard!'

'You can't be sure. Another police car could have seen us and radioed—'

'That cop said I should be more careful when I overtake . . .'

'He's right. I said you should have waited—'

'Shut up! Fucking Porsche driver. Thinks he's such a big shot.'

He started the van. But he drove more carefully after that.

At about the same time, Krause and Engels were in their helicopter on a routine traffic check in the Magdeburg area, but still keeping an eye out for the refrigerated truck, and the Cherokee. The day was speckled with high cloud but, as yet, no rain threatened in the region.

'I wonder if anyone will ever find that truck,' Krause began. 'It must be well across the country by now.'

'Perhaps even across the border,' she said. 'Or hidden somewhere. I saw a film once about a freezer truck. Among the beef carcasses hanging in it were the carcasses of humans split the same way – right down the middle – mixed in among the others. The whole thing was going to a meat factory. One day, they'll mix human and animal genes and breed the result for food.'

'My God, Engels! I've just had breakfast!'

'Don't eat meat.'

'That's all I need . . . a vegetarian observer.'

'I'm not vegetarian. I eat fish.'

The helicopter thrummed its way westwards for a while, before turning south.

'There's a rumour . . .' Krause said.

'There's always a rumour.'

'This one's special. The rumour is that the Berlin hotshots want to steal you from us. Special request. They want to train you to pilot status.'

Engels was very surprised. 'I haven't heard anything.'

'A little bird told me.'

'I know who *she* is. That little blonde in the documents department. God. You men.'

'We're just friends.'

'Hah hah,' Engels enunciated.

'What's your problem, Engels?'

'*I* have a problem? Because I don't sleep around?'

'So? Is it true?'

'Is what true? I just said I know nothing of this. You shouldn't believe everything you hear in bed.'

'I never said—'

'Hold. Something coming in.' Engels touched a hand to her helmet. 'An Autobahn patrol found the Cherokee . . . in a *Rastatte* car park not far from Brandenburg. They must have stopped for the night. Well, we don't have to look for that one anymore. But I think we've lost the truck.'

'I agree.'

'That's something. Sir.'

134

Krause tightened his lips. He fancied Engels and hated the thought that she might be leaving before he'd had a chance with her.

Engels knew it, and also knew she would never allow him that chance. She wondered whether the rumour about Berlin could have substance. Training to *pilot*.

She hoped that for once Katja Fromm, the *rumour bird* in question, had correct information.

The thought excited her.

Day Two: Kommissar Klee's office, 09.30 hours.

Klee was at his desk, finishing his report of the night's incident on his computer, and was preparing to despatch it by encrypted e-mail, directly to Pappenheim in Berlin. He had put the last full stop to it, when his immediate superior, *Oberkommissar* Gräben, entered.

Klee did not have the office to himself. Space allocation dictated that he shared it with two other *Kommissars*, one from the motorcycle branch.

'Finished that report yet, Klee?' Gräben demanded.

The two *Kommissars* paused in what they had been doing to watch interestedly. They took morbid enjoyment in the confrontations between Klee and Gräben, who was the younger of the two and somehow felt inadequate in Klee's presence.

It probably had to do with the fact that Klee had once been a teacher during the DDR times and his professorial manner, accentuated by that moustache, tended to unsettle the recently-promoted Gräben, who was almost young enough to have been his pupil. An excellent policeman, Klee had little time for Gräben's posturings. He had not yet gone home since the night before, and needed sleep. He was not in the mood for Gräben.

'Just about, sir,' Klee replied carefully.

'Just about? It's either finished, or it isn't.'

'It's finished.'

'Good. Have a copy printed and sent to my office.'

'I can't do that, sir.'

Gräben's eyes grew round. *'What?'*

With impeccable timing, the phone rang in the office of Gräben's own superior, *Erster Hauptkommissar* Wilhelm Norring.

He picked it up. 'Norring.'

'Hello, Willi.'

'My God, Pappi! Where did you spring from? Where are you?'

'Berlin.'

'My God!' Norring repeated. 'How many years since we've seen each other? Two? Three?'

'Over three.'

'Still an *Oberkommissar?*'

'For my sins, yes.'

'You should stop giving your superiors a hard time, Pappi. Bad for promotional prospects.'

'Someone has to.'

'Tell me about it,' Norring said in sympathy. 'So, what can I do for you?'

'That business in the woods last night.'

'Ah, yes. Nasty stuff. Not what I wanted on my patch. I was away yesterday and came in this morning to receive the glad news. One of my people, Klee, is in charge of the case. I won't know the full details until I see his report, but he told me that one of your people, a *Hauptkommissar* Müller, made the discovery.'

'That's just it. We have a very strong interest. In fact, Klee's report is to come directly to us.'

'Are you serious about this, Pappi?'

'Very. It comes to us even before you see it.'

Norring was silent for long moments. 'I am assuming you would not be saying this to me unless it was necessary.'

'You know me, Willi. I don't fool around. I promise you will be put in the picture later.'

Norring took a deep breath. 'So, what do you want me to do?'

'Make certain Klee is not obstructed by anyone immediately outranking him.'

'Gräben,' Norring said instantly. 'The little officious creep will want to get his hands on that report so that he can take it to the boss-man himself, and look good. He's very ambitious, and is hoping to get this job one day.'

Pappenheim's laugh sounded in Norring's ear. 'Do you see? I have no one trying to take my job. The joys of low rank.'

'*Oberkommissar* isn't low, Pappi, but I get your meaning.'

'Well? Can you keep Gräben off Klee's back?'

'Leave it to me. But who will keep *my* boss off my back?'

'Leave *that* to me. Thanks for the help, Willi.'

'You owe me a drink.'

'I owe you one. Thanks again, Willi.'

As they hung up, both Norring and Pappenheim knew it would be some time before they actually got together for that drink.

In Klee's office, the stand-off was still in progress. Gräben did not want to believe that Klee had refused his demand.

He stared at his subordinate. 'Are you refusing my order?'

'Not refusing, sir,' came Klee's quiet response. 'I am obeying an order.'

'Whose?'

'I cannot—' The phone on Klee's desk rang. He picked it up. 'Klee.'

Gräben stared impotently at the *Kommissar*.

The other two continued to look on with expectant interest.

'Klee,' came Norring's voice in the *Kommissar*'s ear. 'That report.'

'Yes, sir,' Klee said cautiously.

137

'Is it finished?'

'It is sir.'

'Send it on to Berlin.'

'Yes, sir.'

'And Klee . . . is Gräben with you?'

'Right here, sir.'

'Put him on.'

Wordlessly, Klee handed the phone to Gräben, who frowned uncertainly at him before taking it. 'Gräben.'

'In my office, *Oberkommissar*,' Norring ordered firmly. 'Now!'

'Yes, sir, but—'

'Now means *now*, Gräben!'

'Yes, sir,' Gräben acquiesced tightly. He handed the phone back to Klee.

'He's on his way, sir,' Klee said to Norring, eyes upon Gräben, who glared back at him.

'Thank you, Herman.'

'Sir.' As they hung up, Klee added to Gräben, 'He's waiting.'

Gräben's eyes were lances that longed to skewer the *Kommissar*. 'I don't know what you did, Klee . . . but this is not over!' He strutted angrily out of the office.

'Well,' the motorcycle *Kommissar* said with a laugh. 'If you need a job, Herman, you can always join us on motorcyles.'

Klee grinned at him. 'Green leathers don't suit my complexion.'

They all laughed.

The sound of the laughter reached the departing Gräben, who stiffened his back as he walked on.

The Porsche was now near Arnstein, roughly midway between Schweinfurt and Würzburg, and the rain was still falling heavily. The plume of its tail churned in its wake, strongly reminiscent of that of a speedboat. In her seat, Carey Bloomfield was surprised to find that she was now quite relaxed with Müller's driving capabilities. He was at ease with the machine, seemingly an extension of himself.

'We'll be stopping soon to fill the tank,' he said. 'I always ensure that it is refilled at the halfway mark.'

'If we're stopping for juice,' she began with relief, 'that's good. I need to empty *my* tank.'

'You should have said. We passed many rest places. There are toilets—'

'I can wait till the next gas station.'

'Alright. It's not far.'

Barely minutes later, Müller changed lanes, slowing right down as the 300-metre warning stripes appeared, and filtered into the exit lane that led to the service station. When they had stopped at the petrol pumps, Carey Bloomfield got out.

'I'll go do my business, while you tank up,' she said.

Müller nodded. 'Fine.'

'You're not going to drive off and leave me here?'

'Of course not.'

'Can I trust you?'

'Absolutely. You have my word.'

'Do you trust me?'

He grinned. 'No.'

'At least you're consistent.'

He watched as she hurried towards the toilets. 'I am very consistent, Miss Bloomfield,' he said to himself, unhitching the fuel hose and inserting the nozzle into the car's filler.

She entered the toilets, went straight through and out to the back of the building. She got out her mobile as she huddled against it to shelter from the rain, and dialled Toby Adams.

'This will be very short, Toby,' she began quickly when he answered. 'We're at a gas station between Schweinfurt and Würzburg. We're heading for the base. Warn them I'm coming in so we don't have an awkward situation at the gate.'

'Done. Anything else?'

'No. Gotta go. I'm supposed to be in the john.'

'Watch your step.'

'As always.'

She cut transmission and went back into the toilets.

While she was making her surreptitious call to Toby Adams, Müller received a call from Pappenheim just as he had driven the refuelled Porsche into a parking slot to await her return. He turned off the engine and remained in the car.

'They found the Cherokee,' Pappenheim said immediately. 'In a motel car park.'

'Ah!'

'Not so good, I'm afraid. It was a hired vehicle, and returned yesterday. The hire firm's driver was sent to pick it up in Magdeburg late yesterday, but as he did not have to deliver it in Brandenburg until today, he decided to take a girlfriend out to the motel for the night. As he was still . . . er . . . occupied, he was a bit shocked to be confronted by uniforms.'

'I'll bet he was. What do the company have to say about the person who hired it?'

'An American. He'd hired the Cherokee for a week and dropped it off at an outlet, to await pick-up by the driver. There's a booking for the Cherokee in Brandenburg. The American said he was flying out.'

'Scheduled airline?'

'She couldn't say. She saw no one else with him.'

'Damn! What name did he give?'

'Henry Morgan. If he is what we think he may be, the name could mean nothing. His documents would have been perfect. Even down to the credit card he used to hire the Cherokee.'

'Check it out, anyway.'

'Doing so,' Pappenheim said. 'Klee's report is in.'

'And?'

'Very detailed. Good man, that. By what's in there, the killings were most definitely the work of a pro. Clean shots.'

'And the weapon?'

'Like the first ones, and the ones in Magdeburg.'

'Beretta 92R.'

'That's the one,' Pappenheim remarked with his sometimes ghoulish cheerfulness. 'Yours burning a hole in its holster as yet?'

'I'm dying with hilarity.'

'Just don't die. I am beginning to doubt that we're dealing with a maddened avenging angel.'

'I've been having the same thoughts. Something's nagging at me, but I can't quite place it as yet.'

'Don't force it. It will come.'

'As long as it doesn't arrive too late.'

'But you don't think it's the Americans.'

'They're involved somewhere,' Müller said, 'but I don't quite believe they're going around popping these people. I believe they would only do so in self-defence, although with what they call deadly force.'

'Shoot to kill, in other words.'

'Yes.'

'There's plenty of other stuff in Klee's report . . . times of death, and so on. He suggests the victims were lured. Somehow, I can't see those two types going willingly into the woods with someone whose head they would kick in just for the pleasure of it. On the other hand, that's how our perpetrator works his traps.'

'Exactly.'

'Do you want me to show any of this to the Great White?'

'Not yet.'

'Well, you're in luck. He hasn't graced us with his presence as yet. Seems the function he went to . . . one of those where he networks the high and mighty . . . went on long into the night. Perhaps he's still having his beauty sleep. The joys of high rank.'

'Not getting the promotion bug, are you, Pappi?'

'What do you think I am? Mad?'

Müller smiled into the phone. 'Just wondering.'

'By the way, I've put in an official request for Engels.'

'The helicopter observer.'

141

'Yes. I've offered pilot training. She's bound to accept.'

'Has the Great White approved the request?'

'You have,' Pappenheim replied slyly.

'That should please him. More nails for the coffin he's so busily preparing for me.'

Pappenheim chuckled. 'Luck with the Yanks. How's the babysitting?'

Müller glanced towards the toilets and saw Carey Bloomfield. She looked around worriedly. He flashed his lights once. Her face cleared as she spotted where he had parked. She ran against the rain towards the Porsche.

'Speaking of my cross,' he said, 'she's on her way back from the toilet. Talk to you later.'

'Enjoy,' Pappenheim said, chuckling again as the call ended.

Carey Bloomfield opened the door and got in quickly. 'Woo!' she said. 'Will this rain ever stop? I've got water all over your nice leather seat. Sorry.'

'It will dry out.' He started the engine.

'I thought you'd gone,' she said as she clipped on her seat belt and the car began to move.

'I gave you my word,' he said.

'You always keep it?'

'That depends.'

'On?'

'The other person.' They filtered back on to the Autobahn. 'We'll be going off the Autobahn very soon,' he continued. 'The base is not far from here.'

They drove on until the junction just before Würzburg. Müller left the Autobahn and joined a *Bundestrasse* that headed back north towards Werneck. About 6km later, an American military sign pointed towards the right. He turned on to a minor road that ended a kilometre later at the gated barrier of the base.

The iron-grilled gates were slid open, but the barrier was down. Behind the gates was a sentry hut on each side of the road. Adjacent to the one on the right was a long low building.

Two helmeted military policemen, armed with pistols and submachine guns, stood guard at each hut. A large sign, depicting an attacking bald eagle with a multi-barrelled rotary cannon in its claws, bore the legend:

WELCOME TO
COMBINED ATTACK FORCE ALPHA
Col. WILLIAM T. JACKSON Commanding

Müller drove up to the barrier and stopped.

The two policemen eyed the gleaming Porsche with interest. The one on the right came forward with slow alert steps, weapon ready for use, if need be. He did not blink in the rain and his uniform was so sharply pressed, it seemed as if the raindrops dared not touch it.

He leaned towards Müller's lowered window, eyes staring into a great distance, yet still minutely noting everything. The eyes focused upon Müller's hair and earring. They remained distant, but the disparagement in them was obvious.

'Can I help you, sir?' he began with a firm, detached politeness. 'Ma'am?'

'*Hauptkommissar* Müller,' Müller replied, no less firmly. 'Berlin.'

'Ah. Yes, *sir.*' The policeman had visibly stiffened his stance with the sort of respect he reserved for officers; but he still did not relax his alertness. He would still shoot, if given cause. 'You are both expected. Please go through the barrier and stop by the main guard to check in.'

'Thank you,' Müller said.

'Thank you, sir.' The policeman indicated to his colleague that the barrier should be raised. As the barrier began to rise, he added, 'That is some car, sir. Serious drivers only.'

'I'm a serious man,' Müller said with a fleeting smile, remembering the scrutiny of his hair.

'*Sir!*' The policeman saluted.

The barrier was fully raised and Müller drove through, knowing the policeman's eyes were upon the car.

He pulled into a parking slot before the low building, as directed. The roof had been extended so that the parking area was partially within shelter from the rain. He climbed out just as another military policeman, a black sergeant with a sidearm, came out of the building and approached. With the exception of his colour and the rank, in smartness he was a virtual clone of his colleague. The rain would not have dared touch his uniform either. The sergeant's eyes danced slightly when they contemplated Müller's hair and earring; but he remained politely respectful.

Two Apache attack helicopters thundered overhead in the downpour, with omnipotent arrogance.

'*Hauptkommissar* Müller?' the sergeant began when the throbbing noise had faded. 'My name is Henderson. If you and the lady will come with me, please.'

Carey Bloomfield, taking her bag with her, climbed out. Müller locked the car and they followed the sergeant, who led them to a waiting room with a high counter. The sergeant went behind the counter.

'Do you carry a weapon, sir?' he asked Müller.

'Yes.' Müller did not look at Carey Bloomfield, whom he knew had glanced at him, as if to say, *I knew it.*

'I'm afraid I'll have to ask you to check it in. It is an absolute rule, sir,' he went on when Müller appeared to hesitate. 'Your weapon will be quite safe. It will be locked away there –' he pointed to a bank of solid-looking, numbered steel compartments that lined the wall behind him – 'using two keys. I will give one to you, and I keep the other. The safe cannot be opened with one key.'

'Very well, Sergeant.' Müller withdrew the Beretta and handed it over.

'The 92R,' the sergeant said approvingly. 'Major weapon, sir. People go for the later models . . . but personally, I reckon on this one. Good choice.'

'Thank you.' Müller still did not look at Carey Bloomfield. 'Do you also want my spare magazines?'

'Not necessary, sir. Reloads without a gun is like gas without an engine. Lonely.'

'I . . . I see,' Müller said, intrigued by Henderson's philosophy.

The sergeant took the weapon and put it into safe number 009. He inserted two keys, one above the other. He turned the top key to the left, the lower one to the right.

He removed both keys and handed the one for the lower lock to Müller. 'Your key, sir.' It carried a tab with the number on it.

'Thank you.' Müller took the key and put it in a pocket.

'Your ID, please, sir. I must book you in.'

'Of course.' Müller handed his police ID over.

The sergeant wrote the details into a book on a shelf beneath the counter, then returned the ID.

'Thank you, sir,' Sergeant Henderson said, then went on. 'Your bag, please, Miss Bloomfield.'

'You're putting it into one of these safes?' she asked.

'No, ma'am. But I must check it. Is your ID or US passport in there?'

'Yes,' she replied, handing the bag over.

The sergeant put the bag on the shelf below the counter and opened it to check. His expression did not change when he saw the automatic pistol. He took out an ID, and also wrote something into the book. He put the ID back, shut the bag, and returned it.

He said nothing about the weapon.

'Thank you, ma'am. If you'll both please return to your car. A staff car is waiting. Please follow it *exactly*. It will take you to the Colonel Bill's office.'

'Thank you, Sergeant Henderson. I'll be back for my pistol.'

'It will be waiting, sir.' Henderson gave them a smart salute as they left.

Outside, the staff car was waiting. They got into the Porsche and Müller started the engine. The military car moved off.

'Colonel Bill,' Müller said dryly, slipping into gear and following.

Overhead, another pair of mean-looking Apaches throbbed past towards their landing ramp.

It was still raining.

Seven

Day Two: 10.00 hours.

M üller and Carey Bloomfield stood outside the door of Colonel Jackson's office, accompanied by a female captain. She was no less smart than the military policemen at the gate, but kept glancing at Müller's earring. She knocked once.

'*In!*' the voice from within called briskly.

The captain opened the door and stood back for Müller and Carey Bloomfield to enter.

'Police *Hauptkommissar* Müller, and Miss Bloomfield, sir,' she announced from the doorway.

'Thank you, Captain.'

'Sir.'

'Please come in,' he added to Müller and Carey Bloomfield.

The captain did not enter, but quietly shut the door behind them. The office was spacious, but furnished in the classic utilitarian style of a military unit primed for instant mobility. In front of the colonel's wide desk was a low table with three chairs. On the table was a sealed coffee pot, three cups on saucers with small spoons, sugar, milk, and three side plates. On each plate was a generous slice of Black Forest cake. Small forks had been laid next to them.

Colonel Jackson was a surprise. He was as tall as Müller, and his uniform had achieved the impossible: it was smarter than that of any of his personnel, and his silver eagles gleamed proudly upon his shoulders. His left breast seemed to bear more coloured ribbon than the combined flags of the United

Nations. Above the impressive collection of medals, were the wings of a pilot.

The colonel had the leanness of the consummate warrior. An inheritor of the genes of both black and white ancestors, with a spot of Apache Indian thrown in, his complexion was that of a healthily tanned individual. His cropped hair was almost white, strongly at odds with his youthfulness. His eyes were a piercingly potent grey, and his voice carried an aura of controlled strength.

He had risen from behind his desk and now came forward to greet his visitors, hand extended in welcome.

He first shook hands with Carey Bloomfield. 'Miss Bloomfield.'

'Colonel,' she responded.

Then he took Müller's hand in a brief, but firm grip. 'Glad to have you with us, Mr Müller.' He gave no outward reaction to Müller's hair and earring.

'Thank you, Colonel.'

'Please take a seat,' Jackson went on, indicating the table with the chair. 'I thought we should make this as informal as possible. *Schwarzwälder Kirschtorte*,' he added, pointing. 'I have a passion for the stuff. Hope it's not too early for you.' His accent was educated Mississippi.

Carey Bloomfield looked at the cake with anticipation, before pointedly glancing at Müller. 'Not too early for me. I had an interrupted breakfast.'

'I too, will join in, Colonel,' Müller said straight-faced. 'I also happen to like Black Forest cake.'

Jackson looked pleased. 'Then let us enjoy it.'

He glanced at each of them as they sat down but whatever the thought he had, he did not give it voice.

'We can speak in German, if you prefer, Mr Müller,' Jackson went on as he began to pour the coffee. 'I have a reasonable command of the language. That OK with you, Miss Bloomfield?'

She nodded. 'My German's fine. It's up to *Hauptkommissar* Müller.'

'We will stay with English,' Müller said, giving her a fleeting, tight smile. 'But I am happy either way, Colonel.'

Jackson gave each another quick glance but, again, did not voice the thought. 'Then English it is. You both take sugar and milk?'

They nodded.

When he had finished pouring the coffee, Jackson leaned back in his chair and said, 'Please help yourselves to the cake. As I said, we will make this as informal as possible. Mr Müller, I am impressed that you found us.' He did not take sugar, or milk.

'I used the resources at my command, Colonel.'

'I think it is rather more than that,' Jackson commented shrewdly. 'Many people have resources at their command, but most somehow manage to misuse them. A very few know how to first use their brains, *then* apply the resources. I number you among those few, Mr Müller.'

'That is a fine compliment, Colonel . . . but I merely applied some logic.'

'And played some good old hunches,' Jackson said. 'I recognize a little of myself in you, so I'll come straight to the point. You let me know what you're after, and I'll tell all I am allowed to.'

Müller carefully sectioned off a piece of cake with his fork, and put that into his mouth. As he ate, he decided it was very good cake indeed.

'Which will be how much, Colonel?' he asked when he had finished the piece. 'And this, I must add, is excellent cake. It does not taste like one bought from a bakery.'

'It wasn't. I will pass your comments on to my wife. She will be very glad to hear they came from someone like you.'

'Then please tell her this is as excellent as those my aunt makes. I never believed I could enjoy this particular cake baked by someone else. I am hooked.'

'Praise indeed,' Jackson said. 'You did not assume she was American,' he added with a hint of approval.

'I never assume, Colonel, until I know more. Although, sometimes, I do make educated guesses.'

'More than educated guesses, I think. And so, Mr Müller, while we enjoy my wife's cooking, you'd better fire the first shot.'

Carey Bloomfield, who had been watching with interest as the two men sparred like dominant males over a patch of territory, concentrated on enjoying the cake while listening attentively.

'I am investigating a series of murders,' Müller began, 'which could have serious political and social implications, if the murderer is not found very quickly. So far, we have discovered nine bodies – all male – in less than forty-eight hours, although two of those were killed some days previously.'

The colonel was staring at him. '*Nine* bodies? Who were they? And what have they to do with this base?' The surprise seemed genuine.

Müller described the bare facts of the case to him, giving only as much information as he felt the colonel should have at that time. For the time being, he also left out the part about the small statue of the Black Madonna.

Jackson listened in silence, grey eyes absolutely still.

'And do you believe we have got something to do with this?' the colonel enquired softly when Müller had finished.

'I am here to eliminate the possibility, Colonel,' Müller said. 'One of your people fired a weapon in the street, after two of them had been set upon by those idiots. They then took off, switching cars in the process, and running an elaborate deception to decoy searchers. These incidents, coming so soon after the first discovered murders, followed by the third set of bodies being found where the decoys vanished, puts your people too close to the action to be purely coincidental.'

'So you traced the decoys.'

'Up to the point where the Corvette disappeared, and the Cherokee *and* the truck went their separate ways. We believe the Corvette was loaded on to the container truck – a *freezer* truck, to kill infrared search – near Magdeburg. We've found the Cherokee, hired by a Henry Morgan, who – if my history serves me correctly – was a British pirate who was later knighted and made Governor of Jamaica . . . where the rum comes from.'

The colonel was staring at him, slightly bemused.

'He was at Oxford,' Carey Bloomfield explained, pointedly dry. 'The Henry Morgan stuff.'

Müller gave her a sideways glance.

'Ah,' Jackson said. Again, he looked at each as if he wanted to say something but, again, did not.

'Mr Morgan, who either has a sharp sense of humour,' Müller continued, 'or it's his real name and the humour belongs to his parents, is long gone . . . as is the truck. We believe the people in the Corvette when it went north were also decoys – not the two who were attacked – who were eventually picked up by the Cherokee. They have also vanished. The Mercedes was traced to this base, or we would not now be here.'

Jackson had listened to all this again in complete silence, his only reaction the slightest raising of an eyebrow.

'Goddam,' he said in the same reflective, soft voice. 'But you are good. If you ever want to quit the police and join the US forces, I've always got room for a good tactician. You're a damn good second-guesser, Mr Müller.'

'You flatter me, Colonel. But for me, being a German policeman is a very special profession. I have no wish to change it.'

'Rightly so, Mr Müller . . . and you have my respect for that. Before we go further on this, let me ask you . . . do you intend to take action against the people who used their gun to frighten off their attackers?'

'I am not one of those policemen,' Müller began carefully, 'who believes the potential victim of an attack should first die before defending himself. However, despite my sympathies, under normal circumstances I would say yes. The subsequent investigation would determine the kind of action

151

necessary, if any. But these are not normal circumstances. My primary interest is in the killer – *or* killers – of the people we found.'

'Would your bosses agree with your comments?'

'Not necessarily.'

'You always go up against your bosses, Müller?'

'Not necessarily.'

Suddenly, Jackson's tough expression broke into an infectious grin. 'I know a couple of generals who would reach for the valium at the mere mention of my name; so I know where you're coming from, Müller. Right,' he went on. 'You've been straight with me as far as you can. I'll repay the compliment, but naturally, up to my own limits. To get any further, your top people would have to talk to *my* top people. And I mean top . . . above your police superiors. You hear what I'm saying?'

Müller nodded. 'I think I do, Colonel.'

'Are you prepared to accept those limitations?'

'Do I have a choice?'

'No.'

'Then, obviously, I must accept.'

'Pragmatism too,' the colonel said. 'I admire that in a person. I shall begin, as the saying goes,' he continued, 'at the beginning; which, for me, is twenty years ago. I was a green, young second lieutenant then. My unit was stationed just north of here and our primary mission was to hold the Fulda Gap *by any means and at any cost* until reinforced and then, if possible, punch our way through and create hell behind enemy lines. We knew that our first contact was likely to be with the army of the DDR, reckoned to be the toughest of the first nuts to crack among the Warsaw Pact ground forces.

'But we were fired up by the prospect. Most of us were descended from people who had fought the Nazis on German soil during the Second World War. To us, it would be like putting the ending to an unfinished chapter. It helped that the pictures we had of the DDR army showed us uniforms

152

that looked like variations on the theme of Hitler's army. We would hit them with overwhelming firepower. If they proved as tough as we'd been briefed, then our intended continuous attacks would pulverize them. If they proved less so, it would make our eventual success that much quicker. Therefore, if the politicians acted like children as usual and screwed up and the balloon went skywards, we were ready.'

The colonel paused as the powerful thrumming of Apaches sounded low overhead. He got to his feet and began to pace slowly.

'I am,' he continued when the sounds had again faded, 'something of an enthusiast of European medieval history, particularly the centuries of the crusades.' He stopped just long enough to give them the briefest of tight smiles. 'No surprise there. Despite their dubious reputation, I have always found it possible to admire some among the Templars, the Knights of the Red Cross and the Hospitallers, the Knights of the Black Cross – and, as you know, *they* were mainly teutons. Another group, mostly unknown and most unusual, were the Black Knights from Africa. About six hundred strong, in full chain mail and weaponry; a sizeable chunk of armoured cavalry. *Black* crusader knights, Müller. I wanted to find out more about them, and about the Black Madonna in Magdeburg Cathedral. That cathedral, a building that took three hundred years to build – seventy-six years more than the US of A has been in existence – was worth a look. I was eager to get to Magdeburg.'

Carey Bloomfield darted Müller a sharp glance at this. The colonel's back was towards them at that moment, so Jackson was unaware of it. But Müller did not look in her direction. He kept his eyes firmly upon the colonel.

'Because I wanted to find out more,' Jackson continued, 'in advance of such an eventuality, I went to Würzburg and scoured the bookshops. I found one that had a little information; though this was very limited for my purposes. I was looking at one of the books when someone said: "A very unusual subject. Few people are interested in this." I will remember those words for ever. I turned, and looked at a vision. I make no apologies for putting it like that.

'To me, that day, I looked upon a vision.' Jackson had paused by a window, and was looking out as he reminisced. 'She was small, blonde and perfect, with the brightest green eyes I have ever seen. They are just as bright today. I glanced behind me to see if perhaps she had spoken to someone else. Surely, I thought, she would not waste time with me, a woman like that. She was just eighteen.'

He turned to face them, moved to one side away from the window, and leaned against a wall, beneath a picture of an Apache firing its gun.

'As you may have guessed by my accent, Mr Müller – and I am certain you, Miss Bloomfield will have recognized – I come from the South. Mississippi, to be précise. In those days, though social changes were taking place, certain parts of Mississippi were enemy territory to anyone not carrying a white skin. There were some men in those parts who believed that every white woman on the planet was their own personal property. So, though my intellect strongly refuted such crassness, you can take the man out of the state, but you can't take the state out of the man . . . if you get my meaning,' Jackson finished with deprecating humour.

They nodded, seemingly mesmerized by his narrative.

'Of course, ever since World War Two, many non-white US soldiers found the more relaxed atmosphere of Europe a breath of fresh air,' Jackson went on. 'Ironic, when you consider what's happening now in your country, Mr Müller. But that day in Würzburg, the gods were smiling on me. The vision in the bookshop – as I am certain you've guessed – eventually became my wife. It was not easy to get permission at the time. My unit commander was a colonel whose attitudes on race would have gone down big with those good old dinosaurs from Mississippi.

'He refused point-blank. But the gods were still with me. My immediate commander was a major – a truly civilized man. It also helped that he came from a family who was, and is, financially and politically powerful. His father was a senator at the time. The major went to the colonel, who possessed secret political ambitions, God help us. Imagine a creature like that with political power. The major laid it on the line. I got my permission.'

'The major *blackmailed* your colonel?' Müller asked.

'I would not have put it so baldly, but what the hell . . . Yes.'

'And the colonel's political ambitions?'

'Crumbled to dust, thank God. The climate had changed enough to make his kind obsolete. He was so extreme, he really belonged in the uglier elements of Hitler's army. The major became my best man, and is my son's godfather. I have a son of ten, and an eight-year-old daughter. The major is now one of the two-star generals I've given the valium habit.' Jackson gave another of his infectious grins.

More Apache helicopters temporarily halted conversation.

'The reason I have given you this précis of my life, Müller,' Jackson continued, 'is to explain to you why the good of Germany is also close to me. I don't want to see fifty or more years of hard work by a lot of people put at risk by a bunch of neanderthals. Because they have no real answers, they blame everything on foreigners. They seem to have conveniently forgotten that Germans in other countries are immigrants too. If the people of these nations behaved in the same way, the entire German diaspora would be at risk. Anyone with a German name, or of German descent – no matter how small the link – would be a potential victim; and if all the generations of Germans and their families who have settled worldwide were by some kind of insanity forcibly returned to Germany, you would have to deal with a population quite probably approaching the size of the States. What price the simplistic answers then?

'Imagine no holidays anywhere outside Germany, because of that risk. No Ibiza, no Majorca, no any goddammed where; no business, no sporting contacts, no international relations; an iron ring about your borders, through which no one could get in, or out. A crazy idea. A true madness in the world. But we both know that there are a lot of political crazies around. I have fought them as a soldier and you will have fought them as a policeman. We both must continue to do so.

'My second-in-command has a German name, but he is a third generation American. The family originated in Mainz, and he still has an army of cousins there. I don't want my kids to be under threat because they look a little off-white, or to have their buddies at school call them Nazis, because they have a German mother. My children have an American, and a German heritage. I expect them to respect both. They have already got their American heritage and pride deeply embedded into them; and I want them to have a German heritage that does not include these assholes, who have done enough damage in the past. There is another, better Germany, vast of landscape, that is not barbaric. If people ever threatened my kids or my wife, I'd take their goddammed heads off in a heartbeat. You hear what I'm saying?'

Müller nodded. 'I hear you very clearly, Colonel,' he responded quietly.

'The other thing, Müller, is that I am not the only one getting the shivers over what is happening. I was also not the only one who watched that wall come down with foreboding. I would have preferred that it had remained up, but that the West helped the eastern part to regain its dignity after years of sterile dictatorship *before* being incorporated into the democratic process. If you graft an infected limb to a healthy body, the body will not make the limb better; the *limb* will itself infect the body and, possibly, destroy it.

'You cannot turn citizens of a dictatorship – people who have been traumatized by state terrorism, turned into snitches upon each other and made to distrust even members of their own family – into model democrats in the blink of an eye. It takes years, and quite possibly generations, to do that. Now, in a little more than the tenth year of German unity, what have you got? Mistrust. The days of mistrust are upon us, Müller, and you and I, in different ways, are the sentinels at the gate . . . each to his own task. We are supposed to be the watch, to give warning, to stay the dark forces that are beyond that gate. I have a close friend, another German, and a former *Bundeswehr* officer, who now lives in the States. He was my liaison officer. He quit the army early this year and took his young family over to the US, where he now holds down an executive position with an international company. He didn't want his children to grow up in such a climate, he said.

'I have been authorized to tell you that in cooperation with other organizations, I have been tasked with a fact-finding mission. The objective? To test the extent of the regrowth of Nazism in this country, *and* in other NATO countries. I cannot tell you who these personnel in the field are, although some are German. I *can* tell you that they operate in all the *Bundesländer*, and not all are white. They also have the authority to defend themselves if attacked. The incident that led you here involved a captain and a major under my command. A report of the incident has already been filed, the handling of which has now been passed to higher authorities. They, in turn, will talk to their opposite numbers here in Germany and, together, make a decision. Until I get the order to pull my people out, they will remain active.'

Müller had absorbed all that the colonel had said to him. 'I see. But what if one or more of these people have exceeded their orders?'

'Not a chance.'

'I am after a killer, *or* killers, Colonel. I have enough experience as a policeman to know that "not a chance" does not exist. People cross the line between control and lack of it for all sorts of reasons . . . policemen, soldiers, politicians, even your average citizen on the street. In fact, *especially* the average citizen, otherwise there would be no need for people like me. Someone has crossed that line, Colonel.'

'Not under my command,' Jackson said firmly.

'Am I allowed to question the captain and the major?'

'I am sorry to say . . . no. They are no longer available.'

'I was afraid that might be the case,' Müller remarked pointedly. 'Just as with Mr Henry Morgan.'

'Had those morons not attacked my people, Mr Müller,' Jackson said, 'they would still be quietly going about their business.'

'I am certain of it . . . but, in a way, wasn't the attack the very thing you were looking for?'

Again, the colonel favoured them with one of his tighter smiles. 'Touché, *Hauptkommissar*. Yes, it was a result . . . but with unwanted fall-out, as we have both discovered.'

'You mean, I have stumbled upon a clandestine operation.'

'I am certain your unit runs them all the time,' Jackson countered, relaxing against the wall. 'These people whom we watch, Mr Müller, they imagine themselves to be patriots. But patriotism—'

'—is the last refuge of the scoundrel,' Müller quoted.

Jackson gave a slight nod of recognition. 'I see you know your Dr Johnson.'

'Eighteenth-century English philosopher,' Müller said, as before. 'When the scoundrel is out of ideas and excuses, he wraps himself in the flag.'

'The escape route of dictators, fanatics, and the like everywhere. But the people never seem to learn. They still choose to follow those who feed them easy answers . . . until too late. Then destruction follows.'

Again, the helicopters made their presence felt.

'Hear those choppers, Mr Müller?' Jackson said. 'Not so far from these borders, another scoundrel wants to hang on to power by any means. He has already brought destruction upon his country, and may yet bring more. Elements of this unit were involved in that first dose of destruction and those choppers may yet become part of more destruction, if he fails to see reason. Imagine a possible nightmare, Müller: things get so bad here in Germany that these choppers, or others like them, are used in anger on German soil; or . . . attacks on people whose religions encourage "volunteer" fundamentalist

158

terrorists to respond . . . or who consider the provocation warrants the despatch of official hit teams; and all because some asshole poisons the nation. And that would make me as mad as hell.'

'Then help me find the killer, Colonel, because I would be very angry too. In many ways, I share your views and anxieties. This killer may have very strong reasons for what he is doing. Perhaps he is taking revenge. On the other hand, whoever it is, is playing with fire. I don't want to see that fire burn out of control. I am a policeman. It is my duty to prevent this from happening; and I take this duty very seriously. In a civilized land, it should not just be possible for a person to go about his or her business unmolested. *It is a right without challenge.* I consider my country a civilized land. A short while ago, you said we were sentinels, each with his own task. If this is so, then we must help each other.'

'I cannot help you with your killer,' Jackson insisted. 'You will not find him among us.'

'Magdeburg, Colonel,' Müller said quietly, in a sudden change of tack.

'What about Magdeburg?' Jackson had straightened himself off the wall, and his grey eyes were fixed unwaveringly upon Müller.

'The killer left a small statue of the Black Madonna next to the bodies.'

'And?'

'No "and", Colonel. I am searching for answers.'

'Seems to me, whoever did that has a flair for the theatrical— Now what?' Jackson chopped back his words as Müller stared at him.

Müller glanced at Carey Bloomfield, then turned again to Jackson. 'You're the third person—'

'The third person who what?'

But Müller did not explain. 'Something at the corner of my mind is nagging,' he replied.

'I always find it best to leave it alone,' Jackson advised watchfully. 'Like a zit, let it work its way out.'

Müller smiled ruefully. 'I've had that advice too . . . though not in those terms.'

'It's good advice. Take it.' Jackson turned to Carey Bloomfield. 'You've been very silent throughout all this, Miss Bloomfield.'

'I've learned very early on in this job, Colonel,' she said, 'that it is sometimes much better to watch, and to listen.'

He came back towards the table. 'Wisely said.'

Müller prepared to get to his feet. 'Well, Colonel,' he began, standing up. 'We seem to have taken up enough of your time. Thank you for the coffee and the very excellent cake. And thank you for your candour . . . As far as you were able to give it.'

But Jackson had a surprise waiting.

'I would consider it a great pleasure,' he said, 'if you would both join me for lunch at my home. It will soon be that time. You can then tell my wife, in person, about the cake.' He grinned at them.

'Is that an order, Colonel?' Carey Bloomfield asked with some irony.

'Orders to a *Hauptkommissar*, and a reporter,' Jackson said. 'Well, there's a first time for everything.'

'I accept,' she said before Müller could say anything. 'I still miss breakfast.'

Müller glanced at her. 'Very well, Colonel,' he said to Jackson. 'I, too, accept. Thank you.'

'I'll phone my wife. And call me Bill. No one calls me Colonel at my table, unless I say so.'

Müller and Carey Bloomfield exchanged glances once more – he neutral, she triumphant – as Jackson went to his desk and picked up one of the telephones on it.

He dialled, then looked at his lunch guests in turn. 'Something going on between you two?'

'No!' they said together.

It was still raining when they got into the Porsche to follow Jackson's staff car to the colonel's residence. The low cloud cover was an unendingly dark blanket that had the look of permanence about it; but the Apache helicopters kept on flying. Colonel Bill clearly did not allow a small thing like inclement weather to deter his birds.

'A right without challenge,' Carey Bloomfield repeated as they started off. 'That was some speech, Müller.'

'I happen to believe it,' he said. 'There are some points where Colonel Bill and I meet.'

'And others?'

'I shall have to wait and see. He is not completely off my list.'

Five minutes later, the small convoy pulled up before the base commander's residence. Jackson's wife was outside waiting, sheltering from the rain beneath the roofed porch.

'She's gorgeous!' Carey Bloomfield said to Müller. 'She makes me feel like a sack of potatoes . . . and I'm younger!'

'You're not like a sack of potatoes,' he said.

'That had better be a compliment, Müller!'

'Who knows?'

But they had stopped before she could say anything further.

The colonel got out of the staff car and walked in the rain to his wife. They hugged like first-time lovers. The driver looked firmly ahead.

Carey Bloomfield and Müller got out, and ran towards the house as the colonel's vehicle moved off.

Arm still about her husband, Elisabeth Jackson greeted them with a warmly beautiful smile. She was as small and as well-formed as Jackson had described. Motherhood appeared not to have affected her; and the green eyes had indeed not lost the power Jackson had seen on the day they had first met.

'Thank you for coming,' she welcomed them in German. There were no American intonations when she spoke the language, despite the passing of the years away from her former homeland. 'Please come in.'

She shook hands with them both. Müller noted it was a firm handshake. Small she may be, he decided; but this was no weak woman. He strongly doubted that Colonel Bill, in any case, would have married a weak woman.

The house was spotless, yet without sterility. It looked warm and welcoming, and carried a seamless mix of American and German styles. Jackson closed the door behind them. It was clear from the way the colonel and his wife continued to hold on to each other even as they stood in the house, that the love still burned very strongly.

Müller found it very easy to believe that Jackson would be merciless indeed, in the protection of his family. Killing would not be unimaginable. There was no sign of the children.

'Let's go straight in,' Jackson said. 'It's a light lunch, and everything's ready. We've got the place to ourselves. The kids are on a school day trip. Lousy weather for it, but we can't keep them soft. After you.'

As they were shown into the dining room, Müller was still unsure whether Colonel Bill was a tentative ally, a neutral player or, possibly, a very dangerous foe.

Time, he decided, would tell.

Day Two: Schlosshotel Derrenberg, 13.30 hours.

The rain continued unabated. The Thüringian day, resolutely gloomy, was shrouded by its own endless canopy of low, dark cloud. The sun appeared to have fled for ever. The stream had become a torrent and the water level had reached the bottom lip of the run-off tunnel. It continued to rise. Already, a steady flow was spilling into the concrete tube. The stream's former soft murmur had metamorphosed into a powerful rushing sound that could be heard from the hotel grounds.

Into the gloom of the day came a big, gunmetal grey Mercedes saloon. It pulled up before the hotel entrance. Three men were inside. A white man was at the wheel. In the back were the other two. One was another white man.

The third was black.

162

Bulent Landauer was waiting to greet them. He sent one of the hussar-uniformed staff, carrying a large opened umbrella, to the car.

The black man, wearing a hat pulled low, a long lightweight raincoat the colour of night and soft leather gloves, was the first to climb out. He also wore sunglasses. Landauer made the mistake of assuming that this was just the standard affectation of certain types of black men.

The man hurried beneath the umbrella carried by the staff member, towards the hotel entrance. Once he had been safely deposited, the staff member returned for his companions.

Landauer extended a welcoming hand. 'Bulent Landauer, sir,' he greeted in English. 'Manager. I believe we spoke.'

The black man did not remove his gloves before shaking hands.

'Ah yes,' the newcomer said. 'The man with the Turkish mother. You very kindly put me at ease.'

Landauer smiled, trying to place the American accent, and failing. 'We are here at your service, sir.'

'Is everything ready?'

'All rooms have been cleaned and prepared, and the hotel is now completely free of other guests, as you requested. Schlosshotel Derrenberg is completely at your service.'

'Thank you, Mr Landauer. Now may my colleagues and I check that all is OK? The rest of our group will be arriving this evening.'

'Please do as you wish, sir. If I may repeat, we are completely at your disposal.'

'Thank you, Mr Landauer. That is good to know. Ah. Here come my colleagues.'

The other two men had crowded together beneath the hotel umbrella. They too wore raincoats. Unlike the first man, they carried briefcases. They were not wearing sunglasses. They did not introduce themselves. Their eyes, Landauer thought, were strangely cold. He made another assumption and, thereby, his second mistake. He thought the men were simply disgruntled because of the foul weather.

As they entered the hotel, the black man said, 'Mr Landauer, if it is OK with you, may we first speak in private? My colleagues can find their way around. We can register later.'

'Of course, sir. No problem at all. We can use my office.'

The umbrella hussar returned to his other duties as Landauer showed his guest to the manager's office.

'Thank you, Mr Landauer,' the black man said again as Landauer shut the door behind them, ensuring they were completely private.

Something in the manner in which the words had been spoken made Landauer frown uncertainly. He turned from shutting the door and froze, face paling, eyes widening in disbelief.

The cold muzzle of a pistol was pointing unwaveringly at him.

'I . . . I . . . don't . . . understand . . .' he stammered at last. His eyes began to fill with a very real fear.

'Of course you don't understand, Mr Bulent Landauer,' came the harshly contemptuous retort. 'Why should you?'

The polite diffidence of the black guest had suddenly vanished. In its place was a chilling demeanour that struck deeply into Landauer's very soul. Landauer began quickly to realize he was in the presence of someone who was unremittingly evil, so startling was the transformation. This man would kill him without compunction.

'And now, my little Turk,' the man continued disparagingly, 'to the real business.'

'Why are you doing this? What do you want? I do not understand. You are a black man. You were worried—'

The opened back of a gloved hand slammed with unexpected suddenness against the left side of Landauer's face.

Landauer staggered backwards, eyes watering with the pain of the blow. He instinctively placed the palm of his hand protectively upon the wounded skin.

'Since we're going to spend some time together,' the man told him with cold objectivity, 'rule number one . . . You do not ask questions. Rule number two is the same.'

'I . . . I . . .'

'I . . . I . . .' the man in the black raincoat mocked. 'Lost your tongue, my little Turk?'

'I cannot understand! Why is a black man doing this?'

'You are in blissful ignorance,' the man responded. 'Don't try to be smart. Now, let's get down to business. How many staff are here today?'

Landauer stared at the gun, and did not hesitate. He still held a hand to the wounded cheek.

'Twenty,' he replied.

'Any more coming later?'

'No.'

'Are you sure? Lying to me would be a very bad move.'

'Twenty, twenty, twenty!'

'Alright, Landauer. Don't panic. Twenty it is. Now I want you to get on the hotel speaker system and announce a staff meeting in . . . let's see . . . the famous DDR room. It's a suite, so that should hold all of them.'

'But they will think it strange—'

'*Do it!*'

'The owner—'

'You let me worry about that,' the man snapped. 'I'll be attending to her soon enough. Now, make that announcement! Tell them to leave every room unlocked. And keep *calm*. I don't want them alarmed . . . yet.'

They moved closer to Landauer's desk, which had a terminal for the hotel's speaker system on it. Mindful of the weapon trained upon him, Landauer hesitantly reached for a button and pressed it once.

'This is the manager,' he began. 'Would all staff please go to the DDR suite. This includes the kitchen staff. The representatives of our conference guests would like to discuss their requirements with you. Leave every room unlocked. Please do this immediately.'

165

Landauer switched off, but instantly the unit buzzed and an irate voice came on.

'What the hell's going on?' demanded the voice of the senior chef. 'I've got a lot to prepare. I haven't time to—'

Landauer cut him short by pressing another button. 'I am sorry, Mr Holtmann, but there can be no exceptions. Our clients insist—'

'Bloody rich assholes. Always making stupid demands . . .'

'These rich assholes, as you call them, Mr Holtmann, pay your very high salary. *Without them you'd be making your creations in an imbiss*!' Landauer, driven by his own fear, suddenly yelled. 'Go to the damned suite!' He cut transmission abruptly.

In the kitchen, Holtmann frowned at his own terminal. Landauer was known for his politeness, to staff and guests alike.

'The little Turk must be stressed out by something,' he remarked aloud. 'The German part of him is obviously not in control,' he added with rancour, and smiled.

Those of the kitchen staff within earshot did not agree with his tasteless comments. They liked Landauer; but the senior chef's recommendations could mean the difference between having a job and not having one, so, shamefully, they smiled with him.

'Come on,' Holtmann said to them all. 'As the man said, the pampered yankees pay our wages. Let's go to the suite, as the owner's pet monkey commands.'

In the hotel, the two other men in raincoats had made their way to an empty room and had opened their brief-cases. Within each was not the expected selection of documents. Instead, the cases were special weapon carriers, and in each of them was a machine pistol, silencer, infrared scope and a generous supply of loaded magazines; enough ammunition to hold off a small army. There was an added element: each also carried five small, timed thermo-grenades;

sufficient to start a fire big enough to destroy the building.

The men made their weapons ready with swift, practised ease, then slung them beneath their coats. They did the same with the grenades, shut and reset the combination locks of the cases, left them in the room, and went out.

They made their way on silent feet through the hotel. They seemed to know their way around. They checked each room with swift economy, working their way towards the DDR suite. Each time they heard a member of staff, they hid and waited until the person had gone.

In the manager's office, Landauer stared at his captor.

'Do you want to ask a question?' the man enquired.

Landauer nodded jerkily.

'Ask.'

'What . . . what now?' Landauer asked quickly.

'We wait. And before you ask again, you'll know for what, when the time comes. Now shut up!'

Minutes passed in silence, Landauer seemingly still paralysed by fear. Then a short beep sounded. It was not from one of the terminals on Landauer's desk.

The man put a hand into a pocket of his coat and withdrew a small headset with a throat mike. He plugged the headset into an ear.

'Yes?' he said. He listened. 'Good. Out. Your staff are all in the suite,' he went on to Landauer. 'Phase One complete. My colleagues will see they behave themselves. Now to the next phase. We're going to the owner's quarters, and you will give me the entry code.'

Landauer was astonished. 'How do you—'

The back of the gloved hand was swift and savage in response. This second blow sent Landauer stumbling.

'No questions!' the man snarled. 'Unless I give you permission!'

There are times when hunted prey, cornered, will, with seeming insanity, attack its pursuer. The surprise this causes can sometimes buy enough time to enable the prey to escape.

For whatever reason, Landauer had reached that point. He staggered up and, without pausing, launched himself at his tormentor. With anyone else, it might have worked; but the man he was dealing with was no amateur. Landauer's mad rush was anticipated.

The man dodged sideways. Landauer, not connecting, stumbled again and reached out to save himself. His hands grabbed at the sunglasses, wrenching them off as he fell. They broke. The man in the raincoat swung the pistol. It connected viciously with the side of Landauer's head. With an involuntary cry, Landauer dropped to the floor, grabbing at his head. Blood trickled through his fingers.

'Don't be in such a hurry to die, my little Turk!' the man barked savagely. 'Your time will come soon enough. Get up! Don't make me ask you twice!'

With difficulty, Landauer got to his feet. Then, as he looked at the man, he wiped at the blood that had snaked down his cheek, down along the side of his face, to drip on to the collar of his spotless shirt. He stared at the rings around the man's eyes.

'My God!' he exclaimed softly in a shocked voice. 'Your eyes . . . the skin around them is white! You're not black at all! This . . . this is just skin stain . . . *No!*'

Landauer shrunk backwards as the man came towards him menacingly, weapon pointing.

Landauer stopped with his back against a wall. He waited, expecting the bullet that would end his life.

But the man did not shoot. Instead, he put the muzzle of the pistol against Landauer's forehead.

'This is your last chance, my little Turk,' he said in a tight, low voice. 'Next time, I will pull the trigger. Now, that entry code. No pausing, no thinking. Just give it. *Now!*'

Landauer gave it.

The 'light' lunch at the colonel's house was as enjoyable as it was generous.

They were on the coffee and more of Elisabeth Jackson's excellent Black Forest cake when Colonel Bill looked across the table at Carey Bloomfield, who was sitting opposite.

'Forgotten your missed breakfast now?' he asked. He used German, the language they had spoken throughout lunch.

'Completely,' she replied. She glanced slyly at Müller, who was sitting next to her, and opposite the colonel's wife. 'I don't think I'll be hungry again for a while. That was a great lunch,' she added to Elisabeth Jackson.

'Thank you. Help yourself to more of the cake. You too, Jens.'

Müller raised his hands in surrender. 'One earlier, and two pieces here. I think I should not be greedy.' He glanced at the colonel. 'Besides, I would not like to take all of it, as someone might not be pleased.'

Colonel Bill grinned. 'There you go, EJ,' he said to his wife. 'Another fan of your cake.' He got to his feet. 'I must ask you to excuse me,' he went on to Müller and Carey Bloomfield. 'Duty calls. Please stay as long as you wish. I'll have a car on standby to take you back to the gate. A private word with you, Jens, if I may.'

Müller stood up. 'Of course. If the ladies will excuse me.' He followed the colonel out of the dining room.

At the door, Jackson firmly put on his cap. The peak was positioned in such a way that it practically hid his eyes. Head back, he sighted at Müller along the tip of his nose.

'A German war hero and former First World War U-boat commander,' the colonel began in English, 'once wrote down some interesting words. He listed in turn various minorities who were being persecuted during the time of Hitler, saying when they came for each he did not speak, because he was not one of them. His last line is telling. When they came for him, there was no one left to speak for him.'

'Martin Niemöller,' Müller said. 'Hitler considered him dangerous enough to make him his special prisoner.'

The colonel nodded approvingly. 'You do know your stuff. I could walk out of here and quote those words at the next ten people I see. They would simply stare at me as if I'd just landed from another planet.'

Müller gave a short, dry chuckle. 'And I could ask the first fifty or more on any street. They, certainly, would not have the slightest idea what I was talking about.'

'Well,' the colonel said, '*he* knew a thing or two, that U-boat captain. In later years – after the *Second* World War and on – he became a pacifist. Only someone who knows the hell of war can be a true pacifist. Of course, people said he was old and not all there. Some even called him a commie; but that does not alter the power of those words. People like you and I, Müller, unlike that U-boat skipper, should not wait until they get to us. One other thing . . . Maybe you should concentrate your hunt closer to home. Leopards do not change their spots.'

Müller looked at him speculatively. 'Why do I get the feeling you're telling me more than you should?'

'Am I? The fire you spoke of,' the colonel went on, 'comes from the dark, diseased pits of the human soul. Ensure it does not again consume your country; because, in some malignant quarters, it appears – disturbingly – that the lesson has not yet been learned. Here at CAFA base, a hell of a lot of the people in my command are descendants of those who once came over to this country, and tasted that fire. I am also one of those descendants. My grandfather told me he *believed* the devil himself had come to earth to spread his evil across your land, so terrible were the things he saw. He didn't believe he was fighting human beings, but creatures who had lost their souls.

'He was still of that thought when he died, all those years later. Whatever he saw back then never left him. I was in Kosovo, and I saw things there that will never leave me. The civilized human and the barbarous savage are but a hair's breadth from each other. It takes very little to turn the one into the other . . . Just some evil sonofabitch with a good lie to tell convincingly, and those stupid enough to believe it; or enough of a barbarian to *want* to believe it. My own country

170

has the obscene scar of slavery etched deeply into its psyche and even today, if you scratch it, it bleeds. But my country is also one of many races, and I am proud of that.'

The colonel, standing erect, paused, took a short breath before continuing. His eyes stared probingly into Müller's.

'The virus of racism exists in one form or another in most countries,' he went on, 'but that is no excuse for any country which considers itself civilized to tolerate it. Is there such a thing as the racially pure? I think not. These days, the scientists can trace your genetic fingerprint to its source thousands of years in the past. Among the obvious ones that you can see in my complexion, are also the genes of the Apache Native American in my own blood.

'One of my oldest friends since college – and also formerly an officer of this unit – was so blond, an Aryan fanatic would fall to his knees in veneration. He had a great line in putting racists down. If your hair has the slightest wave, he would tell them, you've got a black gene. Made those assholes mad as hell. Every hair on his head was straight; but guess what . . . he had a black ancestor from way back in the slave days. He died on a mission in some wretched country, risking his neck for people who don't give squat. When I see some of the archive films taken during the time of Hitler, I find myself wishing I had some kind of time machine and could take my entire command – Apache gunships included – back there with me so that I could hit those bastards so hard, I'd knock them back into the stone age where they belonged. Of course, we can't turn back time; but who knows . . .

'There are those who will misuse and abuse the hard-won democratic rights of others, to enable them to destroy democracy itself. They even possess the gall to label their own vile organizations as democratic. This is at once a subversion, *and* a perversion. Such a constitutional abuse should be considered a crime against humanity. It *is*, in fact – if you think about it for more than half a second – a constitutional crime. Your country needs people like you, Müller . . . and *we* all need each other, or the whole goddammed shebang ceases

171

to work. So remember, *Hauptkommissar* . . . sentinels at the gate.' The colonel paused again. 'Definitely nothing going on between you and Carey Bloomfield?'

The suddenness of the change of subject caught the *Hauptkommissar* slightly unawares.

'Definitely,' Müller replied.

The colonel gave a slight nod, and didn't look as if he believed it. He held out a hand for a firm, brief handshake.

'A pleasure meeting with you, Mr Müller,' the colonel said. 'It's a dangerous world out there and even though you know that, watch out. Don't sit with your back to any windows. Sentinels at the gate,' he repeated.

He gave Müller a sharp salute, and went out.

Müller heard the shutting of a car door. The driver of the staff car would have been instructed to return at a certain time and had been punctual. The colonel was not a commander who would tolerate anything less than absolute punctuality.

As the car drove off, Müller, pondering upon the colonel's words, went outside to stand on the porch. It was still raining. Another car was already on station; clearly the one Jackson had arranged to lead them back to the gate.

As he stood there, Müller felt his nagging thought crystallize. Perhaps it had been Colonel Bill's parting words; but whatever it was made him reach swiftly for his mobile, to call Pappenheim.

'Where are you?' came Pappenheim's voice immediately.

'On the base, at the colonel's house. Just had lunch.'

'*Lunch*? You're close pals already?'

'He's an enigma, Pappi. He could be a dangerous friend, or an even more dangerous enemy.'

'Sounds interesting. Right up your street, in fact.'

'Thanks for nothing. I'll tell you all about him later. We can also put a temporary hold on this line of investigation. There *is* an operation running. The people in the car are under his command; but I'll tell you all about that too, when I'm back. First, there's something I want you to check on.'

'Fire away.'

'It's some years ago . . . an old file, so you'll have to dig deep. You and I hadn't even met then.'

'Your misfortune,' Pappenheim said shamelessly. 'Digging is my speciality . . . The deeper the better.'

'Find out all you can about a DDR killer who got away before the wall came down; the one who hunted out the escapees.'

'Oh-oh.'

'What?' Müller demanded.

'Do you know who was on that case? A certain person who was a young *Kommissar* at the time.'

'The way you've just said that brings just one name to mind: the great, unloved Kaltendorf.'

Pappenheim gave an exaggerated sigh. 'Don't know how you do it. Right again. But, to continue . . . The Great White's never got over it. It would kill him if this new business leads to the same killer, and *you* get the bastard. I think Kaltendorf would faint from loss of blood . . . because all his blood vessels would have popped in sheer rage. But hold on, Jens . . . We're looking for a *black* man; even though Kaltendorf would just love to implicate you. As far as I know, the DDR didn't have black hit men hunting out escapees. So why the interest in a *white* killer?'

'Humour me.'

'I recognize that little phrase. Something more I should know?'

'I'm not sure as yet myself, Pappi. It's a mixture of things – things you, the colonel, and Miss Bloomfield have said, plus a little thought that's been nagging at me. Just find out everything you can about that old killer; everything out of the ordinary – profile, habits, *modus operandi* . . . *every* little thing; any piece of information on the files . . . even connecting links with any Stasi files you can get at.'

'When you have covered all the things possible and nothing makes sense,' Pappenheim said, almost to himself, 'try the impossible.'

'And now you're paraphrasing the famous, fictional detective in the deerstalker hat, Pappi?'

'That's where you're headed,' Pappenheim said unrepentantly. 'Hope you know what you're doing.'

'And *I* hope I do.'

'Since we're now dealing with impossibilities, you might as well have a little joy put into your life.'

'Now I know it won't be.'

'The Great White was in Magdeburg at the time of the killings.'

Müller said nothing.

'Hello!' Pappenheim called. 'Knock-knock. Anyone there?'

'Are you certain?' Müller at last enquired.

'Does the Pope say Mass? I double-checked. His function was in Magdeburg. Another political sliming . . . and he does own a Beretta.'

'*What*? How do you know?'

'I know many things, oh great *Hauptkommissar*,' Pappenheim intoned.

'Pappi . . .' Müller said warningly.

'A gift from an American police friend years ago, when the GW made a trip to Chicago. I found that out today.'

'I won't ask how . . . But it still doesn't necessarily mean—'

'What's this, Jens? Not feeling sorry for that piece of slime, are you?'

'No. I just don't want to rush to judgement.'

'He would not do the same for you. He's still hoping you'll fall flat on your—'

'I know.'

'Perhaps I'll discover he let that DDR killer escape,' Pappenheim said hopefully. 'Which would explain a lot.'

'Whatever it is, I want to know as fast as possible.'

'By yesterday?'

'The day before that.'

'Sounds familiar. I'll do all I can.'

'Think about this, Pappi. Why *not* a white man? Or a

woman, for that matter? We both know that people have in the past dressed up to look like men, or women, to confuse possible witnesses. Why not a white person masquerading as black? All it would take is a little make-up stain for the face, and a pair of gloves. The only eyewitness report we've got so far comes from a dying man, in pain, and scared out of his wits.'

'An intriguing concept. I take it you don't want the GW to know any of this.'

'Are you crazy? Of course I don't.'

'Just checking,' Pappenheim said with relief.

'Alright, Pappi. Call me the moment you have anything.'

'Will do. Babysitting still going well?'

'Arrgh!' Müller said.

Pappenheim's chuckle ended the call.

Eight

Day Two: Schlosshotel Derrenberg at about the same time.

The man with the blacked-up face had forcibly taken Bulent Landauer to the short connecting corridor, and had gained entry using the code he had extracted from the terrorized manager.

'You're going to stay here for some time while I get on with my business,' he told Landauer conversationally in a low whisper. He was now speaking perfect German. 'The question is . . . will you cooperate without giving me trouble? Or will we have to do this the hard way?'

'What . . . what do you mean?' Landauer asked in the same language, wisely keeping his own voice at whisper level. It mattered little to him that his captor now spoke German with native fluency. All he wanted was to come out of this alive.

'What do I mean? You have asked a question without my permission, but we'll let that pass . . . for now. What I mean, my little Turk, is that I want you lying here on the floor quietly, soundlessly, silently. In short, I want no warning noise whatsoever, from you.'

'I . . . I will be silent. I promise!'

'Of course, you promise. The problem with that is . . . I am a very untrusting person. I always assume I am being lied to . . . unless I can prove otherwise, to my own satisfaction. I think you are lying to me, my little Turk.'

'No! I'm—'

'Keep your voice down! You continue to be suicidal!'

'I'm not lying,' Landauer pleaded in an urgent whisper. 'On my life . . .'

'Your life is already hostage; but I am glad to hear it. However, untrusting person that I am, I need more assurance. Sit down on the floor, and open your mouth.'

Landauer's eyes grew round in the soft lights of the corridor as he looked at the pill the man was holding in his gun-free hand.

'Don't worry,' the man said. 'This is not cyanide. I plan something special for you, and I won't be cheated out of it by a cyanide pill. This will just put you to sleep until I am ready to come back for you. Now sit down, and *open your mouth.*'

Landauer sat down hesitantly, eyes staring at the pill in quiet terror.

'Don't worry,' the man said again soothingly, as if to a child. 'You can take my word for it. This is not poison. Open wide. A little wider . . . That's it.'

Before Landauer could try to avoid it, the man had popped the yellow pill into his mouth. Then a powerful hand grabbed his lower jaw, forcing it shut as two fingers of the same hand squeezed his nostrils tightly, blocking all air. Landauer gulped in an effort to breathe. The pill went down.

The man released him quickly, and straightened. Landauer was gasping.

'There,' the man said, looking down. 'That wasn't so bad, was it? And stop hyperventilating. That's not the pill. You're simply panicking. In a few moments you will feel drowsy, and a sense of floating will come to you. You will feel at peace with the world and, before you realize it, you will be asleep.'

The man watched indifferently as Landauer struggled to bring his breathing under control.

Then the manager's eyes began to blink lethargically as Landauer fought a losing battle to stay awake. Whenever the eyes came open they stared at first fearfully, then desperately, and finally blankly at the man, as the drug took hold. At last, the eyes remained closed and Landauer slowly tipped over to one side as he slumped to the floor.

'This will keep you quiet long enough for my purposes,' the man said, staring emotionlessly down at the unconscious manager. 'I'll be back for you.'

He went over to the second door and keyed in the second code. The door came open and he stepped into the owner's residence.

Swiftly and with practised silence, he began a search of the ground floor. He found Aunt Isolde, alone in the kitchen. She was in the act of eating a slice of smoked salmon. She paused to look at the door, startled to see there a black man in a long black raincoat, and wearing a hat.

She slowly put down her fork. 'What are you doing in my house?' she began sternly, then noted the white skin around the eyes. She frowned for some moments, before recognition dawned. '*You*!'

'No welcome,' the man said calmly, 'but certainly recognition. Good of you to remember me.' He brought out the pistol, but did not point it at her.

'How can I forget,' Aunt Isolde snapped. She looked at the gun in the man's hand. 'What are you going to do? Shoot me?' She did not seem afraid.

'It might come to that,' he said easily, 'but I have something much more spectacular in mind. And please don't give me any trouble. I am not alone, and you have the welfare of your staff to consider.'

Her face paled. 'What have you—?'

'Questions, questions. Why does everyone always ask so many questions? Rule number one: you will be told what I want you to know, *when* I want you to know it. Rule number two is the same. So please remain seated. We've got some time to get reacquainted.'

The man went over to the table, picked up a fork and stabbed a slice of salmon, which he put into his mouth.

'It just melts in the mouth,' he said appreciatively. 'But then, it is as one would expect of you.'

She looked at him with contempt, and said nothing.

'You will lose your arrogance,' he told her coldly, 'before this day is over.'

Day Two: CAFA base, Colonel Jackson's home; 14.00 hours.

Müller put his mobile away and went back inside. As he entered the dining room, both women looked at him.

'Has Bill gone?' Elisabeth Jackson enquired in German. 'Was that his car leaving?'

Müller nodded as he regained his seat. 'And I'm afraid we too, must soon leave. We should be getting back to Berlin.'

'You men and your professions,' she said with an understanding born of long experience. 'It's the same with Bill.'

'The job has to be done,' he said.

'The exact answer I would have got from Bill. At least you will stay long enough for some more coffee . . . and some cake, yes?'

'Coffee yes, cake . . .'

Elisabeth Jackson was smiling at him, eyebrows raised.

'Oh well,' he said, capitulating.

The smile was triumphant as she turned to Carey Bloomfield. 'Carey? And don't tell me you're watching your weight. There's no weight to watch.'

'I won't. I like my food. Yes, please.'

'Thank heavens. I can't stand those women who pick at their plates like birds.'

'You won't get that from me,' Carey Bloomfield said. It was like a vow.

At the end of another enjoyable half hour in the company of the colonel's wife, Müller decided that courtesy had been served.

Elisabeth Jackson was there before him. 'I can read the signs,' she said to him pleasantly. 'You're eager to get on with your business.'

'Am I so obvious?'

She reached across the table to place a hand briefly upon his, and to give it a soft pat. 'There is no reason to feel awkward. I do understand. It is the same with Bill. So, thank you for coming to lunch.'

'Thank you for inviting us. The pleasure was ours.'

They all stood up together.

'Then I hope we'll see you again. Both of you.'

'Miss Bloomfield may be back in New York,' Müller said, 'but I will definitely return.'

'Just a minute, Müller,' Carey Bloomfield put in. 'I'm not leaving you to that cake all by yourself.'

Elisabeth Jackson gave each a sideways look. 'Is there . . . something . . . ?'

'No!' they both said together, as they had done with Colonel Bill.

At the guardhouse, Müller retrieved his automatic from Sergeant Henderson.

'Hate to see it go, sir,' Henderson said in English as, with obvious reluctance, he handed over the weapon.

Müller gave a tight smile as he took the Beretta from Henderson. 'Can't leave it with you, Sergeant.'

'Real shame, sir. It's a beauty . . . in perfect condition. Like new. Some of the guys could learn from you about how to look after their sidearms.'

'Thank you for the compliment, Sergeant,' Müller said as he placed the Beretta back in its holster. 'A weapon that doesn't work when you want it to leaves you feeling – as you said – like gas without a car . . . Very lonely indeed.'

'Amen to that, sir.' Henderson saluted. 'Watch your back, sir.'

'I always do, Sergeant. I always do.'

Henderson accompanied Müller to the Porsche. Carey Bloomfield had remained inside the car while Müller had gone in to collect his automatic.

The sergeant studied the car with a neutral expression, but his eyes were lively with interest. He went round to the passenger side and leaned forward as Müller got in behind the wheel.

Carey Bloomfield lowered the window slightly. Though the rain spattered the sergeant's cap and his uniform, the water seemed to roll off without moistening the fabric.

'Be lucky, Miss Bloomfield,' Henderson said to her, 'and have a nice day.' He glanced up at the doom-laden cloud cover. 'As much as you can in this.'

'Thank you, Sergeant Henderson. I'll do my best. And you have a good day too.'

He stood to attention and saluted. 'Ma'am.'

The sergeant stood in the rain and held his salute as the Porsche moved off. He lowered his hand slowly, watching as the car went through the raised barrier. Then he walked back to the guardhouse. Above his head, four thundering Apaches in line astern winged over, curving towards their landing points.

He did not look up at the glowering sky, nor did he hurry.

'Are we really going back to Berlin?' she asked.

They were on the *Landstrasse*, heading for the Autobahn.

'Yes,' Müller replied, 'but first, we'll stop off to see Aunt Isolde. Besides, she expects to see you. You did not say goodbye properly. Remember?'

'I remember,' she remarked pointedly. 'I missed breakfast.'

'You made up for it at Colonel and Mrs Bill's.'

'Are you trying to say I stuffed myself?'

'I would never be so churlish.'

'That's some answer.'

He grinned at her as they approached the Autobahn junction.

'So, what did the bold colonel tell you, when he asked you to walk with him to the door?' she went on.

'Oh . . . he said a few interesting things.'

She stared at him. 'And that's it?'

181

'That's it.'

'God. Do you ever give anything away?'

'When it comes to information . . . hardly ever.'

'Tell me about it.'

'But you should be pleased,' he reasoned as they joined the Autobahn and headed in the direction of Schweinfurt. 'You got plenty in the colonel's office . . . exactly the same as I. You were there. You heard.'

The sharp response she was about to make was cut short by the ping from the navigation/communication console. A message came onscreen. *Call*, it said.

'Pappi,' Müller explained. 'It's a good time. The *Tankstelle* we stopped at before is close by. We'll pull in there to top up with gas, and I can call him.'

'Good ol' Pappi,' she grumbled. 'Always calls at just the right moment.'

At Schlosshotel Derrenberg, the rain continued to pound dementedly and the water level in the stream was still on the rise.

The man with the blacked face continued to make himself at home. He still kept on his hat, raincoat and gloves. He had polished off two more slices of the smoked salmon, and was in the process of spearing another with the fork he had taken. He had sat down opposite Aunt Isolde, the gun lying flat on the table, but close enough to his hand for a rapid grab if necessary. The fresh slice of salmon vanished into his mouth.

Aunt Isolde surveyed his actions with eyes that continued to hold contempt.

'This is truly superb salmon,' the man said through his mouthful. 'Help myself to coffee, shall I?'

'Why not?' she snapped. 'You seem to have helped yourself to everything else . . . my hotel, my home, so why not the food as well?'

He wagged an admonishing finger at her. 'Tut-tut. Such outrage.' He reached across for a cup and helped himself from the pot of freshly-made coffee. 'Expecting anyone? There are more cups here on the table than you need.'

'I have many friends. I am always expecting someone to call.'

He took his time pouring the coffee, before saying more.

'What about family?' he asked with a sly suddenness. 'You've got a nephew, haven't you? The star policeman.' He used the word 'star' with heavy irony. 'The one who likes to masquerade as a common man by not using his title. He comes here from time to time, does he not? Have you seen him recently?'

It was a tribute to Aunt Isolde's self-control that she did not react as expected.

'It's not a masquerade,' she replied haughtily. 'He believes in what he's doing.'

'I'm sure he does,' the man wryly countered.

'You're the one who's masquerading,' she went on. 'Running around with a blackened face.'

'Now, don't *you* tell me I have a flair for the theatrical,' he said easily, taking no apparent offence. 'And I'm not just running around. This is a deadly serious business, I assure you. So, where's your favourite nephew?' He laughed suddenly. 'Probably chasing his tail. And I left him so many clues . . . even on his doorstep, so to speak.'

'What do you mean?'

He stared at her, the mask of his face forbiddingly powerful. 'You really have no idea, have you, of what I'm talking about?'

'Why should I?'

He laughed once more, a short, harsh bark. 'So, he hasn't told you anything of substance. Perhaps he was too embarrassed. Not far from here, in some woods . . .' He stopped. 'No. We'll leave that for later.' He took a sip of coffee. 'Mmm. Coffee's good too.' He regarded her over the rim of the cup. 'I know he found them.'

'Found what? You're talking in riddles. Stop being so damned theatrical.'

But the darkened face merely smiled at her.

Müller pulled off the Autobahn and on to the exit for the service station.

'Will we be stopping again before we get to Aunt Isolde's?' Carey Bloomfield asked as the Porsche stopped at the pumps.

'No,' Müller replied. 'It's non-stop till we get there.'

'In that case, I'm off to the you-know-what. I've been holding on because I didn't want to ask at Colonel Bill's.'

He gave her an amused look. 'Why not? He would not have shot you for asking.'

'Hey. I didn't want to. OK?'

'OK, OK.'

Müller got out, and went round to top up the tank. He watched neutrally as she climbed out.

'Won't be long,' she said.

He nodded, eyes on the fuel hose as she hurried towards the toilets, staying close to the building, sheltering from the rain as much as she could. When he had fuelled and paid he moved the car to park away from the pumps, then, staying behind the wheel, called Pappenheim.

'Talk to me, Pappi,' he said as soon as Pappenheim came on.

'Which do you want first? After the drought, there's a sudden deluge of information. I have many strands.'

'Give them to me in any order you choose.'

'Where's the baby?'

'Gone to the toilets.'

'Then we'll start with her. The information is still apparently normal—'

'*Apparently*?'

'Well, she's been to the usual, journalist places around the globe . . . but mainly to crisis areas . . .'

'Nothing very odd there. Some journalists specialize in crisis reporting.'

'They do indeed, but usually, you can read their work.'

'Meaning?'

'Meaning I have not yet found a source that can give me an example of her published work. There are no archive examples. There's always an example somewhere – even on the Net these days – of a published work, by just about anybody who has actually had one published.'

'What about her newspaper?'

'If she has anything to hide, making a further enquiry there would only alert her. I decided to try other ways.'

'So, what are you really telling me, Pappi?'

'What your gut's been telling you for some time: watch your back. If she really is what she says she is, then she's just a nuisance getting under your feet and she'll be gone in a few days.'

'And if she isn't?'

'Watch your back,' Pappenheim repeated.

'I've been given the same advice twice already today, but I'm certain each of these advice-givers had different reasons.'

'Well, you've got mine now. If she's no journalist, she's tagging you for a specific purpose. Perhaps you broke the heart of some distant relative and she's planning to pay you back,' Pappenheim added, laughing. 'You know . . . *revenge.*'

'Been watching TV soaps again?'

'I should have the luxury of the time to do so,' Pappenheim said dryly. 'Next item,' he continued. 'Kaltendorf . . .'

'*Kaltendorf?*'

'Oh yes. He had a really close meet with the DDR killer. So close, in fact, the DDR man had a gun against the Great White's forehead, and pulled the trigger.'

'Christ!'

'But the gun misfired. Can you believe it? So close, so close,' Pappenheim murmured dreamily. 'No more GW . . .'

'As he's still alive, the killer must have let him go.'

'Exactly what he did. The man laughed in Kaltendorf's face, told him it was his lucky day, and left the poor bastard shaking like a jelly as he made his getaway. I don't think Kaltendorf ever got over that . . . which explains a lot.'

'So, in effect, Kaltendorf had the killer and lost him.'

'Personally, I think the killer played with him, suckered him into the situation and would have killed him, but for that misfire. Then, with a flair for the theatrical, he let Kaltendorf go. Much sweeter than simply killing him. Look how it twisted him. Something like that never leaves you, I guess.'

'You've faced guns in your time, Pappi. We both have.'

'Yes . . . but we're not the GW. This was a blatant affront to his pride, as he saw it then, and still does. It would not surprise me if the incident still recurs in his nightmares. I think he hates you because, in a way, you must remind him of the killer. You keep puncturing his pride.'

'You're not trying to tell me you believe he would commit crimes, just to implicate and destroy me, because I *remind* him of a killer who once let him live?'

'I am saying no such thing.'

'Where is he now?'

'Not here. In fact, he hasn't been around to remind me to remind you he wants that personal report . . .'

'*Flair for the theatrical . . .*' Müller said to himself. '*Close to home.*'

'What?'

'Flair for the theatrical,' Müller repeated. 'You've said it again. I keep hearing that phrase, and it's jogging hard at my memory.'

'Which was why you asked me to check out that DDR killer . . . and with good reason. According to the files, both ours at the time and those of the Stasi I've been able to . . . er . . . prise, he has been described as someone like that. His Stasi bosses didn't like it because they considered him insubordinate, and too autonomous; but as he was so damned effective, they let it pass. This remind you of anyone you know?'

'I don't have a flair for the theatrical . . .'

186

'Perhaps not . . . in your terms. But I know someone we both know, who thinks the description I just related fits you. Close for comfort, or what? The DDR killer,' Pappenheim went on before Müller could make comment, 'used to leave little calling cards: a note, a comment for someone to pass on, a bullet by the body or bodies . . .'

'Like the remark to the dying man, or the small statue . . .'

'Precisely.'

'The question still remains. Why would an ex-DDR killer stain his face, then go out killing shave-heads? *Why* . . .' Müller paused. 'Why not, if— Good Christ!'

'I believe,' Pappenheim said, 'we are of the same mind, but will not speak of it. There's nothing that indicates he's not still active . . . except that, these days, he could be self-employed . . . if you get my meaning.'

'Oh, I get it,' Müller said grimly.

'If he *is* self-employed and if he *is* our man, it would be interesting to find out who's paying him. I can think of all sorts of people who would like to see this country go down the tubes, including those who would use the excuse to call for a strong new Germany . . . Need I go on?'

'No need at all. I can see exactly where that kind of situation would lead. History repeating.'

'Exactly. A new war and, this time, the end of Germany . . . for all time. So much for asshole patriots.'

'Not a nice vision, Pappi.'

'I'm not here to give nice visions . . . just to tell it as it is.'

'Cassandra . . .'

'Was a troubled, pubescent young woman, and this is not Troy . . .'

'. . . who told it as it would be.'

'That's the trouble with those who foresee,' Pappenheim said with a chuckle. 'Never any good news.'

Müller heard Pappenheim's long draw on his cigarette.

'There's more,' Pappenheim continued.

'There's always more.'

'Cynic.'

'No. Policeman.'

Pappenheim gave a short laugh, and coughed slightly. 'Our DDR killer – if it is he – vanished from Europe for a while. No information on his destination, or destinations.' Pappenheim coughed again.

'What's up, Pappi?' Müller asked. 'Smoking catching up with you more than usual today?'

Pappenheim coughed once more.

'OK, Pappi. This can't be just your cigarettes, Alarm Condition One, warning of lung pollution. Tell me the bad news.'

'According to Stasi files, the killer was a frequent visitor to a particular luxury nest – in DDR terms – for Party favourites. He is known to have given a few out-of-favour members early exits from the planet. You don't want to know where that particular establishment was.'

Müller felt a chill descend upon him. 'Your voice has already told me, Pappi.'

'Sorry, Jens. I could be wrong,' Pappenheim went on hopefully. 'The man could be long dead. He must have had a lot of enemies; many people wanting revenge after the wall came down.'

'But you could also be right. We can't afford to count him out.'

'What are you going to do?'

'On our way back to Berlin, we'll be calling at the place in any case. No harm in checking that everything is OK there, even if we could be on the wrong track. Find Klee and put him on standby, just in case; but keep it all low-key.'

'Will do.'

'Close to home indeed.'

'Going cryptic on me again?'

'Something someone said.'

'Well, if you need cheering up, here's something else from the Stasi files. They kept tabs on our great unloved, then *Kommissar. They* accused *him* of having a flair for the theatrical too. Must be someone else they're talking about. But, if true, it could be the reason the DDR man wanted to take him down so badly. Pride. No room for more than one top dog, I guess. He succeeded more than he knew. He gave us a big cross to bear. Perhaps the DDR man is dead and our perpetrator really is Kaltendorf. Perhaps all those years of secret humiliation have finally snapped him.'

'God knows, I don't like that man, but it wouldn't make sense, Pappi.'

'How many crimes do you know that make sense? But there could be another reason for Kaltendorf to lose it so badly . . . In addition to his great love for you, of course.'

'I'm all ears.'

'I think you're just about ready for this. The situation demands it . . .' Pappenheim stopped.

'This century, Pappi.'

'His daughter.'

'*What*! Kaltendorf has a *daughter*?'

'Thought that would knock your socks off.'

'But this is crazy. Are you sure?'

'I would not mistake about something like this,' Pappenheim said indignantly.

'OK, Pappi. Cool it. I'm not doubting your sources of information. But the Great White with a daughter is like . . .'

'I know . . . like politicians keeping their promises once they've got your vote: hard to believe. But it really is true. He's been keeping it a very deep secret. It still is.'

'I don't even dare ask how you found out.'

'One of the best ways. Pure accident. I went into his office some time ago, after one of his imperial summons. I hadn't gone immediately, so he wasn't expecting my arrival. He was looking at a framed photograph. He put it quickly away into a drawer, locked it, then yelled at me for not knocking first. He looked so guilty, it hooked my interest. I noted the drawer for future reference.'

'What a surprise.'

'First opportunity I got, I had a look.'

'Should you be admitting to me you broke into our superior's desk, Pappi?'

'I'm admitting nothing. There is no sign of forced entry. The photograph of a young girl was lying face down. At first, I had an unsettling thought. The GW interested in young girls? Then, as if by magic, the frame came apart in my hands . . .'

'Of course it did . . .'

'There was a note on the back . . . in French . . .'

'*French*?'

'As in "Marseillaise". "To my dear Papa, on my sixteenth birthday. See you again, soon. All my love, Jeanne-Marie."'

'I can't imagine anyone calling the Great White "dear Papa".'

'Neither can I, but I swear to you it's true. She's a beautiful child – must be getting close to seventeen now – and is about the only redeeming thing about that man. On the other hand,' Pappenheim added quickly, as if afraid he was going soft on Kaltendorf, 'not so long ago, people who loved their own children had no trouble killing those of others. Not much redemption there.'

'But what has Kaltendorf's secret daughter got to do with this case?'

'Aha . . . Thought you'd come to that. At the back of the photo is an address in France. Cap Ferrat.'

'Nice address.'

'Indeed. I did some checking. I have a contact in the French police who has a contact in Cap Ferrat . . .'

'Pappi, it wouldn't surprise me if you told me you had a contact in Tonga . . .'

'Funny you should say that . . .' But Pappenheim was chuckling again. 'I haven't reached there yet. The officer in Cap Ferrat knows the girl's family well. Seems *her* grandfather on the mother's side was also a policeman . . . colonial gendarme on Réunion; that's a little French island in the Pacific . . .'

'I know where Réunion is, Pappi.'

'Anyway,' Pappenheim went on unabashed, 'the grand-father met and married an exotic young woman from the island . . . *she*, by the way, had a white father – civil servant – who went native, as they used to call it in those days – and very beautiful by all accounts. Shows where the young girl got her beauty. Certainly not from the Great White. They came back to France when the grandfather retired from the service, with a teenaged daughter who was born out there. The GW met the daughter in Nice when he was on holiday in the south of France and, according to my informant, fell like a ton of bricks for her.

'He went back there each holiday he got; sometimes, even for a weekend. She never came to Germany. Then she got pregnant. Whatever the reasons, they never married. The child also remained in France. Kaltendorf's love went off to the island to visit her relatives there. She had never been back since coming to France, and they took the young girl with her. While out there, she, the mother, drowned.

'Ostensibly an accident; but my informant says it was an open secret that it was suicide. It seems Kaltendorf's family did not approve of the match, and his balls were too weak for him to stand up to them. The grandparents took over the care of the child. As you can imagine, the GW is not their favourite person. He dotes on the girl to make up in some way for his lack of courage, I believe. Again according to my informant, despite everything, the girl truly loves her father. So who understands these things? He has brought her to Berlin on two occasions. I believe that, for all the reasons I just gave, he would do anything to protect her from our more unsavoury citizens.'

'Including this series of murders?'

'Perhaps she was once out on her own and got threatened. As I said before . . . we both know some people do things for the most warped of reasons. The Great White hates and envies you; he nurses a burning sense of humiliation dating back to the time the DDR killer let him live, and you are a daily reminder of it; he hates himself for lacking the courage to save the woman he loved; so the only thing of real value he has left is that young girl. Would he go over the edge for her? Given his history . . . I would say yes. A secret hunt like that would make him feel brave, as well as drop you in the shit for good measure. He'd be getting rid of all his ghosts.'

'It's still conjecture, Pappi . . . but I follow your reasoning. I'll lock nothing out.'

'I could be completely wrong . . . but, at this stage, anything is possible.'

'None of the choices are pleasant . . .'

'If you wanted pleasant, you shouldn't have joined the police,' Pappenheim said with a laugh and a drag on his permanent cigarette. 'If my family had your family's money, I'd buy me a yacht, fill it with beauties, and laze in one of the sun traps of the Mediterranean, or the Caribbean.'

'No, you wouldn't.'

'No, I wouldn't. No hope for us then.'

'None at all, Pappi. We're the damned.'

'Welcome to the club.'

'What do you mean "welcome"? I'm already in it.'

'Oh yes,' Pappenheim said, chuckling. 'I forgot. Baby still in the toilets?'

'Yes.'

'She goes often, that one,' Pappenheim remarked.

'Hey, I didn't build her . . .'

'That's right. Someone else did.'

'Now who's being cryptic?'

'I can't even spell the word. I'll put Klee on standby, but no movement till I hear from you.'

'OK, Pappi. And *no* sirens. I'll get back to you.'

'And what's that sound?'

'What sound?'

'Oh . . . it must be the rain on your car. Wouldn't you really like to be in a sun trap . . . ?'

'Pappi!'

Pappenheim ended the call with a laugh.

*   *   *

While Müller had been talking to Pappenheim, Carey Bloomfield had made contact with Toby Adams. As before, she was hunched against the back of the toilets to keep out of the rain, and the news was less than welcome.

'Nothing at all?' she asked.

'Nothing,' he replied. 'No news. Nada. Your best bet is to stay your present course.'

'I want the bastard,' she said grimly.

'Keep your cool, Carey. I know he killed your brother . . .'

'He *butchered* my brother,' she corrected, with a snarl so savage, Müller would have been astounded, had he been there to hear it.

'I understand how you feel . . .' Adams began, in an attempt to mollify.

'With all respect, Toby, you *don't.*'

'I guess not. But don't get emotional on this. Emotions can get you killed. *We* want him. That's the purpose of your assignment. This is not a private hunt.'

Adams' voice, while patient and concerned, carried with it the distinct tones of an order.

'I won't lose it,' she said.

'I'm glad to hear it. Now you'd better get back to your policeman. If he's as smart as you say, you shouldn't use the toilet routine again for a while.'

'It won't be necessary, now we're on our way back to Berlin.'

'Alright, Carey. Watch yourself.'

'Of course. Is it raining up your way?'

'Dry as a bone.'

'Down here it's like the last goddam day of the world.'

'See that it isn't yours.'

'I'll make sure.'

When they ended the call, she re-entered the toilets to leave by the front entrance. She ran in the rain to where Müller had parked, and got in.

'Sorry,' she said. 'More water on your leather seat.'

'It will survive,' he said mildly as he started the car.

She peered through the windscreen. 'Jesus. Is this deluge *ever* going to stop? The day looks like night.'

'Then I'll turn it back to day,' he said, switching on the powerful headlights. 'We're going to have to travel fast. I want to get to Aunt Isolde's quickly.' He moved off, heading for the Autobahn feeder lane.

'You mean we're going to make like a speedboat in all this water?' She peered again through the windscreen. Trucks going past were streaming waterfalls of spray.

'Don't worry. I'm—'

'Yes. I know. A fully qualified pursuit driver. I'm not worried.' She looked on with equanimity as Müller slid in behind a monster truck that looked like an office building on wheels, to quickly move into the overtaking lane. 'Heard from Pappenheim?' she added.

She had posed the question almost as an afterthought and glanced behind the car. Already, a high tail of water was billowing in the wake of the Porsche. A speedboat indeed.

'Have you been in touch with anyone while you went to the toilet?' he countered.

'No,' she lied easily.

He did not glance at her. 'I heard from Pappi,' he said, but did not explain further.

She responded to that with a surreptitious, sideways glance of her own, but made no comment.

He quickly reached for and pressed a button on the communications console. The screen changed to show a telephone number beginning with 036647, the Saalburg area code, each digit blinking as the unit dialled.

She stared at the screen. 'Someone I know?'

'Aunt Isolde. Just warning her we're on our way. I can do this hands off. There's a small microphone behind a grill on the dashboard. All I have to do is speak when the connection is made.'

'Except when it's to Pappi.'

He did not react as the unit made the call.

*   *   *

At Schlosshotel Derrenberg, the man with the blacked-up face had helped himself to most of Aunt Isolde's smoked salmon. He was still sitting, his automatic still close to hand; and though she continued to silently fix hard eyes of contempt upon him, he was totally unmoved.

'My colleagues will have completed their work by now,' he said conversationally, pulling slightly at the left-hand cuffs of coat, jacket, and shirt to display an expensive-looking watch. It was a chronograph with a titanium wristband. 'Nice watch,' he went on, pushing the sleeves back. 'Got it off one of my adversaries . . . no . . . prey would be a better term. He had no further use for it.'

'You're a thief as well,' Aunt Isolde snapped. 'Robbing the dead.'

'I wouldn't put it quite like that,' he said cheerfully. 'I call it a trophy. I won. He lost. Having safely herded all your staff into the DDR room,' he continued, 'my colleagues will have planted their timed firebombs . . . Well, to be more precise . . . timed versions of phosphorous grenades in strategic places throughout this building . . .'

Aunt Isolde was staring at him in horror, face going grey. '*What?*' She had risen angrily to her feet. 'You intend to destroy my home? How dare you! *How dare you, you . . .*'

His gloved hand moved with the swiftness of a striking snake to grab the automatic, which he pointed unwaveringly at her. The gloves were of soft leather and were like a second skin. They would give no hindrance at all to his use of the gun.

'Oh, I dare,' he told her softly. 'Now *sit* down!' His voice had suddenly become a cold snarl. 'Or I will shoot you. This is neither a threat, nor a promise. It is a fact. *Sit down!*' he repeated.

Aunt Isolde did not move. Her eyes stared right back into his, daring him to shoot. His finger began to tighten on the trigger, and just as the realization dawned within her eyes that he would indeed shoot, the phone rang.

The phone was fixed to a wall. Both their heads snapped

round to stare at it. The man's finger relaxed from the trigger.

'Saved by the bell,' he said with a cold smile. 'Literally. But don't try to answer it,' he warned. 'Let it ring. You're a busy woman. You've got the hotel to run. You can't always be available.' He laughed softly.

The phone kept on ringing.

'I should answer it,' she said.

He shook his head slowly and gave her a short, admonishing wave with the gun.

'Whoever it is will become suspicious,' she insisted.

'Good try . . . but no. All the phones throughout the hotel work. Do you know why? Suspicions are more likely to be raised if the phones were cut. My colleagues have ensured that the answering service is in operation. So . . . are you expecting someone?'

'I've told you before,' Aunt Isolde began distantly, as if forced to speak to a bug she would rather squash beneath a shoe. 'I know many people. I am always expecting someone to call.'

'Friends? Relatives? Business associates? This is your private residence. So someone close would have your private number. A family member? Your policeman nephew, perhaps?'

'You're the one with all the answers.'

The phone continued to ring insistently.

'If I had gone out,' she said, 'or there were no staff around to take the call, an answering machine would. I never switch it on when I am home.'

'Many people do.'

'I am not "many people".'

The phone stopped.

'There you are,' the man said. 'Whoever it was has given up.' He saw the light of hope vanish from her eyes. 'Too bad,' he said, smiling. 'Now *please* . . . sit down. I am not yet ready to shoot you.'

*   *   *

Müller glanced at the number on the screen.

'No reply,' he said. 'She must be in the hotel. I'll try the management office.'

He was about to overtake a dark-coloured saloon when a white Golf ahead of it suddenly pulled out.

Müller hit the brakes.

'Jesus!' Carey Bloomfield shouted. '*Is he blind?*'

The Porsche slowed massively without the slightest hint of a swerve, even on the streaming road surface. Müller put the powerful beams on full, warning the Golf driver with an unmistakeable signal. Then he pressed a button to the left of the central console. The orange of the indicator lights, the red of the triple brake lights, the red rear and white front fog lights, the white of the reversing lights, all began to flash. On the lower section of the nose of the car, two small panels on either side retracted to reveal a pair of small but powerful, high-intensity flashing blue lights.

The Golf darted back into its lane with the alacrity of a scalded cat.

'His lucky day,' Müller said. 'I haven't the time to pull him over.'

Carey Bloomfield was staring through the rainswept windscreen. '*Blue* lights? I'm *seeing* blue lights?' She glanced at him. 'You've got *blue* lights on this car?'

'Among other things . . . yes.'

'What other things?'

He didn't reply. He let the full complement of lights continue to flash. Cars stayed out of the way, leaving the fast lane clear.

She twisted round to look back. The white Golf was fast receding. 'You've got a problem with white cars.'

'Perhaps you should ask the drivers of certain white cars about *their* problem,' he suggested.

'Back in the States, *I* drive a white car . . . and don't you dare say anything.'

'I won't.'

'That's even worse,' she said.

'Only doing as you asked.'

He pressed the call button on the console once more. The number for the hotel management office came onscreen as the unit dialled.

The number rang twice, then the pre-recorded message began in German. 'We thank you for calling Schlosshotel Derrenberg. We regret there is no one to take your call at the moment, but please leave us your name and number after the tone, and we will call you back as soon as possible. We look forward to welcoming you at Schlosshotel Derrenberg.'

The message was repeated in American-accented English, in French, and in Italian.

Müller's expression gave nothing away as he pressed the call button for a third time. The new number was for the hotel reception. Two rings, and the same message came on. He ended transmission.

Carey Bloomfield glanced at him. His expression still gave nothing away, but she felt a distinct increase in the Porsche's acceleration. She watched as he selected the CD player. The first of the randomly selected titles from the Tom Petty album *Into The Great Wide Open*, began to play. 'Learning to Fly,' Petty sang.

The car seemed to streak along the suddenly empty fast lane, as other traffic hurriedly got out of the way of the flashing blue lights bearing down upon them. Now that there was no back-spray from vehicles in front, the windscreen remained reasonably clear and the road ahead could be seen for a long distance.

'Your blue lights are working magic,' she said.

He said nothing.

She glanced again at him. Though his face continued to remain expressionless, there was a stillness about it that clearly signalled a distancing from her. She sensed that, though previously he had tolerated her presence with a kind of world-weary resignation, a definite change had come over him. Since the lack of response from Aunt Isolde, the total, hardened policeman had taken over as if he had suddenly put on a new mantle.

She did not attempt to disturb him further. She had noted that the car was travelling at a far greater speed than at any time previously. She glanced at the speedometer, wished she hadn't and decided it was best to settle back in her seat, watch the empty lane ahead, and listen to the CD.

The therapy worked. Soon, the sound of the Porsche's engine seemed to fade and only the music could be heard. The speed of the car gave the impression of being rocketed along at warp velocity, without actually touching the road.

At the Schlosshotel, the man with the blacked face got a call from one of his men.

'Yes?' he responded curtly.

'Two calls came in . . . one to the management office, one to reception. Neither registered on the telephone screens. All others have been hotel business, and all the phone numbers showed up.'

'Right. Thank you.' The man turned to Aunt Isolde as he ended the conversation. 'It seems your caller did not give up, after all. Whoever it was called the office, then the reception desk. In each case, the number did not register.'

'So? Why should this have anything to do with me?'

'Some phones can be programmed not to register, when the caller does not wish to reveal his or her identity. And these calls came from someone who knows all your numbers. I think it has plenty to do with you.'

'And some phones don't register at all, programmed or not.'

The rings about the eyes in the black face seemed to glow a pale white. The eyes themselves, the lightest of grey, appeared to become lifeless.

'I think I should warn you, as I warned your little Turk,' he said very softly, 'that I am not the best person to play games with. In such cases, I have a very low patience threshold. *Someone* who needs to speak with you urgently has been calling. That person – whoever he, or she, may be – was determined enough to try at least three times . . .'

'It may not be the same person . . .'

'I warned you! Don't . . . play . . . games with me. *Three* phone calls that don't register? I'm certain the main unit in this house has not registered them either. So, unless there's been a sudden rash of people with non-registering phones calling your *private* number, your hotel management, *and* the hotel reception in quick succession . . . Do you see where I'm heading?'

Aunt Isolde did not reply.

'So . . .' he went on. 'Whom could it be?'

'I've no idea.'

'You have a wide circle of people, as you've said.'

'Where should I start? And why should you worry if you're going to kill me, and burn the place down?'

He stared at her speculatively. 'You've got guts. I'll give you that. You're accepting your fate very calmly.'

'I'm accepting nothing. If I had a gun, I'd kill you for what you're intending to do: burn my property, burn the innocent people in that room . . .'

'*No* one is innocent,' he snapped. 'I've seen more than enough in this life to convince me.'

'And you're the least innocent of all.'

'I am a product of my environment. I was made into what I am.'

Aunt Isolde's mouth turned down in disgust. 'The old excuse.'

'No excuse. The truth. If that phone rings again, answer it. For your sake, give no indication that anything is not as it should be.'

'But you said—'

'I've changed my mind. Whoever is calling will not leave things be, if there is still no answer. Trust me. There was an insistence about those calls. The person will call again.'

'If you're worried, why not get on with what you intend to do and clear out of here?'

The eyes in the black face surveyed her as they would a specimen viewed through a microscope. 'Must be the British influence of your former husband. Stoicism in the face of disaster, I think it's called.'

'I can't stop you,' she said philosophically.

'That . . . is certainly true. But I am not quite ready to leave. Everything has to be in place. Besides, I have the distinct impression you're desperately waiting for something to happen, or perhaps *someone* to arrive.' He gave the soft laugh. 'I like to watch the hope live and die in your eyes. You would be surprised to know of the number of people in whose eyes I have seen this happen.'

'I would not,' she said coldly. 'It is clear you enjoyed playing with those unfortunate—'

'*Unfortunate!*' He laughed again, this time harshly. 'Many were people you would have found repugnant. What *they* did to others in their time would have made you vomit. Corrupt, mendacious, treacherous . . . Don't shed your tears for such vermin. Save them for yourself. You will need them.'

Carey Bloomfield stared at the wet road, wondering how Müller continued to keep firm control of the Porsche at the high speed at which they were now travelling.

She gave him one of her surreptitious glances. He held the wheel lightly, it seemed, making the barest of corrections, at one with the car. Sweeping bends were taken with hardly any drop in speed. The Porsche seemed glued to the wet road. Behind it, the high tail of following spray billowed like a vast plume on the hat of a cavalier at full charge. The flashing blue lights, mixed in with the others, continued to clear an unrestricted path for them. The powerful headlights splashed bright daylight upon the gleaming road surface.

Tom Petty was now singing 'All or Nothing' on the CD.

Müller's face continued to show no emotion. He seemed to be as much engrossed in the music as in driving the car.

Continuing to feel reluctant to disturb him, she went back to studying the seamlessly flowing ribbon of wet road. The darkness of the day was beginning to look more and more like the onset of real night, instead of the earlier gloom of the heavy and unending cloud cover. The brightness of the powerful headlights carved a swathe through the rain and the dark, and the flashing lights threw up darting, multicoloured specks against the plummeting, impacting raindrops as the car fled along the road.

The music stopped suddenly.

'Yes?' Müller said. He did not look in her direction. 'You wanted to say something?'

She debated within herself about whether to tell him about a growing suspicion in her mind.

What the hell, she thought. *Why not.*

'Anything in particular worrying you?' she asked.

'I worry about many things.' He did not reduce speed.

'Come on, Müller. I know you're worried about Aunt Isolde. Why?'

At least two kilometres went by before he spoke.

'What gives you that impression?'

'Oh, come *on*, Müller! You just called the place three times . . .'

'To warn her we're on our way.'

'Jesus!' she exclaimed in exasperation.

'Keep *Him* out of it.'

'You're so goddammed frustrating sometimes, Müller!'

Another two kilometres of silence passed.

'I am not worried about Aunt Isolde,' he finally said.

'Oh sure. And hens have teeth. That's why you've got the blue light show, and we're going for the speed record between here and the Derrenberg.'

The reaction to her comments was the CD coming back on. Tom Petty was 'Into the Great Wide Open'.

The Porsche fled on, pushing the rainy dark ahead of it.

Nine

At the Schlosshotel Derrenberg, the man had risen to his feet and had gone to a window, taking his gun with him. He moved in such a way that Aunt Isolde was always within the tracking arc of the weapon.

'Strange day, isn't it?' he remarked calmly, as if they were having a perfectly normal conversation. 'It is like night out there. The rain looks like it's never going to stop. Global warming, do you think?' he added as a joke. 'An easy reason these days, to explain the unexplainable.'

Her contemptuous eyes followed his movements, but she made no comment.

'Your mysterious caller has not tried again,' he went on in the same conversational tones. 'Surprising. But perhaps he, *or* she, is giving it a little longer, hoping to get an answer next time. Even so . . . I don't like surprises. I am never comfortable with them.'

'Is someone paying you to do this?' she asked.

His characteristic, soft laugh lived briefly. '*Paying* me? In a way, I suppose, it *is* a kind of payment . . . but not in the crude way you mean. Oh . . . I have been paid very well indeed for my services over the years; and I am worth every mark, pound, or dollar . . . or most other currencies, except perhaps the rouble these days. It's not that I am prejudiced, but one should protect one's requirements for old age.' The soft laugh came again. 'I do very good work; but this . . . is personal.'

'Against *me*?'

'Only in an indirect sense, but yes, you are part of it.'

'I don't understand . . .'

'Why should you? You would not begin to understand.'

'Is it revenge, for some unknown reason?'

'That too. But the reason is not unknown. At least, not to me.' The man turned from the window, ensuring his back was not exposed to it. 'You could also say,' he went on, 'it's a revolt against political cupidity and stupidity. You have been wondering why I put this stuff on my face. I have been hunting the hunters, and I have made certain that my prey believe they are now being hunted by their victims and, by implication, so do the police. When my colleagues and I have burnt down this . . . effete monument to the class culture, with you and your staff in it, I will also make certain that this act will be seen as having been committed by the formerly hunted.

'Acts of arson against them responded to by an act of arson against your precious, bourgeois palace. You who will die in tonight's flames will be seen to have been sacrificed in reprisal, for what has been done on several occasions to *them*. The politically opportunistic, mendacious, and power-hungry will eagerly seize upon these acts to raise the eternal foreigner question, in order to buy votes. And somewhere from within the extreme cesspools of politics there will be an unthinking, siren cry for strong government. Out with the foreigners, and we will have no more problems. Where have we heard *that* before? Nero burnt Rome, and blamed the Christians. The people believed the lie, because they wanted to. Many individuals in history and up to recent times have followed in his wake, blaming others for their own acts of vandalism as we, surely, both know. I am merely continuing the long, and ignoble tradition.'

'You are despicable,' Aunt Isolde said, at once shocked and horrified. 'You're trying to bring chaos to this country. You want to create conflict.'

'But of course,' he said, as if to a child with learning difficulties. 'And your deaths will serve to fan the flames

204

because the people – selfish as they are – are so easily fooled. I should know, after all. And please don't tell me I won't get away with it. I can see by your expression that's exactly what you're thinking.'

'Germany has been scarred enough by people like you . . .'

'Not like me at all.'

'But *why*?' she asked. 'Why seek to destroy your own country?'

'*My country*?' he snarled with a vicious suddenness. 'This soft, self-absorbed place is not *my* country. *My* country was destroyed when the wall came down! Sold cheaply, and bought cheaply. This, is *not* my country!'

Then, suddenly, some understanding of what was driving him began to dawn upon her.

'You're missing it,' she said in a hushed voice. 'You're missing the power you once had. You're as hungry for power as all the politicians you despise so strongly.'

'Yes,' he admitted harshly. 'I had power; but I was no self-serving politician. I had a duty to perform, and I was very good at it. You could say I was one of the executive arms of government.'

'You mean you murdered under the orders of a dictatorial regime.'

He smiled thinly. 'Call it what you will. Even highly placed Party officials respected and, best of all, *feared* me. I was a police colonel, but even the generals in the military watched their step when they knew I was around. And don't think I was a Party animal. I never bought into all that claptrap; but I had my position in a world that was structured in a way that everyone clearly understood.'

'And do you really believe it was such a worker's paradise?'

'I have just told you. I never bought the propaganda, even though I was part of the world it created. There are many like me – on both sides – who wish that wall had never come down. And as for people like you, with your class culture—'

'Which you envy . . . and that's the real reason you're using *my* home to make your sick point.'

It was the wrong thing to say. The man went suddenly very still. The gun pointed with a frightening steadiness. For the second time, Aunt Isolde expected him to forget whatever plans he had for her and pull the trigger. She stared at the gun with morbid fascination, but was strangely unafraid.

'*Envy*?' he snapped at her. 'Why should I envy *you*? Aah . . . I see. You believe that because my grandfather was the product of a useless von Röhnen emptying himself into the body of a young serving maid, I *envy* your title? Or perhaps you think that because my grandfather – himself a von Röhnen genetically, but unrecognized because of the manner of his conception – was kept a common soldier during the war to serve under the command of officers far less intelligent than he was, I hold a grudge?' He laughed at her. 'It is the nature of your class to hang on to such conceits.

'And do you know what they said at the time? That his mother – *my* great-grandmother – was a common slut who gave it to anyone available. No mention of the fact that she was a virgin when von Röhnen first took her – and continued to do so, abusing his position of power so that he could have her any time he pleased.'

'So, you're paying me back for something that was done before I was even born?'

'Don't be ridiculous. You're important for my current purposes, but not *that* important; but look at the situation in which you now find yourself. I hold command over your life and the fate of this –' he waved a hand briefly – 'this grandiose building, in the palm of my hand. Does having a title make one any less mortal?'

He did not wait for a reply. Instead, he moved the gun away slightly, and glanced at the watch he had taken off one of his victims.

'It is half an hour since that persistent caller rang.'

'Nervous?' Aunt Isolde taunted mildly.

'Not at all,' he answered, remarkably taking no offence. He smiled at her.

Outside, the swelling stream had now risen halfway up the overflow tunnel.

The Porsche Turbo was now just twenty minutes from the Autobahn exit that would eventually take them to the Schlosshotel. Carey Bloomfield was still wondering how they had managed to make it safely this far, at this speed, in such weather conditions. It was, she thought, a tribute to Müller's skill and the sure-footed progress of the car itself. Despite her anxieties, she was impressed with both. The CD, still in shuffle mode, had come to the end of 'King's Highway' and had selected 'You and I Will Meet Again' for the second time.

She glanced at Müller. All his attention was on the black ribbon of wet road ahead of them. The expression on his face continued to give nothing away.

She did not disturb him.

'You seem to be waiting for something,' Aunt Isolde said.

The man looked at her. 'Am I? I thought *you* were hoping for someone to arrive. My distaff, distant cousin . . . your nephew the star policeman, perhaps? Or am I *his* distaff cousin? Yes. That's it. I am the distaff one. I come from the wrong side of the blanket, as they used to say in those prejudiced days. Are you waiting for the Herr Baron to arrive on his white charger to save you?'

'So, you hate him too.'

'Sorry to spoil your fun, but I don't hate him. But he would be the icing on the cake. I would take him down as I took down his boss years ago. The idiot Kaltendorf. He made the mistake of thinking he was as good. I made a fool of him for his pains. He never got over it. Lost his nerve after that. Better than killing him, which I could easily have done.'

'And now, you want to humiliate Jens-Müller too.'

'I left clues all over the place for him,' the man complained with a perceptible degree of petulance. 'A little slow, your nephew the baron.'

'Don't underestimate him.'

'Don't worry. I *never* underestimate. The question exercising my mind at the moment is whether those calls were his. If so, where did he call from? Is he on his way here? And again, if so, when will he arrive? My problem is that I never like staying in one location for too long. Do the job, and leave. But if he is coming, I'd hate to miss him. I want him to witness the event I'm leaving for him: my own celebration of ten years or more since the death of my country. How will he feel, do you think, when he sees this place go up in flames, with you inside?'

'He will come after you, whatever hole you crawl into.'

'Oh will he?' The man sounded eager. 'Then he's got more backbone than Kaltendorf. Must be the breeding. Being a baron or whatever obviously helps.'

'Earlier, you called me ridiculous. Well . . . enjoy your ridicule of Jens-Müller; but he'll wipe that smile off your face.'

His smile broadened. 'Dear, dear Aunt Isolde.'

'Don't call me that,' she snapped. 'You don't have the right.'

The smile vanished. 'The final bravado of the doomed,' he said.

In the DDR room, Holtmann looked at the assembled staff.

'That's it,' he said. 'I'm not hanging around here any longer. I have work to do. We've been left in here like idiots waiting for someone to say move. If those people want to talk, they can find me in the kitchens. Who's coming?'

'Perhaps they're having long discussions with the manager and the owner,' someone suggested. 'Guests are funny people. They have all sorts of demands. We were told to wait. We should. Anyway, we're being paid for doing nothing, so why worry? Besides, it's lousy outside. It's a good break from running after fussy guests.'

There was general laughter.

'And these lot are American,' someone else began. 'We all know how fussy *they* can be. Bring me a Waldorf salad,' he went on in a jokey New York accent. 'You don't know how to make a goddammed Waldorf salad? What kind of a place is this, anyway?'

Exaggerated groans accompanied the performance.

But Holtmann was not to be deflected. 'You can all waste time in here if you wish, but I'm leaving. And the kitchen staff are coming with me.' It was an order.

He went to the door and grabbed at it. It didn't move.

'It's locked!' he said in outrage. 'What the hell is this?'

'But it wasn't locked when . . . who was it . . . checked . . .'

'That was a long time ago!' Holtmann snarled. He banged on the door with his fist. 'Hey! *Hey! Open the damn door!*' He kept banging on it, while the others in the room stared at him.

Several moments later, they heard the swipe card. Then the door opened.

'What the—' Holtmann's outraged voice began, then it died abruptly as if someone had squeezed his windpipe.

One of the men was standing outside. He saw what the man was holding.

'A gun!' Holtmann cried in a hoarse whisper. 'He . . . he's got a gun!'

Startled gasps from within the room followed this revelation.

The man crooked a finger at the senior chef, beckoning him.

For someone who was in a hurry to leave scant moments before, Holtmann had suddenly lost all desire to do so.

The man was not patient. He stuck the machine pistol in Holtmann's face. The meaning was clear. A terrified Holtmann went hesitantly out. The door slammed shut behind him.

'What—' Holtmann began.

'*Shut up!*'

Holtmann kept his mouth shut.

'Look,' the man with the gun said.

Holtmann looked down. Something black and elliptical, with a top that had a red, blinking light, was attached to a supporting wall.

'This,' the man told him, 'is a firebomb. It senses movement. I temporarily disarmed it when I came to the door. It will reset itself in a few minutes. Go back in there and tell your colleagues to *shut up, and don't move*, or they will all be blown to hell with you. Got that?'

Eyes fearful, Holtmann nodded urgently.

'Good. Now let's go back. Any more banging on that door or any other noise whatsoever . . . and *boom*!'

Holtmann allowed himself to be meekly herded back. The door was again locked.

The man made a call to his boss.

The man with the blacked-up face stared at Aunt Isolde as he answered.

'Yes.'

'This is Two,' came the voice in his ear. 'A slight annoyance. The head cook,' 'Two' went on disparagingly, 'started banging on the door. I took him out and gave him a lecture. Frightened him enough to make sure they will all remain quiet from now on.'

'What did you do?'

'Told him a story about the grenade sensing movement. They won't dare breathe . . . even when the place catches fire. They'll roast in peace.' 'Two' laughed at his own macabre joke.

The man gave his familiar soft laugh. 'Well done. By the way, check outside from time to time. We may have a visitor.'

'Expected arrival?'

'He may not come at all. This is insurance.'

'Will do. We should leave soon.'

'We shall.'

210

'Two, out.'

Müller turned off the flashers as they approached the Autobahn exit. The secret blue lights were once more hidden
behind their unobtrusive panels. He also turned off the
CD player.

Carey Bloomfield instinctively took a soft, deep breath of
relief as the car began to slow down, realizing that she had
unwittingly tensed herself during the high-speed dash.

'Feeling more relaxed now?' Müller asked with more than
a hint of dryness as he fed the car into the exit.

'I was OK,' she replied guiltily. 'Really.'

He made no comment, but she sensed he was smiling as
he turned on to the road that would eventually take them to
the Schlosshotel.

As they came round a bend that seemed particularly
familiar, she recognized the spot where he had earlier found
the bodies as it flitted by on the edge of brightness made by the
headlights, the passing foliage gleaming with wetness from
the still heavily falling rain. He did not glance at it, she noted.

He had already cut speed considerably and as they drew
nearer their destination, the Porsche was cruising with the
barest of sounds from the engine.

'They shouldn't hear the car at all, with all this rain,' he
suddenly remarked. 'And the stream will also be making a
lot of noise. We should be OK.'

'*They*?' she repeated. 'Who's *they*?'

'Did I say that?'

'Yes, you did.'

'A figure of speech.'

'Oh, sure.'

He did not elaborate, and continued to drive at cruising
speed. He switched on the small front driving lights and
turned off the headlights. The smaller lights, mounted flush
lower down, were still more than bright enough for driving,
even in the dark of the rain; but they gave less warning to a
possible distant observer.

'Why did you do that?' she asked.

'Caution,' he replied.

'Why do you need to be cautious? We're just going to your aunt, whom, if I remember correctly, you're not worried about.'

'Humour me.'

'That's some answer.'

'It's an answer.'

They came round the final bend, and the turn-off for the Schlosshotel appeared. Müller turned into it, continuing to drive at a crawl. The sound of the rain on the car was now far louder than that of the engine. The lights of the place could be seen speckling through the tall trees, and cast a subdued glow beyond them. The building itself was still hidden behind the screen of woodland.

Müller now turned off all lights on the car. The glow from the lights of the building gave sufficient illumination for his purposes. He slowed the Porsche to walking pace until the Schlosshotel itself came into full view; then he pulled off the driveway and into the shadows, and stopped the car. He turned off the engine. As it made cooling noises, the sound of the rain on the roof came through powerfully. In the background, an even more powerful sound could faintly be heard.

'The stream,' he said. 'It's risen quite high. I know the sound.' He looked at her in the gloom of the car, his face ghostly in the eerie glow of the communication screen. 'I'm going to have a look around. If everything is fine, I will call you on the car's system. All you have to do is talk to it.'

'Yes, sir. Any more orders?'

'This is not a game, Miss Bloomfield.'

'Carey.'

'Miss Bloomfield,' Müller repeated emphatically. 'Give me ten minutes by the timer on the console screen. If you do not hear from me by then, hit that button . . .' He indicated a fingernail-shaped button. 'It will give you a direct link to Pappi. He will know what to do. I'm leaving the keys. Take the car, and get out of here as fast as you can.'

'You're trusting *me* with your precious car?'

'I am trusting you with my precious car. And please, Miss Bloomfield, just once . . . do as I ask without questioning . . .'

'Sir, yessir!'

Müller sighed.

'Müller?'

'Miss Bloomfield?'

'You'll get that nice suit all wet and dirty.'

'The dry cleaners will make it just as good as new.' Müller reached for the door catch.

'Müller?'

'*Miss* Bloomfield . . .' Müller began with a touch of exasperation.

'I don't know what you feel is wrong out there, but watch your back, and don't get any holes in that nice suit.'

Müller paused. 'Thank you. I always do, and I'll do my best not to . . . And please, if it becomes necessary, get out of here. And don't use the CD. As little noise as possible . . . just in case.'

'You got it.'

'I hate those movies where the man tells the woman not to move and she *always* does so, gets into a lot of trouble—'

'—and he has to spend time saving her. I've seen those movies. I hate them too.'

He gave a curt nod, opened the door and climbed out into the rain.

The sound of the stream surged briefly through the dark to be muffled once more as he quietly shut the door. She watched as he moved into the shadows of the wood, and saw enough in the ambient light to observe that he had pulled something out of his jacket. She knew he had drawn his weapon.

'Not worried, eh, Müller?' she said to herself softly as he seemed to vanish. 'Strange behaviour for a man who's not worried.'

She decided she'd wait for five minutes before calling Toby Adams, just in case Müller was playing some kind of game and would double-back to the car, to catch her out in the middle of the call.

As she peered out at the wet darkness, she sensed a malevolence out there; waiting.

Müller, meanwhile, was making his way cautiously and silently towards the building, using all the cover available. The grounds were extremely familiar to him, enabling him to make relatively easy and secure progress. The sounds of the rain and the stream completely masked his passage so that he was able to reach the staff quarters without being seen, or heard. The route he had taken enabled him to avoid the need to cross the stream by the footbridge. This would have brought him closer to the main building, and he did not want to risk it.

He had tried to make as dry a passage as possible, but Carey Bloomfield would have smiled ironically, he decided. His suit was seriously wet and had collected some dirt in the interim; but still some way from being soaked through. He hoped to make it inside before that happened.

From his position, he surveyed the area in front of the hotel. What he saw confirmed his gut feeling that something was definitely wrong. Though the Derrenberg had an underground garage for both staff and guests, it was normal for there to be a number of vehicles parked near it. Only one stood there, directly in front: a dark Mercedes saloon.

Where were the conference guests and *their* cars? Not all parked away by the hotel staff, surely. And where was the doorman in his hussar uniform?

Müller was just about to make a dash for the pedestrian entry to the residential courtyard, when a movement caused him to freeze in the shadows. A man in a raincoat had come to the hotel entrance. Müller's eyes zeroed upon what the man held, ready for use.

A silenced machine pistol.

Müller considered warning Carey Bloomfield, then immediately decided against it. She might make too loud a noise

214

starting the car and the alarm would instantly be raised, with possibly fatal consequences for anyone held inside; Aunt Isolde included, if she were indeed there. He would have to first get into the building, in order to establish exactly what the situation was. Lives, he knew, could so easily be lost by acting in haste. Both he and Pappenheim had seen it happen when operational action – not under their command – had been wrongly judged. He was not about to make a similar mistake.

He had already given Carey Bloomfield the ten-minute margin. She knew what to do, as did Pappenheim, when he received the call.

Müller remained where he was, watching as the man with the machine pistol took a slow look around. The man's head turned with the precision of a radar antenna. This was no amateur.

When the man's gaze reached the area where Müller was hiding, the tracking head seemed to hesitate briefly. Müller was certain he had been spotted; but the head continued to track until at last, apparently satisfied, the man turned to re-enter the hotel.

Müller let out his breath slowly, hoping he had been wrong about being spotted. A true professional would have behaved exactly as the man had. No outward reaction, save for the slightest of hesitations, which someone without Müller's skills would have missed completely.

In the man's place, Müller decided, he would have done exactly the same, then come out unexpectedly, in time to catch whoever it was making a dash for new cover. Müller remained where he was.

Right on cue, the man came rapidly out once more, gun pointing. He held that stance for long moments.

Müller again held his breath and did not move.

The man remained so still, he could have been a statue; then, abruptly, he lowered the weapon, and went back inside.

Müller still did not move.

A long minute passed. The margin he had given to Carey

215

Bloomfield was ticking away and he had still not gained entry. It was time to move. If the man came out yet again, he would have to take him on the run. But he hoped that would not occur. The sound of his own automatic would give the very warning he did not want those with the guns inside to hear.

He chose his moment and made a swift run for the pedestrian gate. He arrived without drama and quickly tapped in the code on the backlit keypad. He also added a single digit to the code, to temporarily disable the security lighting. The lock hissed softly open, and the gate swung smoothly and silently. He went through. The gate swung back just as silently and clicked softly shut. The lights did not come on.

Blinking in the rain, Müller suddenly pressed himself against the building. The lights in Aunt Isolde's private kitchen were on. A shadowy movement from within threw an elongated replica on to the courtyard, inside the splash of light which marked out the borders of the window. The shadow wore a hat.

Müller remained where he was, hoping the person to whom the shadow belonged would move soon. The keypad was already resetting the security lighting system, and they would soon be flooding the courtyard. He had to be inside before that happened; but the person by the window seemed determined to remain there for ever, looking out at the darkened courtyard. Fleeting seconds were like years.

Then, at last, the person moved.

With great relief, Müller went to the door he had used the night before and again tapped in the code, praying the noise of the lock would be as unobtrusive as that of the gate.

It was. He had beaten the lights, and he was in.

In the kitchen, the man with the blacked-up face had moved from the window as he received a call from one of the other men.

'This is Two.'

'Yes.'

'I just had a look outside. Thought I saw something.'

'And?'

'I'm not sure. I want to do another check with the infrared scope. I think I might check out the grounds . . . just in case. Could have been some small animal. But, after what you said, I still think I should check it out.'

'Do it. Good idea about the scope.'

'The rain might degrade it, but I should still be able to get something. Always assuming there's anything to get.'

'Do it, anyway. Did you hear any vehicles?'

'No. Nothing.'

'Alright. Get back to me when you've done the outside check.'

'Two, out.'

The man turned to Aunt Isolde when he had finished speaking to his number two. 'One of my colleagues believes he spotted something . . . or some*one*, I should say. You heard our conversation, so I'm certain you've got the gist.'

'What do you expect from me?'

'Nothing. I have all I need. However, my people are not given to exaggeration. If he says he believes he spotted something, I take that very seriously indeed. He seems to feel he may have been mistaken, but, like a good professional, he is checking further. I do hope, for your sake, it's just some night-time animal looking for a meal in this foul weather. On the other hand, if it is your star policeman nephew – my *cousin* – lurking out there playing the hero, things could get interesting.'

There was distinct anticipation in his voice. He smiled at her.

Aunt Isolde looked stonily back at him.

In the Porsche, Carey Bloomfield called Toby Adams precisely five minutes after Müller's departure.

'As usual,' she began as soon as Adams had responded, 'this has to be quick, Toby.'

'Something in your voice,' Adams remarked astutely. 'Where are you?'

'Parked in the dark, near the hotel.'

'*Near* the hotel? Where's Müller?'

'Out in the woods somewhere . . . gun in hand.'

Adams was silent for some moments. 'What the hell's happened?'

'That's what I'm going to find out almost as soon as we've ended this call.'

'You're going out there *after* him?'

'I'm going out there after someone . . .'

'But we have no trace . . .'

'Perhaps we'll find one here. By the way, Müller ordered me to stay put and, if he wasn't back, or in touch with me, within ten minutes, I'm to contact Pappenheim, then get the hell out, using his car.'

'He *trusts* you with his *Porsche*?' Adams exclaimed before he could stop himself.

'Thanks for the vote of confidence in my driving, Toby.'

'Um . . . what I mean . . .'

'I know exactly what you mean, Toby. If you ever buy a Porsche, I won't ask you to lend it to me.'

'Carey . . . just take it easy,' Adams said, neatly dodging the subject. 'If you feel you must go out there, remember . . . no emotion. You're dealing with someone very dangerous.'

'Don't worry. I'm dangerous too.'

'Just you watch it. As I've said before, I don't want to see a body bag.'

'And I don't want to be in it. So, we're on the same track.'

'Carey . . .'

''Bye, Toby.'

She ended the call before he could say more, then looked at the console. Four minutes to go before Müller's deadline. She pressed the button he had indicated.

'Yes, Jens?' immediately came Pappenheim's voice at low volume on the car speakers.

'This is Carey Bloomfield.'

The immediate silence this produced indicated the level of Pappenheim's astonishment.

'Miss Bloomfield,' he said at last, voice distant and unfriendly.

'Keep your shirt on, Pappi. You know I would not be using this unless I'd been instructed.'

'So, where is he?'

'He told me I was to contact you,' she said, ignoring the question, 'and that you'd know what to do.'

'I know it. Where is he?' Pappenheim repeated.

'Out in the woods by the hotel. He told me to get out after I'd contacted you. He left me his keys.'

'The keys to his *Porsche*?' Pappenheim said in further astonishment, this time ironically mirroring that of Toby Adams.

'Thanks,' she said dryly. 'That's twice now.'

'Twice what?'

'Not important.'

'So? Are you going to do as he's asked?'

'No.'

'That does not surprise me.'

'What do you mean?'

'Miss Bloomfield, whoever you are – *whatever* you are – you're not a journalist. This leaves me with a problem. Do I trust you for now?'

'Or?'

'Or do I have you picked up?'

'Whatever you think I'm going to do, you'd be too late.'

'I know it. Therefore, I must risk that you are not a danger to my boss. If you are . . . I will find you, wherever you may go. Even if I have to resign from the police to do it.'

'Remind me not to get on your bad side, *Oberkommissar* Pappenheim.'

'It is definitely not a good place to be.'

'Then I had better let you get on with what Müller wants you to do.'

'We'll be seeing each other again, Miss Bloomfield.' It almost sounded like a warning.

'Perhaps,' she said, and cut transmission.

She quickly got her bag and took the big automatic out of it. She rapidly checked it. Deep within the bag were strips of lightweight canvas material that she speedily put together to become a shoulder harness with an open-pouch holster. She removed her jacket, put the harness on, then the gun into the holster. She left the jacket off.

'What the hell,' she muttered to herself. 'I'm going to get wet anyway.'

Besides, the jacket could itself become a hindrance under the circumstances.

There were two spare magazines, which she clipped to the harness. She reached across and took the keys out of the ignition and put them into a side pocket. If left alone for a certain length of time with the ignition key out, the car would lock itself and enable its alarm system.

'Ready as I'll ever be,' she said, and climbed out into the rain and the dark.

Müller's ten-minute deadline was up.

Müller looked down at his shoes.

He had wiped them as best as he could on the mat. From a small storeroom sited near the door for that very purpose, he had quietly taken a cloth and wiped off all excess moisture and dirt, replaced the cloth and shut the storeroom door. It looked as if it had never been disturbed.

He checked behind him. He had left no wet footprints on the narrow Persian rug that covered the hallway which led to one of the doors to the kitchen. His clothes were wet, but not dripping. Hopefully, he would be leaving no trail for anyone coming to this area to spot after he had passed. Within the shoes, his feet were dry.

Gun held two-handedly, he made his way cautiously towards the kitchen. The ten minutes were up. He hoped Carey Bloomfield had done as he'd asked.

In the hotel section, the man called Two contacted the third man.

'I'm going outside for a quick check around,' he said. 'You watch things in here, especially those idiots in the DDR room.'

The third man was currently patrolling the conferencing area.

'Right,' he confirmed. 'Don't let the rabbits get you.'

'Very funny.'

Two, infrared scope now mounted on his weapon, went to the hotel entrance and trained it on the spot where he thought he'd seen something. A tiny red bloom was there. It was just a trace.

Too small to have been a man, he mistakenly decided, even allowing for the fact that the wet weather would have cooled the spot and so degraded the return. Yet his instincts nagged at him.

He went out into the rain. The sound of the swollen stream came powerfully.

Carey Bloomfield made her way towards the building with the practised skill of someone used to clandestine movement. She used available cover with an efficiency that would certainly have surprised Müller.

'Shit,' she said to herself softly as the continuing rain began to make itself felt through her clothes. 'This is Noah's-Ark weather.'

Though she moved swiftly, it was not done in haste. Every metre of ground she covered was first carefully checked out. She had almost reached the footbridge, when she saw in the lights of the hotel, the man with the gun move into view. She could easily identify the weapon's configuration.

'Shit!' she again said to herself in a low whisper. 'Infrared scope.'

She had long dropped flat, pressing herself into the ground and hoping that if he trained the machine pistol in her direction, the bloom of her body heat would not register strongly enough for him to become suspicious. Suddenly, she was very thankful for the heavy rain. Getting wet through was no longer annoying.

From her position, she could still just about see the man. She did not move.

She watched as he came slowly towards the stream, weapon sweeping in slow tracking arcs, but never pausing in any particular quadrant. Every so often he would turn round suddenly, as if hoping to catch someone in surreptitious movement. This pattern continued until he reached the edge of the stream. So far, the tracking weapon had not paused in the area where she lay.

She had her own weapon in hand, held flat against her right thigh. He was close enough for her to get off a couple of killing snap shots, if he spotted her. She hoped she would be quicker than he was. His surprise should give her the edge.

Like a predator in ambush, she waited for her moment of action.

Müller was close to the door of the kitchen. He had flattened himself against the wall, gun raised, waiting to make his entry. He heard the man with the blacked-up face talking, and felt the shock of recognition go through him.

'Not long now, *Aunt Isolde*,' the man said, deliberately making goading use of the forbidden form of address. 'We'll be leaving your monument to class as a bonfire that will be seen for kilometres; a fitting tribute to mendacious politics, flawed unity, and the death of my country.'

'Does that make you feel powerful?' Aunt Isolde asked scathingly.

Müller decided this was the best moment to enter. The voices had clearly positioned each speaker. Aunt Isolde was not as close to the man as he had at first feared. He would have a clear shot.

He darted in, braced himself against the inner wall, gun pointing unerringly at the man in the raincoat.

'*Not . . . one . . . move!*' he ordered with soft emphasis.

'*Jens-Müller!*' Aunt Isolde cried in surprise, relief, and pleasure.

The man did not move, but his gun was already pointing at Aunt Isolde.

'Ah . . . my cousin, the brave, noble baron, or graf,' the man said with unnerving pleasantness. 'At last. I wondered if—I *hoped* you would come. I am impressed. One of my men thought he'd spotted something, but you've clearly fooled him. Very neat. At least, you are smarter than Kaltendorf. And I did leave you some clues. Did you like the unlovely presents I left in the woods, not far from here?'

Müller kept his gun trained on the man. '*Put down the weapon, Dahlberg!*'

'Oh, do call me Baron . . . or perhaps Graf? No? I am a von Röhnen, you know. Just like you. We are family. We share the same genetic—'

'Herman Dahlberg,' Müller interrupted formally, staring coldly at the blacked-up face. 'You are under arrest. Put down your weapon!'

'Or what?' Dahlberg enquired mildly. 'You'll shoot me? In time to prevent me from killing your nice, annoying aunt? In time to prevent this entire edifice from blowing up and consuming, in the flames, the staff locked in the DDR room?'

'*What?*' Müller asked, horrified. His gun did not move. 'Aunt Isolde . . . is this true?'

'I'm afraid it is,' she replied. She instinctively began to move towards Müller.

'No, no, *no*, Aunt Isolde!' Dahlberg admonished in his eerily pleasant voice. 'I will shoot you dead before the very eyes of your heroic nephew. Do spare a thought for the poor man. The sight of your brains going all over the place would surely have a devastating effect upon him.'

Aunt Isolde stopped moving as if she had been turned to stone.

'You are sick!' Müller said tightly. His gun still did not move.

'The *world* is sick, Cousin. Otherwise, you and I would not be here in this situation. Think of all the strands in our lives that have led us to this . . . inopportune meeting. Only a sick world could have produced the varying influences that have led us to this very spot. And now that we are here, what are we to do? We have a stand-off. There is no way you can kill me and save your aunt. Not the remotest chance in hell.' Dahlberg's voice had suddenly become chillingly hard.

'Aunt Isolde,' Müller began quietly, eyes firmly upon Dahlberg. 'Do you know how many of them—'

'Just three, I think. But I can't be certain . . .'

'Forget it, Cousin,' Dahlberg said to Müller harshly. 'It is immaterial for your purposes how many of my men there are. What you've got to ask yourself is whether you can do anything to save your Aunt Isolde, before I kill her.' Dalhberg's gun was held at full arm's length, pointing directly at her head. 'As I've said . . . a stand-off.'

Outside, in the rainy woods, Carey Bloomfield's moment did not come. The man with the infrared scope on his machine pistol suddenly turned and began searching elsewhere. Eventually, he moved out of sight behind a corner of the building.

She remained where she was. Like Müller, she expected a trick. She waited, the seconds ticking away. A full minute passed, and there was still no sign of the man. She gave him another thirty seconds. Still nothing.

She would have to risk moving.

She turned her head slowly, until she could see the shape of the footbridge. It was not within direct lighting, and the back-glow from the lights in the grounds gave sufficient, though the illumination was not strong enough to show more than a silhouette. She was thankful for that. She remembered what Müller had said about the floodlight and hoped it was not triggered by movement.

She would have to move *now*.

'Shit,' she muttered, not liking the idea at all. She was still not sure of what the gunman was up to.

But she couldn't wait for ever. She rose with a fluid motion and set off for the footbridge at a fast run, dodging and darting behind every available cover, and at varying bursts of speed.

The man had been hiding behind a corner. He decided to pick a moment to train the scope on the spot across the stream where he had seen a weak bloom. He caught Carey Bloomfield in full flight between two areas of cover and was startled to recognize in the scope the curves of a woman. His moment of hesitation gave her the chance to make it to new cover.

The man was in a quandary. Should he warn Dahlberg? He pursed his lips. This woman moved well. She was good; but not that good. He could take on a woman without needing to raise the alarm. He would first kill her and, having got the proof, *then* tell Dahlberg.

Carey Bloomfield made another dash. She reached the bridge and felt relief when the light did not come on. She was halfway across when something hummed close past her head. She had not even heard the shot!

Silenced, she thought as she threw herself flat and rolled the rest of the way, expecting a fusillade to follow her. *I'm a goddammed beacon of warmth in that scope.*

But no further shots came. She knew, however, he was still waiting; but where? With that scope, the advantage was all his.

She crawled off the bridge and something thumped into it near her left foot. He can't be that bad a shot. The bastard was playing with her.

She made a decision which filled her with trepidation, bringing back as it did a particularly unpleasant childhood memory; but it was her only way out.

She was close enough to the racing stream. She put the

automatic back in its holster, and lowered herself into the turbulent water, gripping the edge of the levee wall with both hands. It was unexpectedly cold and the shock nearly made her lose the hand hold. She began to pull herself slowly against the current, working her way towards where she judged the mouth of the run-off tunnel would be. She could then use the lower lip to brace her feet, and so wait there for the next move by the gunman. The trouble was, her childhood nightmare returned with a vengeance.

Her father, a military doctor with the US Air Force and stationed in Florida, had taken his family on a camping holiday near the coast, in a huge motorhome. She and her brother had taken their mountain bikes, and had gone riding through some woods. She had hit a small log and had been thrown into a creek. Unfortunately for her, she had disturbed a cottonmouth. The annoyed snake bit her. She screamed, and her brother dropped his bike to drag her out. The snake was still wrapped about her leg. Very bravely, he grabbed the animal by the head, and with a hunting knife he always carried on camping trips, sawed off the snake's head. It was a big snake for the kind, over five feet long and jet black, in startling contrast to the white lining of its mouth.

Their father – who thoughtfully always carried antivenin supplies on camping trips – had thoroughly schooled them about snakebite, and her brother's subsequent actions undoubtedly saved her life. The viper's haemotoxic venom was extremely painful, and this had made her cry out in both fear and the violence of the pain.

The nightmare of the incident came rushing back as she felt the water swirl about her. Were there vipers in Thüringen and, especially, *had any been swept into this stream*? She tried to forget the cottonmouth as she slowly worked her way, hand over hand, against the powerful current. Every time something borne by the water touched her leg, she had to stop herself from screaming. The man was up there, waiting. Could he see her hands in the scope?

No bullets smacked the ground. Perhaps it never occurred

to him that she would go in. And if he had spotted what she'd done, perhaps he thought she had been swept away.

Carey Bloomfield struggled against the current, trying hard not to breathe too loudly with the exertion of her progress. At last, she felt a change in the direction of the water: the *run-off*.

Inching one foot forward, she braced it against the edge of the overflow tunnel and used that purchase to bring the other foot to bear. Her trainers, low-soled and pliable, gave her a firm grip, even below the surface. Now she was lying in the water, feet jammed against the tunnel, with just one hand gripping the edge of the levee wall. Praying she was not going to be dragged into the tunnel itself, she again drew the pistol out of its holster.

'Hope you enjoyed the trip,' a smug voice said above her.

She did not pause. In a sweeping motion her gun arm came up, like a striking cottonmouth, dripping water. In that instant, she saw all she needed to. The man was standing directly above her, gun pointing. But she was faster.

The Beretta barked sharply twice into the wet darkness. The man was so astonished, he never got off a shot. Both bullets hit him beneath the jaw, tearing upwards through his head. He toppled into the stream, gun falling out of slackening hands. It slammed painfully against the side of Carey Bloomfield's head, before sinking into the water.

She stifled the cry she felt being wrenched out of her, and nearly lost her one-handed grip on the wall. Then the man's body, propelled by the stream, banged into her. She felt his arms wrap slackly about her, and she wanted to scream aloud.

He's dead, she thought. *He's dead*!

What if in his dying throes he dragged her into the tunnel?

Head throbbing from the blow from the falling gun, she fought the panic she felt rising and made herself put the Beretta back into its holster, thus freeing that hand. The body was still being pressed against her by the force of the stream. The run-off was working too well.

With difficulty, she pulled herself out of the torrent, all the while having to disentangle herself from the gunman's body. In the darkness of the water, she imagined it to be a giant cottonmouth and fought a hard battle with her mind, against the return of the nightmare. At last, she was free. The body, cleared of the obstruction, was swept into the tunnel. The gunman had been too sure of himself.

She lay on the ground, soaked and breathing deeply, nightmare receding.

'Jesus,' she whispered. 'Oh Jesus.'

In the kitchen, they heard the double report of the Beretta, even through the closed, double-glazed windows; even through the sound of the rain. It was an aberration amongst the sounds of the dark outside.

Dahlberg took three swift steps to position himself close behind Aunt Isolde. One arm went about her neck and his gun hand held the weapon against her temple.

'If your men are out there,' he said to Müller in a hard voice that lacked all emotion, 'that was a very bad mistake. I shall have to modify my plans, but you will still not save Aunt Isolde.' He paused suddenly. 'But for a moment,' he went on, 'you looked very surprised . . . so perhaps this was not of your making, after all.' He rubbed the pistol against Aunt Isolde's cheek. 'Tell me,' he said to her. 'Did we miss someone? Has someone with a gun been hiding, waiting for a chance to start shooting? A security man, perhaps?'

She didn't speak, but her mouth moved.

'Oh, I'm so sorry;' he said with exaggerated solicitude. 'I'm not allowing you to breathe properly. There. Is that easier?'

'There's . . . no one,' she said hoarsely. 'We don't have . . . armed security . . . People . . . who need them usually . . . bring their own. And, as you falsely booked the hotel, there's . . . there's no one else.'

Dahlberg looked at Müller, whose gun was still pointing. 'Not your men, and no one from the hotel. We have a mystery, Cousin. What are we going to do about it? I'd better check. Two!' he said into his mike. 'Two! What's going on out there?'

'That shot did not come from any of my people,' Müller said. 'I have no one else here. Perhaps your man shot at a rabbit, thinking it was me.'

'He's using a machine pistol,' Dahlberg said curtly. 'Two! What the hell are you doing?'

There was no reply.

'Perhaps his radio's out,' Müller suggested helpfully.

'Shut up, Cousin! I'm not in the mood. *Two!* Answer!'

Müller was as baffled as Dahlberg and wondered who had fired the shots and what, as a result, had happened to the man called Two. He also wondered just how much greater the danger to Aunt Isolde had become because of it.

'Three!' Dahlberg was barking sharply. 'Did you hear those shots?'

Three had been prowling deep inside the hotel and had not heard anything.

'What shots?' he asked.

'Two is out there,' Dahlberg snapped. 'Go and check!'

'On my way.'

Dahlberg turned to Müller. 'Are you going to keep pointing that gun at me? If so, you'd better follow. We're moving. I think it's time we left this place, don't you? And you've still got about twenty or so people to try and save from being roasted alive. Who would be a policeman, eh?' Dahlberg laughed softly. 'Which way out is convenient for you?' He began moving, taking an unwilling Aunt Isolde along. 'You're going to get wet, *Aunt Isolde*. I need you to discourage your nephew, my *cousin* the noble baron, from doing something stupid . . . like trying to prevent me from getting away. Sorry I can't allow you to get your coat. But there it is. Coming, Cousin?' he added to Müller.

229

'I am coming,' Müller replied evenly, 'and I won't lower the gun.'

'As I thought,' Dahlberg said imperturbably. 'And if you've got a phone on you,' he continued warningly, 'I'd advise you not to call anyone. I'd shoot Aunt Isolde immediately.'

'And I would shoot *you* immediately. You would not be going anywhere.'

'Yes. But she'll still be dead.'

Ten

C arey Bloomfield had risen to her feet and was making
her way towards the front of the hotel, keeping close to
the building, gun in hand. The wet clothes, clinging to her
body, made soft rasping sounds as she moved. Her trainers
joined the chorus by making low, squelching noises. She
felt cold, but was determined not to let it affect her. Every
time her movements took her into the rain, it felt warm by
comparison.

'So, where's everybody?' she muttered, noting the strange
lack of vehicles as she drew closer.

She took her time, being careful not to expose herself as
she worked her way towards the entrance. She paused when
she saw the big Mercedes, but there was still no one in sight.
Where were the gunman's friends?

And where was Müller?

The gunman addressed as Three was making his way towards
one of the lifts that would take him to the ground floor,
although he could easily have used the stairs. The entire
building was itself on three floors only.

As he moved, he kept turning round to check, sweeping with
his machine pistol in the same manner as had Two. He reached
the lift, and pressed the button to call it up. It was the same one
Two had used, and it had remained on the ground floor. Three
kept up his turning routine, as he waited for the lift to arrive.

*   *   *

Carey Bloomfield reached the hotel entrance safely as the lift began to rise. She did not hear it. As she entered the hotel, she wondered how to make it past the reception desk and to the management office without leaving wet footprints, or a trail of water droplets. She could still see the dried-out, slightly muddy outlines of another set, presumably belonging to the man she had just killed.

Then she saw a magazine rack close by, just inside. Several were high-gloss style magazines. Careful not to step on to the highly polished marbled floor, she reached over to remove two examples. She quietly put them on the floor, spines towards her intended route, then placed a foot on each. The wet soles of her trainers acted temporarily like glue and held each magazine in place. She then snow-shoed her way across.

The polished surface of the floor and the glossy covers of the magazines made progress quick and easy. She reached the management office safely, then turned to look back along her trail. No footprints. She thought she could see a few drops of water glistening in the lights of the reception area but hoped, if anyone saw them, they would believe the water had been left by one of their own.

Then the lift pinged as it arrived.

She ducked into cover, and waited. Now would be the test of whether she had made a safe entry. She did not want to have to use the gun for a second time, before she knew more about the situation within the building. The shots by the stream appeared not to have generated any frantic activity; but shooting within the hotel would reverberate loudly enough to wake the dead. That would certainly bring the gunman's friends running.

She heard the lift doors hiss open. Rubber-soled shoes made squeaky noises on the marbled floor. The lift doors hissed shut, but the lift remained. She shivered slightly, hoped she was not about to get a chill, or to sneeze. She felt her nose itch, wrinkled it to stop the irritation, and thought about something else. The sneeze did not come.

The squeaky noises moved towards the entrance, and faded.

He had not spotted the droplets of water.

She remained where she was for some more moments, before taking a cautious look.

There was no one to be seen.

'I think we'll use the small corridor into the hotel,' Dahlberg said in conversational tones, as if they were all going on a pleasant journey.

They moved slowly out of the kitchen, Müller and Dahlberg watching each other like hawks ready for the kill. Dahlberg's gun was still against Aunt Isolde's temple, and Müller's Beretta was still pointed in a two-handed grip at Dahlberg.

'Now, Cousin,' Dahlberg continued in the menacingly soft voice he liked to affect. 'Which of us opens the first door? All three of us know the code. I think you're elected.'

'I'm not going in ahead of you.'

The eyes in the blacked-up face stared coldly. 'You're playing with dear Aunt Isolde's life.'

'I've told you . . . if you kill her, I'll shoot you. I'll empty the magazine, load another and empty that too, for good measure. They'll need a crane to lift you out of here.'

The eyes did not blink. 'I can see that you mean it. You are certainly tougher than Kaltendorf. We are alike, you and I.'

'Not in a million years.'

'Oh yes, Cousin. More alike than you would care to believe. I'll tell you what. Let *Aunt Isolde* punch in the numbers. We'll go in ahead of you. You know if you shoot me in the back, at this close range, the bullet from the Beretta will go through me and into her. I will also still have time to fire into her head . . .'

'Stop talking and get on with it!'

'Oh, we are the hard policeman. You heard the man, *Aunt Isolde*,' Dahlberg ordered, deliberately stressing the name because he knew it annoyed her. 'Let's do it.'

They crabbed their way to the first door of the small,

connecting corridor, Dahlberg keeping an almost choking armlock about her throat.

With difficulty, she tapped in the code. The door swung open. Dahlberg tried to shove her through, staying locked to her, intending to shut Müller out. But Müller had expected the move. He was right up against Dahlberg's back, gun touching the lower spine.

'I might just get away with it,' Müller told him, 'if I shoot you there. Your spine will be shattered from its moorings.'

Dahlberg made a noise that sounded like cheerful resignation. 'One to you,' he said. 'I must remember not to underestimate you.'

'It can be fatal.'

'But you should not underestimate me, either, Cousin . . .'

'Stop calling me that . . .'

'But I am . . .'

Aunt Isolde's sudden, hoarse cry, when she saw the prone Bulent Landauer, interrupted them both.

'Oh, Bulent!' she exclaimed, voice almost squeezed to a whisper by Dahlberg's grip.

'Ah, yes,' he said. 'Your little Turk.'

Landauer was conscious and his eyes widening with the horror of both the recognition of Dahlberg, and of seeing Aunt Isolde being held hostage. So fixed were his eyes upon Dahlberg, he did not see Müller following behind.

What happened next was so unexpected, Müller was completely caught out.

Dahlberg's hand moved away from Aunt Isolde's head with startling swiftness. The arm pointed downwards. A single shot echoed within the small corridor. Then the gun was once more against Aunt Isolde's head.

But a lot had happened within that fleeting moment in time. A man had died. Bulent Landauer had not even been able to scream when he had seen what was about to happen, because of the tape Dahlberg had previously fixed across his mouth. The bullet had taken him clean through the heart.

Aunt Isolde began to struggle, making high keening noises in her throat.

'*Stop that immediately!*' Dahlberg snarled. 'Let this be a warning to you both. I am deadly serious. I will not hesitate to kill you, *Aunt Isolde*. What has just happened to your little Turk is a warning to you to *behave*. And a warning to you too, Cousin,' he snapped at Müller.

Müller felt a chilling horror descend upon his mind. He did not take his eyes off Dahlberg to stare at Landauer's body. He and Landauer had known each other for years. While not best pals, there had still been a kind of warm friendliness between them. Müller felt his mouth tighten. There was no way Dahlberg was going to get away with anything.

'You evil, *evil* man!' Aunt Isolde exclaimed when Dahlberg's stranglehold about her neck had relaxed sufficiently to enable her to speak, though still with difficulty. 'Why did you do that? What had he ever done to you?'

'Don't try to appeal to my conscience, or my better nature. I have neither. *Now, move!* The second door.'

From her hiding place, Carey Bloomfield had heard the shot and identified where it had come from.

She did not move, wanting to first ascertain the cause. It was also possible that the man who had just gone out would have heard, and would come running.

She waited, gun ready, to see what would happen next.

What happened next was the opening of the door to the connecting corridor, close to the management office. She shrunk further down into cover, but could still see clearly from her vantage point.

First came Aunt Isolde's reluctant feet, followed by the rest of her body, tilted at a backwards angle. She was being pushed and almost carried through the doorway. Carey Bloomfield stared as the man holding on to Aunt Isolde came through. The long, black raincoat, the arm about Aunt Isolde's throat, the gun at her head, the hat, the black-stained face beneath the hat. Then came Müller, watchful, gun trained upon the man.

Carey Bloomfield felt her heart beat with pain and joy; pain because of what the man had done to her, because, even beneath the stain, the face lived within her nightmares. Joy, because after years of searching, she had at last found her quarry. He was the biggest cottonmouth ever, and she was going to kill it. Today.

She rose out of her hiding place, Beretta pointing in a two-handed grip.

'*Dahlberg*!' she screamed. It was a cry both of anguish and exultation.

Whatever else he was, Dahlberg was cool, and quick. He must have been astonished to hear his name called by her; but he moved with the swiftness of the snake with which, in her pain, she had identified him. Swinging round so that Aunt Isolde's body was between him and Carey Bloomfield's gun, he was calmness itself.

'I know that voice,' he said, as if welcoming a long-lost friend. 'How nice to see you again, Captain Bloomfield. Full marks for tenacity, and for doing your homework. Recognize the watch?'

'*Captain*?' Müller said.

He had also moved swiftly out of the corridor and had positioned himself to one side so that he continued to cover Dahlberg with his gun. He shot glances of astonishment at the big automatic in the hands of the soaking wet person he had last left in the Porsche, with instructions to get out of the area.

'*Captain*?' he repeated.

'Ah, dear Cousin . . . the surprise in your voice is illuminating. So, she didn't tell you. Captain Bloomfield and I are old friends.'

'I'm no friend of yours, Dahlberg,' she squeezed out through gritted teeth. '*You stole my brother's watch, you piece of shit*! And it's *Major*.'

'Major . . . You have moved up in the world. Your brother's watch . . . Ah, yes. He had no further use for it. I always knew you were good, but you're even better than I thought. It must have been you who got poor old Goertzler. Until today, no one had got the better of him. Have you any idea how many people he has killed?'

She stood there, feet braced, gun pointing, eyes hungry for revenge. '*Fuck you, thief*! I gave my brother that watch. I'll get it back off your dead body.'

'Such rage, Major . . .' Dahlberg commented rather calmly, all things considered. He was being covered by the guns of two people who were ready to shoot him dead. 'What are you going to do? We seem to have been in this situation before. Are you going to shoot me through my hostage this time? Too bad you were unable to do so the last time this occurred. Look at her, Cousin. Doesn't she look quite fantastic in wet clothes? I would love to work on that body.'

'Your tricks won't get to me this time, Dahlberg,' she said harshly.

Müller, intrigued by the exchange, glanced at her once more. Her metamorphosis had been so complete, he was finding it difficult to recognize the person who had spent the last forty-eight hours in his company; and this despite the fact that he had already suspected her of being more than a journalist.

'You can't execute him,' he now said to her firmly.

'You keep out of this, Müller!' It was a snarl from someone who would not be deflected. '*I want him*! And I am *darn* well going to get him. No escape for you this time, you bastard!' she raged coldly at Dahlberg.

Dahlberg was still calm, clearly considering his options and planning to make good use of them.

'Do you see, Cousin?' he said to Müller, as if they were somehow partners. 'She is hungry for my blood. You're the policeman and this is . . . for the sake of argument . . . your territory. Will you allow her to execute me?' He was looking hard at Carey Bloomfield as he spoke. 'The last time she and I had such a stand-off, we were in Israel . . . though not in an area, shall we say, necessarily friendly to Americans; especially American *Jews*.' He used the word as if it made him ill just to say it. 'Her brother was where *Aunt Isolde* now happens to be. Of course, he was rather more the worse for wear.

'You see, I'd had the pleasure of his company. I needed some information . . . *he* was a major then . . . but, stubborn man that he was, he simply would not give it; even when I had shaved off pieces of his skin until they looked as delicate as one of Aunt Isolde's slices of salmon. He screamed, of course; but still he would not talk. I was beginning to think I would have to remove every square millimetre, when the sound of firing interrupted our pleasant chat.

'A rescue attempt, led by the brave major's sister, the then captain, *against orders*. Her mission had not been sanctioned. It had been a strictly private affair. She found her brother and I, very much as you now see *Aunt Isolde*. Her brother begged her to shoot *me*, through him. He was in a sorry state, I have to tell you, that poor, brave, but extremely foolish *jewboy* major. "*For God's sake, Carey,*" he begged. "*Shoot me and take the bastard.*"

'But, of course, she could not. He was her brother, after all. In her place, *I* would have shot. But, she isn't me. Her brother begged and begged and *begged* . . . but, all the while, she just stood there, gun pointing but quite useless . . . just as now. She let me take him out of the room. I shot him as soon as I was clear. He was just a mass of red flesh, anyway. He wouldn't have lasted. Had I had more time, I would have salted him. *That* would have made him speak. Then again, perhaps not. The shock of the pain from the salt might have killed him.'

Müller had listened to Dahlberg's calm narrative with revulsion. He glanced at Carey Bloomfield and saw the film of tears in her eyes. Her lips were pulled back from her teeth in a feral hunger; and the gun still did not waver.

'Please, Carey,' Dahlberg mimicked in a passable approximation of her brother's voice. 'For God's sake. *Do it, do it!*'

In her mind, she saw her brother's ravaged body, and

heard his voice. Her finger began to tighten on the trigger.

'*Do it, Carey. Do it!*'

Müller looked on in horror. She was going to shoot!

'*Do it, Carey!*' Dahlberg goaded. '*Do it!*'

'*Müller!*' she bawled suddenly. 'Behind you!'

Müller was uncertain whether this was a desperate trick to divert his attention so that she could kill Dahlberg, irrespective of the danger to Aunt Isolde; but then he realized that she had swung her weapon away. The Beretta roared twice in rapid succession. A cry and a heavy fall indicated she had hit her target. Something clattered to the marble floor.

'Don't even think it!' Müller barked at Dahlberg, who clearly wanted to seize what he'd thought was a chance and was about to try on Carey Bloomfield, what he'd done to Bulent Landauer.

Dahlberg remained in his old position.

Carey Bloomfield moved swiftly across to the entrance, where 'Three', who'd heard the shot in the corridor and had been surreptitiously trying to get a shot at Müller, was lying flat on his back. The machine pistol was some distance from his outstretched, fluttering hand.

She unceremoniously dragged him by one foot into the reception area, smearing his blood on the marble floor. He was severely wounded, and was going nowhere. She picked up the machine pistol, removed the magazine and threw the weapon behind the reception desk.

She again trained her automatic on Dahlberg.

'Thanks,' Müller said.

'You're welcome.' She did not take her eyes off Dahlberg.

'We're back to square one,' Dahlberg said, smiling. 'The major has another problem. *Her* people would like me *alive*. I have plenty of information they would greatly wish me to give to them. As you can imagine, my information is quite encyclopaedic. So . . . who's going to shoot me, *through Aunt Isolde*? Because it really is the only way.'

He smiled with chilling self-assurance, as if he had presented them with an impossible problem to solve, and began to manoeuvre towards the entrance.

'As you seem to have decimated my forces, Major,' he went on casually, 'it is time to make good my escape. It will be interesting to see which one of you will have the guts to shoot.'

They followed, their guns trained upon him.

'What about your crony?' Müller asked. 'Leaving him to his fate?'

'The major shot to kill. If he isn't dead, he soon will be.'

'You're all heart,' Carey Bloomfield said tightly.

Dahlberg gave his soft laugh. 'I don't have one.'

He manoeuvred Aunt Isolde in such a way that if either of them shot at him, she would be hit, perhaps fatally.

Like wild animals searching for an opportunity to strike, they went out into the dark of the rainy day, which had seemingly turned to night without once pausing for the sun.

As they drew closer to the big Mercedes, two shots rang out. Müller had shot two of the tyres. The hiss as they deflated, seemed almost as loud.

Dahlberg's head snapped round. '*That was not clever!*' he shouted at Müller.

'I said you would be going nowhere.'

'Do you *really* think so?' The eyes within the pale circles in the blacked-up face were hooded patches of darkness. 'You forget. I know this place. Many a Party guest came here, but never left the way he came; sometimes alive, sometimes not. *I* saw to that. I always have a back-up escape route. And, since you want to play games with me, let us play this final game. *Come on, Aunt Isolde!*'

He began to drag her, half lifting her towards the stream by the hold about her neck. The gun remained firmly pressed against her temple. He was clearly hoping to be borne away by the stream, far enough for him to climb out and escape to wherever he had left his back-up.

'Your nephew, the bold policeman, wants to play games

240

with me, and the major wants revenge for her brother; but neither of them dares shoot. Do you see? They are *weak*. I would have long ago shot through you. But not they. *Weak*.'

He kept up the monologue as all four headed towards the rushing stream. They threw ominous shadows as each light was passed, flitting apart then merging, then going through the entire sequence over and over.

Aunt Isolde struggled to get away, but to no avail. The grip round her neck was getting tighter as Dahlberg's desire to escape increased his determination to ensure she could not. She was his unwilling suit of armour. As long as he had her, he was safe from the bullets that would take his life.

Then, just as they reached the stream, three things simultaneously conspired against Dahlberg: the wet ground, the constantly struggling Aunt Isolde, and the rising bank. For the briefest of instants his foot slipped, and though he recovered with lightning speed, it was enough for Aunt Isolde.

She slumped, apparently from lack of air.

Her body was suddenly heavy, and the change in weight made Dahlberg stumble. Instinctively, he threw out his gun hand to balance himself. He could not have helped it. His grip around Aunt Isolde's throat eased and her body weight rolled her sufficiently away to leave his chest exposed.

Like hunting pack animals waiting for their opportunity, Müller and Carey Bloomfield struck.

Müller was faster. He fired three rapid shots. Each followed the other in a tight group that struck Dahlberg above the left breast, throwing him backwards.

Carey Bloomfield's characteristic double-shot burst hit him slightly above Muller's, because he was already falling and the angle was thus more acute.

'*Nooo*!' he shouted in impotent rage, and actually tried to bring his gun to bear.

But the arm was already weakening and could not raise itself high enough. The gun fired uselessly but rapidly, so great was the power of his fury. His legs finally gave way and he fell into the stream, five Beretta rounds in him.

Carey Bloomfield ran to the edge while Müller went to Aunt Isolde, who had made a miraculous recovery.

Carey Bloomfield watched the dark, amorphous shape as it floated away. The biggest cottonmouth had at last been slain. The body reached the run-off and was swept into the tunnel.

Beretta still in hand, she turned her face up to the rain and shut her eyes, feeling cleansed as the heavy drops fell upon her. Her brother had at last been avenged.

Dahlberg was still alive and aware of what was happening when the rushing water fed him into the tunnel.

It bundled him along at great speed. He tried, desperately and ineffectually, to brake his progress by attempting to stretch his arms to each side of the concrete tube. His frantic efforts to survive in the enclosed blackness were to no avail. His strength was fast receding, and useless against the power of the water.

The gruesome irony of his situation must have etched itself deeply into his dying mind; for he had himself personally despatched many unfortunates that way, some still alive when he had put them in.

For some time, there had never been any blow-back within the run-off. The excess water was always free-flowing; with good reason. What no one – including Dahlberg – knew, was that the end of the tunnel had long been silted up by river deposits and that a section of it had, at that far end, collapsed into an underground chamber; a good 100m straight down. At the bottom was a protruding rock over which an underground stream, more powerful than the one above that fed into it, made its way to an unknown destination. Goertzler's body had already taken that route.

Despite the pummelling he was receiving from the water hurtling him through the tunnel, enough consciousness remained for Dahlberg to be aware when the ground suddenly dropped away beneath him.

'*Noooo!*' he tried to scream again; but this time only a weak, gargling sound came out of a throat already filled with blood and water.

It finally ended for him when his falling body slammed with sickening force on to the waiting rock, breaking his back. The underground stream then bore him away into the depths of the darkness.

'Major Bloomfield!'

She turned, wiping at her face and brushing her hair back with her free hand. Müller was standing next to Aunt Isolde, gun pointing down.

'We've still got work to do. There are bombs in the building. Did you warn Pappi?'

She nodded, putting the automatic back in its holster.

'And the keys to my car?'

For an awful moment, she feared she might have lost them in the stream; but they were still in her pocket.

'In my pocket,' she replied.

'OK.' He looked thoughtfully at her. 'I'll talk to you later,' he promised sternly. 'Check that man you shot. Pray he's still alive. We need to know where those bombs are.'

She began to say something, but Müller was already on the phone to Pappenheim, instructing him to send in a bomb-disposal unit to follow Klee's team.

As she hurried back to check on the man in the hotel lobby, fast-approaching lights could be seen. There were no sirens and no flashing blue lights; but it was Klee's team arriving. The first car reached the hotel entrance just as she got there.

'And here's the cavalry,' she muttered.

Klee jumped out, stared at her, at the harness she wore, and at the gun in its holster.

'The *Hauptkommissar?*' he asked sharply.

She said nothing, merely pointing in the general direction.

As Klee turned to look, and as more vehicles arrived, he saw Müller hurrying towards him.

'It's alright,' Müller said to his subordinate as Klee glanced in the direction of the departing Carey Bloomfield and Aunt Isolde.

'What the devil happened here, sir?' Klee asked.

'Devil is the right word. We've got bombs to find. Tell your people. I'll brief you.' Müller returned his Beretta to its holster.

Klee's moustache seemed to dance at the news. 'Right, sir. The message just came through that the bomb squad are on their way. And if I may say so, you look wet.'

'You'll soon look like me if you stand here in this wretched rain and don't get on with it.'

Klee grinned. 'Yes, sir.'

The man that Carey Bloomfield had shot had been found to be still alive; just. But they managed to get the locations of all the bombs from him before he died. His name was Wolfgang Nierich, and he had been a former member of a secret DDR special – and greatly feared – police unit. The unit, much hated, had been commanded by Dahlberg.

The trapped staff were freed from the DDR room and Holtmann surprised everyone by being severely shocked by Landauer's murder. He was filled with remorse. Unkind staff whispered it was more likely to be guilt for the way he had spoken about the manager, especially as he himself had stared into the muzzle of one of the guns and had been less than brave when his moment of truth had arrived.

After he had finished with Klee, Müller found Aunt Isolde – who had taken refuge in the staff building until the bombs had been disarmed – now in dry clothes and distressed by the cold-blooded murder of Landauer, sitting alone in the kitchen.

'Are you OK?' he asked her gently.

'I'm fine,' she said a little vaguely. 'But what do I tell Bulent's family?'

'The only thing you can.'

'But not that he died trussed up like a chicken.'

'No.'

'Such a waste.'

Müller nodded. 'Yes. That was a sudden recovery you made out there,' he observed after a while.

She gave him a tired smile. 'I was good, wasn't I? I could see you dared not shoot and even Carey, despite that terrible story of what happed to her brother, found it very hard. Dahlberg might have shot us all, and got away with it. I had to do something. I wasn't sure, but I had the impression he lost his footing slightly. I decided to risk it. It was the only thing I could think of.'

'It worked. It gave us the chance. Where is she, by the way?'

'In her room. I made her get out of those wet clothes, as should you.'

'I'm drying out already. About Major Bloomfield . . .'

'Poor girl. She's been carrying a load for years. She was crying . . . with relief, sorrow, you name it. Don't be hard on her, Jens-Müller.'

'She used me.' He sounded angry. 'She used me to get to Dahlberg. Done her homework, he said. She had. Her people knew of the connection with this house, and of his link to our family. They planted her on Kaltendorf, who then fed her to me, as they already *knew* he would, given his attitude towards me. I feel like a damned pawn . . .'

'Don't be so hard on yourself. You are one of the best of the best. That is why Kaltendorf has so much trouble coming to terms with the way you work. Carey did what she did, *because* she hoped you would find Dahlberg. And you did. You worked it out and got back here in time. Those killings would have continued until he had achieved the results he wanted.

'But she *saved* us . . . the staff, my home. If she hadn't disobeyed your instructions to leave, you might not have got the chance to get him without getting me killed in the process. He *knew* it, and would have killed me, just as he killed her brother in the terrible way he did. And this house – *our* house

– would have been burned to the ground, with twenty staff and Bulent in it. Even if you had survived, you would never have forgiven yourself, and he would have destroyed you just as he has Kaltendorf. I know it's hard to admit that, despite your own reservations, she still caught you by surprise . . . but even so, Jens-Müller. Even so . . .'

Aunt Isolde paused, looking at him with fondness.

He said nothing, and stood up to go to the window where he had first seen Dahlberg's shadow. Every so often, the lights in the hotel grounds beyond the courtyard threw ghostly silhouettes into the wet night as someone passed across their beams. Klee's people were still at it.

'The rain seems to have eased,' he said. 'If I didn't know better, I would say it has been waiting for Dahlberg's end.'

'That's not so hard to believe . . .'

'Come on, Aunt Isolde . . . I'm a policeman. I don't believe in such things.'

'Whatever,' she said, giving him no argument. 'The point is that you and Carey have stopped him. You have ended the nightmare he planned for Germany.'

Müller stared out at the darkness.

'I'm not so sure,' he said quietly. 'He only hoped to succeed because there is already something malevolent out there that he can tap into. He didn't create it. He was *using* it. Colonel Jackson said something about how he felt when he saw the old films of the war. When *I* see them, I find myself asking how could we, an advanced people, have allowed such creatures to take over our country. Sentinels,' he added, almost to himself.

'What?'

'Something else the colonel said.' Müller turned from the window and did not elaborate. 'Dahlberg kept going on about being a von Röhnen,' he continued. 'Was he really one of us?'

'Genetically, part of us. Yes. But in every other way, not part of us at all. We didn't make him, Jens-Müller.'

Müller again turned to the window. 'Didn't we?' he asked

softly. 'The rain really does seem to be stopping,' he went on. 'And don't say it . . . because I don't believe it.'

'I'm not saying anything.'

He smiled tiredly and turned back to her. 'Which is even worse. I know you. Alright, Aunt Isolde,' he continued. 'I'll take another leaf out of Colonel Jackson's book. I will leave it to Major Bloomfield's people to talk to our people. *They* can sort it out among themselves. And I think I'll take a short holiday.'

'Where to?'

'Somewhere without so much rain, I hope. The south of France. I want to look at the face of humanity before it was corrupted.'

'I'm not sure I understand what you mean.'

'I'm not sure I understand myself.'

Day Three: Berlin, 14.00 hours.

Müller carried Carey Bloomfield's travel bag into the airport concourse. The smaller one was slung over her shoulder.

He had driven her there and, during the journey, she had switched on the CD. Tom Petty's album was still selected, and 'You and I will Meet Again' had come on. As they now walked across the concourse, neither spoke, seemingly occupied with their own thoughts.

For her part, the death of Herman Dahlberg had been like a heavy weight lifting off her shoulders. A long journey had come to an end. But Toby Adams had been less than pleased with the news. An invaluable source of intelligence, both historical and contemporary, he insisted, had been lost. She had been unmoved by his protestations. As Müller had shot first, Adams could hardly have accused her of going against operational orders. Her brother David had been avenged for his terrible death, and that was what mattered in the end.

She remembered how her father, on seeing the mangled remains in the body bag, had conspired with her in ensuring her mother never got to see what had been left of her only son.

'Get the bastard who did this!' her father had told her in an abnormally controlled voice at the time; but the hot tears had been in his eyes.

She had achieved that goal, and it felt good.

Müller's own thoughts were ambivalent. He was still unsure of how he should feel about the way she had used him. Yet, at the same time, he could not deny that her presence and capabilities had, without doubt, turned a very dangerous situation into a recoverable one.

Aunt Isolde continued to remain unswerving in her conviction that Carey Bloomfield's presence had saved the Derrenberg, and her own life with it. And even Pappenheim, after having read Müller's report of the incident – despite his earlier suspicions of her – had been impressed by the way she had handled herself, especially by the way she had taken out both Goertzler and Nierich. From Pappenheim, that was praise indeed.

'Hope you haven't got the gun in there,' he at last said, seemingly as an afterthought.

'I haven't.'

'Good.'

They stopped at a check-in desk. When the documentation was over, she turned to him.

'In the end, I didn't get the watch. Time to go.'

'No . . . and yes.' He held out a hand. 'Major . . .'

'Damn, Müller! Just this once. The name is Carey . . .'

He continued to hold out the hand.

In exasperation, she shook it. 'See you around, Müller.'

'See you.'

She turned and went through to the airline gate without looking back. He remained where he was until she had gone out of sight; then stayed at the airport until her plane had taken off.

On the aircraft, she looked down at the ground from her

window seat, as it curved away from Berlin. The song was still playing in her head. There was a definite moistness in her eyes.

Saint Jean Cap Ferrat, south of France, three days later.

Despite the bad weather plaguing most of Europe, the Cap Ferrat day was dry. Müller walked in the warmth of the sun up the rising, tarred driveway. At its end was a magnificent pink villa, perched atop a promontory with the bays of Villefranche-sur-Mer, and Beaulieu-sur-Mer on either side. It was a spectacular location. The building, a labour of love constructed by a strong-willed young baroness at the beginning of the last century, was now a museum.

There seemed to be many visitors. Beyond the edge of the right-hand section of the drive, the ground dropped precipitously for tens of metres. It had been partitioned into parking spaces, with a low wall bordering it to protect the incautious. Several cars were there. Though he had driven down from Germany, Müller had left the Porsche at his hotel, choosing instead to walk.

He paused to look out across the calm blue of the Mediterranean at Beaulieu. Despite the lateness of the season, several big motor yachts were at anchor. He smiled when he remembered Pappenheim's comments about yachts and beauties.

He walked on, and went through the museum shop to gain entry to the no less spectacular gardens, all the baroness's own handiwork. Pappenheim had, through his contacts, discovered that Kaltendorf's daughter frequently went there, to sit alone on one of the benches. It was a favourite place, and one that she always visited with her father whenever he came to see her.

Müller went through to the gardens. After a brief look around, he saw a young girl sitting by herself, reading. She was the girl Pappenheim had described from the photograph in Kaltendorf's desk. She was indeed beautiful. Though he knew it to be a fact, Müller still found it hard to believe that Kaltendorf was her father.

Müller did not disturb her.

'Beautiful, isn't she?' a voice said behind him.

He whirled. 'How did *you* find me?'

'I found you before.'

'Major—' he began.

'Carey,' she corrected.

'We've got to talk,' he said.

'Sure.'

They walked across the gravelled path to the opposite side of the villa. A terrace like the flying bridge of a ship seemed to hang in mid-air. They stepped on to it, and looked out over the deepwater inlet of Villefranche. More exotic yachts, like graceful white swans, were riding at anchor upon the mirror-like surface.

'You couldn't stand the idea of my having some more of Elisabeth Jackson's cake in your absence,' he suggested.

'That must be it.'

'Thought so.'

Briefly, their hands touched; then touched again.

The girl did not look up from her book.